Serguei

PHARAOH'S
DAM

Bychkov

BOOKSIDE Press

Pharaoh's Dam © 2022
Serguei Bychkov

All rights reserved. No part of this publication may be reproduced, distributed, or transmitted in any form or by any means, including photocopying, recording, or other electronic or mechanical methods, without the prior written permission of the publisher, except in the case brief quotations embodied in critical reviews and other noncommercial uses permitted by copyright law.

ISBN:
Paperback   978-1-77883-000-6

The views expressed in this book are solely those of the author and do not necessarily reflect the views of the publisher, and the publisher hereby disclaims any responsibility for them.

BookSide Press
877-741-8091
www.booksidepress.com
orders@booksidepress.com

CONTENTS

Foreword vii
Chapter 1: Jochebed[1] 1
Chapter 2: Moses 4
Chapter 3: Ochos 9
Chapter 4: Nain 11
Chapter 5: Malis 14
Chapter 6: Fooige 18
Chapter 7: Pharaoh 20
Chapter 8: Bahan 23
Chapter 9: The High Priests 25
Chapter 10: Hosea 30
Chapter 12: Love 34
Chapter 13: Goodbye Love 37
Chapter 14: Moses' Choice 39
Chapter 15: Ram.Son of Pharaoh 42
Chapter 15: The Death of Egypt 44
Chapter 17: The Beginning of Everything[1] 47
Chapter 18: Father and Son 50
Chapter 19: The Capital 53
Chapter 20: Mack and Buck 55
Chapter 21: The World Flood 58
Chapter 22: Poison for Pharaoh 63
Chapter 23: An Assassination Order for the Head Priest 66
Chapter 24: Exam 69
Chapter 24: Fire 76
Chapter 25: The Bow and the Arrow 79
Chapter 26: The Assassination of the High Priest of Egypt ... 81
Chapter 27: Heart Surgery 85
Chapter 28: Moses the Chief Priest of Egypt? 88

Chapter 29: Dinner at Pharaoh's 92
Chapter 30: That Sweet Word Freedom..............................96
Chapter 31: Escape from the Palace....................................99
Chapter 32: Ram's Death 101
Chapter 33: The Wedding..103
Chapter 34: The Funeral of Pharaoh's Son 108
Chapter 35: Execution of Ochos 111

--- PART TWO. ---

Chapter 1: Exodus..116
Chapter 2: The Shepherd of the Sheep 119
Chapter 3: Aaron and His Family.......................................122
Chapter 4: Nature's Blow...125
Chapter 5: Eternal Immigrants...128
Chapter 6: Hosea 132
Chapter 6: The Army or the Jewish Community?..........137
Chapter 7: Headquarters of the Revolution 140
Chapter 8: The Ideologist of the Revolution 143
Chapter 8: The Hut...150
Chapter 9: Volunteers...157
Chapter 10: The Collapse of the Revolution 167
Chapter 11: Moses' Law...177
Chapter 12: The Stable Boy's Assistant 182
Chapter 13: Brothers...186
Chapter 14: The Calm Before The Storm 198
Chapter 15: Crossing of the Red Sea 206
Chapter 16: The First Battle 209
Chapter 17: Moses' Triumph...213
Chapter 18: The Hero of Egypt..216
Chapter 19: The Return...221
Chapter 19: The Battle with the Amalekites 226
Chapter 20: Aaron's Sons...230
Chapter 21: Eleazar...239
Chapter 22: Korah 242
Chapter 23: The Fratricidal War..249
Chapter 24: Aaron's Death 254
Chapter 25: The Enemy of the People...............................258

Chapter 26: The Reckoning. 262
Chapter 27: Nain's school.. 269

FOREWORD

The book is written in the adventure genre in the form of a journalistic investigation and tells about an event that happened in Egypt 4500 years ago - Jewish exodus from Egypt. The events described are supported by references from the bible, which quite accurately and truthfully describes the life of the Egyptian people at that time. According to the plot, the Pharaoh decides to dismantle the Great Pyramids and build a dam from this material that blocks the Great Nile. But at this important moment for Egypt, the unquenchable thirst for power forced the adopted grandson of Pharaoh Moses to make a coup in order to reign on the throne. Intrigues, hired killers and the rest of the arsenal of adventurers who want to fish in troubled waters are used. Unfortunately for the Pharaoh, natural phenomena suddenly fall upon the country, putting Egypt on the brink of starvation. At the cost of huge sacrifices, the rebellion is suppressed, and the rebels, led by Moses, flee from the punishment of the Pharaoh into the desert, where they suffer hardships for many years, paying for participation in the rebellion. The book describes the characters of this story, which are very similar to you and me living today. These are adventurers of all stripes, hungry for power and money, and ready to serve at least Satan for this. These are the patriots of the Motherland, sparing no effort for the prosperity of the country. By and large, this book is about a great youthful love for a girl and the love of the heroes of the events described for the Motherland, and all the events described breathe love. They *say that beauty will save the world. No, friends, love will save the world, because without love, beauty is an empty phrase! Enjoy...*

CHAPTER 1:

Jochebed[1]

The older people get, the more often they remember themselves as young. When they see children, they remember their childhood. When they see teenagers, they remember their youth. Seeing the old, they realize with regret that life is actually very short and very soon they will become the same ruins with wrinkled faces and a set of diseases and illnesses, from which there is no cure, and from which every year there are more and more.

- Ah, how fast time flies! - thought Jocheved. - It seems only yesterday she was young, full of strength and hope and love. Especially love! Thinking back on her past, she did not think of reproaching herself for all that she had done without thinking, against God, against the customs of the people around her, against modern morality. She believed that love was always above it, and for as long as Jocheved remembered herself, so long had she lived by love. She was constantly drawn to plunge into another love affair, not caring what people would say or think of her, or what her father would think of her.

And her father gave up on his beloved but wayward daughter, seeing that his influence on her was having no effect. As a result, she lost her virginity early, had a reputation for (to put it mildly) abnormal behavior, and got married when all hopes of creating a family had gone up in smoke.

– Oh, those were the days, – Jochebed recalled, pulling herself up voluptuously, – That's what life is for, to experience everything. Who's going to need me, the old me? After all, life is short: before you're born, it's time to die.

Of course, she was worried when all her girlfriends and acquaintances married and had children. She either envied or reassured herself, enduring the stares of her neighbors and her father's displeasure; – A holiday will come to my street, too.

She has fallen completely madly in love with her nephew Abram[2]. Their ages were unequal, and the experienced Jochebed had little difficulty in turning the young lad's head. Using years of accumulated arsenal of affection, Jochebed drove Amram crazy, but apparently overdid it and went too far in her affair. She became pregnant and everyone knew it.

A huge scandal erupted. The assembled family council, giving in to Amram's fervent pleading and cursing the prodigal Jochebeda to the utmost, decided to marry them. It seemed that with the birth of their daughter Mariam[3] and then their son Aaron[4], Jochebed finally calmed down and became a normal family woman. But only the grave can mend a humpbacked man, and as soon as Amram sailed off to sell grain on Kaptor Island[5], she instantly found a replacement of him. It was a love one could only dream of! It was a firework of feelings, a feast of body and soul! But, soon the fruit of this feast of the soul, and more importantly of the body, stirred in Jehovah's womb. She had to wear long and wide clothes to hide her growing belly, and at the end of her due date, Jochebed secretly gave birth to her son Moses[6] in the house of Shifrah's provincial grandmother[7]. Fearing another scandal and Amram's imminent return, she, not caring much, placed the baby in a papyrus basket and set him adrift on the waves of the Nile, on the waves of life.

1. Jochebed is a biblical figure, Amram's aunt and wife. The Bible, Exodus.6:20. Numbers 26:59
2. Amram is a biblical figure, the nephew and husband of Jochebed. The Bible, Exodus. 6:18.
3. Mariam is a biblical figure, sister of Aaron and Moses.
4. Aaron is a biblical personality, the brother and chief ideologue of Moses.
5. Kaptor is the ancient name for the island of Crete.

6. Moses is a biblical personality. According to the Bible he was born 3,570   years ago.
7. The obedient grandmother of Shiphrah is a biblical person. The Bible, Exodus 1:15

CHAPTER 2:

Moses

What a grace to live in a palace and be the grandson of the Great Pharaoh[1]! One gesture was enough for the servants to move and do whatever the soul wanted. Everyone loved him, and even Pharaoh himself often pampered his favorite grandson. He often took Moses and his own son Ram with him during his inspections of Egypt's cities and temples, teaching him government and other wisdoms of royal life.

But to be honest, Moses did not like the great grandfather, and he hated his son Ram[2] with all his soul. Even though they were the same age, even though they grew up together, even though they were considered by everyone to be inseparable friends, Moses hated him. He could not forgive Ram for his origins. Ram would be Pharaoh and Moses would not, and this had oppressed him ever since the torah when he realized the difference between the son and the grandson of Pharaoh. He showed no real feelings for his uncle-peer, and not a living soul in Egypt suspected it. Only in private did he dream that Ram might have an accident. In his jealous, inflamed mind there were many reasons for his death: from some terrible, incurable disease, from a poisonous snake bite, from a fall from a horse. The main thing is that he should disappear forever. Only then could he, Moses, claim the Pharaonic throne.

Oh-oh! He would not be like his grandfather, who could call up a mere Egyptian during inspections and talk to him as an equal. Why on earth would he do that?! Who were these people to talk to Pharaoh himself? They're just roadside dirt that's disgusting to get your feet dirty on.

As recently as yesterday Moses was present at Pharaoh's conversation with a miserable and insignificant tax collector from the Upper Nile[3], and he, the dog, dared to disagree with Pharaoh himself (!!!) about the amount of the tax for this year. Not just disagreed, but gave his thoughts on the matter.

- Who needs your ideas, you scum, - Moses wanted to shout, but Pharaoh calmly listened to him... ...and agreed!

Moses was all over the place.

- What kind of Pharaoh are you? Show your power, order him to be chopped to pieces and then no petty official would dare argue with you anymore!

But he is not Pharaoh... and he never will be. As much as it pains me to accept it, what can you do?

... It was a beautiful evening, and Moses was waiting for the priest from the temple of the Sun God Ra[4]. Three days earlier, the middle priest Mow had requested a secret audience, hinting at top-secret circumstances Moses needed to know. With a mind prone to intrigue, Moses sensed something unusual in this request and consented.

Finally Hovav[5], a loyal and faithful servant, reported the arrival of the priest. With a slight movement of his hand Moses allowed him to enter, and removed the servant.

The priest looked about 50 years old. His twinkling eyes and face betrayed excitement. He bowed low to Moses and froze, hesitant to begin a conversation. Moses sensed the tension and, to ease the situation, offered his guest something from his table, which the obliging Hovav set for Moses, as usual at this time. Mow refused with a wave of his hand and said in a quiet, uncertain voice, as if afraid of hearing it that according to the records in the Main Temple of the sun god Ra, which are a state secret, he, Moses, is not the grandson of the Great Pharaoh. According to the records he is a Hebrew boy and the adopted son of Pharaoh's daughter Adith[6]. After saying this, the priest took a deep breath and stood anxiously waiting to see what Moses would answer him. A whirlwind of thoughts and feelings raced through Moses' mind during the few seconds the priest spoke. At first, anger filled his mind in an all-encompassing wave. What is this wretched freak talking about? He, Moses, is not the grandson of Pharaoh?! He is not an Egyptian, but a worthless Jew?! He should be executed on the spot for saying that!!!

And Moses raised his hands to clap his hands, calling for the guards.

But the next thought burned him harder than his anger: - what if everything the priest had told him was true...? It couldn't be!!! What about his hope of ever becoming Pharaoh someday? For then he would lose that right forever! Moses froze, put his hands down, and began to think feverishly, trying to understand why the priest had told him all this. After waiting a few tense minutes, the priest, having made up his mind, suddenly took a step toward Moses and whispered, like a disturbed snake, he said:

- Only a few people know this terrible secret: Pharaoh, the Head Priest of the Temple of the Sun God Ra, and your mother. That's all, - he said nonchalantly, and then he made a sad face and continued: -But no one is eternal on this earth Moses. All of us will die someday. Even the Great Pharaoh is. - May the gods make his life eternal, - the priest murmured, raising his hands in the air. Then he took another step toward Moses, and so he came very close and looked around and whispered with only his lips:

- If suddenly it happens that the Great Pharaoh and his son die, (which is quite possible), only the chief priest of the temple of the god Ra will be an obstacle on Moses' way to Pharaoh's throne. So, why the Head Priest shouldn't die suddenly and carry the secret of Pharaoh's grandson's origin to his grave? Consider, Moses, that there may be some sense in the words of your servant Mow, - he spoke and added:

- I will destroy all the records of your birth, and I will be as silent as a fish in the Nile, Moses. I will be silent as a mute from birth, in the hope that the new Great Pharaoh with the beautiful name Moses will appoint me Head Priest of the temple of the God Ra.

Moses was silent; he was amazed. Kill the Great Pharaoh and Ram!? Wow!!! ...But how could the priest guess his secret and passionate desire to be Pharaoh? Or maybe it was a provocation? Then who is and why decided to test me? The Pharaoh is? I don't think so. Grandfather loves me. But he's not my grandfather, according to this priest. What about Ram? Not again. Ram loves me as a brother and best friend, and he is too open to play such games, much less with me.

Pharaoh's personal security chief, Ochos? It is possible, but unlikely. Without Pharaoh's command he will not test or even provoke Pharaoh's grandson, for that you need grounds, and they do not yet exist.

Saying to himself, "Not yet," Moses realized that he is almost ready for Mow's proposal and his soul is eager to do so. But how does he want to do it?

- I have reliable people all over Egypt, - the priest continued, realizing that Moses was waiting for the sequel, - very reliable people. They are dissatisfied with Pharaoh and their position in society. They have no hope for his son, and it makes no sense to wait for him to come to power. Ram is an exact copy of his father and is unlikely to change anything when he comes to the throne. We pin all our hopes on the new man on the throne. A man, who is clever, resolute and generous to his loyal assistants. In our deep conviction, such a man is you, Moses, and we pin all our hopes only on you.

Moses put aside his fears and resolved to try his luck. He was well aware of what awaited him in the event of failure, but his desire to become Pharaoh, his desire to gain unlimited power, drowned everything else.

- What exactly do you offer? - He asked the priest directly.

- We take over the Head Priest; he can die tomorrow, if you wish. It is more difficult with Pharaoh and his son. The guards are so tight that it's almost impossible to do it. Yes, what can I tell you about it? You know it better than I do. But we have an idea, and not a bad one. You have to do it by yourself!

- Me??!! - Moses exclaimed. - No way! Not because I feel pity for them, but because afterwards I shall be executed as the last tomb robber.

- Of course they will, - the priest said, - if they find out who did it. But that's the point, Moses, that no one would ever suspect Pharaoh's grandson of committing such an atrocity. Listen carefully. You know that all the food and wine is tested for poison before it is served at Pharaoh's table and there is no way for you to do anything before that, but after the test is done, you can put poison in Pharaoh and his son's wine. You are beyond the suspicion of the guards and could very well do it unnoticed. By the time the trial is over, if anyone suspects you, it will be too late: you will already have been declared Pharaoh and can influence the investigation, and I am sure that you will find the murderer or even several murderers.

-Think about it, Moses. The day after tomorrow Pharaoh is going to visit our temple, and if you come with him, that will be a sign to us that you agree. Then we'll give you the poison and take care of the old dead nag, - Mow finished, alluding to the Head Priest.

Then he went to the table and boldly poured himself some wine.

- To the rising of a new star in the sky of Egypt! - said Mow, and with visible pleasure drank every drop.

- I have to go, Moses, - he said, glancing at the jug of wine, as if he wanted another drink but did not dare to overstep the permissible limit, and, not getting permission to do so, went out.

- Maybe I'll see you the day after tomorrow, - he said slyly at parting.

Moses shook his shoulder nervously and mechanically picked up the old papyrus, which the priest had allegedly brought on his behalf. Turning them in his hand, he tossed them aside.

He had a decision to make, and Moses pondered for a long time, sitting down on his bed...

Should I go with Pharaoh to the temple? Or I have to go to Ochos?

1. Pharaoh is a biblical figure. The Bible does not tell us his name. It is supposed to be either Thutmose3, Ramses the Great, or Menefta.
2. The son of Pharaoh is a biblical person. The Bible also does not specify his name.
3. Upper and Lower Egypt were two independent states. Pharaoh Menes conquered Lower Egypt (about 5200 years ago) and united them into one state. Memphis became the capital of the united state.
4. According to their religion, the god Ra created the earth, people, animals, and plants.
5. Hovav is a biblical figure, Moses' brother-in-law. The Bible. Num.10:29
6. Pharaoh's daughter is a biblical person. The Bible does not give her name.

CHAPTER 3:

Ochos

Whatever happened in Pharaoh's palace was reported to the head of the personal guard, Ochos. For many years he had served Pharaoh faithfully and was his eyes and ears. In fact, he was only called the head of the personal guard, but in fact he served as the head of internal and external security of Egypt. This job left a mark on his character, and in time he became silent and suspicious. And there was no point in gossiping about it when he had a lot of work to do. Egypt is a large country, the Jewish population alone is about 5 million people1, 40 Noms[2] and all this economy needs an eye on it. Ever since there has been a society and a state, there have been people seeking to exploit them for their own benefit.

Whether it is a common thief from the market of Memphis or a cunning governor, who wants to become a pharaoh. And there's no need to speak of external enemies.

...Today he had a report that Moses had been visited by Mow, head of the archives of the main temple of the Sun God Ra. He reportedly brought Moses some old papyri and stayed with him for half an hour.

Ochos pondered. Moses had never been known for his eagerness to study anything on his own. Why, then, did he need the old papyri, what did he want to know, and, indeed, was that the real reason he had come to the palace of the priest?

Ochos had no reason to suspect Moses, and he asked himself all the questions rather out of the habit of double-checking everything and everyone. He had no beef with Mow either, so he could forget about this visit. He could, but obeying his old habit of double-checking everything, he ordered him to follow the priest.

1. From the author. According to the Bible, there were 603550 Jewish men over 20 years old who came out of Egypt. The Bible. Num: 2:32. If we assume that the family consisted of 5 people, then the number of Jews who left Egypt must have been at least 3 million.
2. Nome - A region or district of Egypt. During the time of the Great Pharaohs, Egypt was traditionally divided into about 40 Noms.

CHAPTER 4:

Nain

Nain was in a cheerful mood. And not just jolly, he was in the best mood imaginable. Of course he was. He had spent the evening with his Fooige. Though it was too soon for him to call her his own, there was hope.

She lived nearby, across the gardens, and for as long as Nain could remember, he had liked this girl. He didn't notice the others; they just didn't exist for him. In his dreams and in his dreams, she was the only one. Well, just some kind of trouble, that's all!

Slim and, of course, the most beautiful in the world, she had always mocked his advances. Both when they were children and, especially, when they grew up. Sometimes it seemed to Nain that she was just mocking him, and his heart was bursting with grief and hopelessness.

Yesterday, when he had worked so hard to get the lilies out of the water, to muster up all his courage and bring them, secretly, from everybody, to her feet, she had laughed and said that she did not like lilies and that he should have given them to Verna.

Verna, their merry neighbor, was the widow of the drowned fisherman Tsuriel. After her husband's death, she was distressed with her little twins, but she didn't kill herself much, and she was often seen in the company of men who paid for her cheerful character.

Nain blushed at this innuendo and was ready to fall to the ground. He was about to throw the damn water lilies into the cucumber bed and leave, when she suddenly blushed and looked at him earnestly and said that she would come to the Nile after sunset.

- And give me the lilies, - she said, taking the flowers from the hands of a stunned and happy Nain, and turned and went to the house.

Nain was in seventh heaven! He ran home and, first of all, hugged his mother, whispering to her that she was the best mom in the world and then began to spoil his little brother Boby. The mother, who knew very well that they would turn the whole house upside down in such a merry mood, chased her sons out into the yard, where they had a game of catch-up. While chasing Boby, Nain slipped, lost his balance, and, splashing, flopped noisily right into the duck's trough. He wanted to slap his brother, but when he heard his mother, who was watching from the porch, burst into laughter and Boby squealing with delight, he laughed.

Not forgetting for a moment that tonight he would see Fooige, Nain washed his face and decided, without waiting for sunset, to go to the Nile. To the Nile meant to the wharf. The boys were always here, swimming, fishing, and seeing the boats off and on. It was always crowded, and Nain knew that Fooige would not come here, but to a place about fifty feet away, where the women did their laundry. After sundown, it was a well known date spot, and all the couples in love would meet there, as if there were no other secluded places around.

It seemed to Nain that the sun would never go over the horizon today. It was as if someone had nailed it to the sky, and so it froze in the sky in one place and could not move, and no matter how much Nain begged him to hurry up and set, it was as if the sun laughed at him and dragged across the sky like a cart pulled by a lazy donkey.

Nain's hair didn't listen either, no matter how Nain arranged it in front of the brass mirror. It stuck out in different directions like the feathers of a disheveled duck after a dog attacked it. Unhappy with his appearance, Nain cursed and told his mother he was going for a walk. She waved at him, as usual, and Nain left the house, satisfied that even his knowledgeable and understanding mother had no idea where he was going. All would have been well, except that Boby clearly did not want to leave him alone, hoping to continue the games. To get away from him, Nain had to let him take his fishing rod. Old neighbor Odis, with whom Nain had loved to fish as a boy, had taught him how to work horsehair so that it would not tear how to make hooks out of bone and the tackle would never fail Nain. Boby, excited about this opportunity to fish with his brother's rod, quickly grabbed it and, fearing Nain might change his mind, disappeared from sight, flashing his heels toward the wharf. Nain headed the same way, but before he reached it, he turned right to the place where the women were washing their laundry. He hoped no one was there, but he was wrong. Three women were leaving the beach, putting the laundry into baskets.

- They were obviously about to leave, Nain thought with satisfaction, but at that moment one of them (it was Verna) spotted Nain.

- Hey, chevalier, - she shouted, clearly wanting to draw Nain's attention to the other women, - aren't you here on a date with me?

She obviously guessed the reason for his appearance here, and with a sly wink at the other women, said slyly:

- Take off your underpants: I will wash them in a jiffy if you help me. Do not be afraid, come closer: we will not bite. At least not me.

She stood up and looked at Nain with a cheerful grin.

Nain ducked to the side and ducked into the reeds. He could hear the woman's laughter.

- I'm sorry I ran into them, - thought Nain sadly, as he made his way along the papyrus[1] to the nearest path.

CHAPTER 5:

Malis

Nain was naively mistaken in thinking that his mother had no idea about anything. Yes, as soon as he appeared at home, as his face, his eyes radiating happiness, Malice immediately knew what was going on in his soul. She had long seen that he was in love, she knew with whom, and when he went for a walk, she finally realized that he was going on a date. Had Nain made up his mind to date Fooige after all?

Fooige was the daughter of her best friend Moline, and they had dreamed more than once that they would someday become related. Fooige, Moline claimed, also loved Nain, but something wasn't working out between them.

- What if he's not going on a date with Fooige? - Malis was suddenly worried. What if some daredevil dickhead had crossed her path? There are plenty of girls.

I'll go over to Moline's, - she thought, - and see where Fooige is. If she went, or had gone, too, for a walk to Neil's, that was all right. Well, if she didn't, trouble.

- Hey, Moline, - Malice called, coming into the yard, - are you at home or in the garden?

- Yes, I am. Come in, neighbor, - Moline answered her.

Once inside, Malis saw her friend hovering by the stove.

- Sit down, Malis, now we're going to have dinner. The sun is going down, so now Serbai will come. My hubby will never be late for dinner. After saying that, Moline began to set the table, and Fooige helped her.

- Hasn't yours arrived yet? - Moline asked about Bahan, knowing that he had been summoned to the capital to see Pharaoh himself.

- It's too soon for him to be home, - Malice answered. - He must return tomorrow.

When she saw that Fooige was home, Malis was upset, and Moline, taking it as a concern for Bahan, said:

- Don't worry, everything will be fine, this is not the first time he has been called to the capital.

- Mother, - she said to Moline, - have you seen my favorite hairpin?

- I haven't seen it, - said Moline.

- I must have dropped it on the shore when I was rinsing the laundry. Once more, sighing sadly, she waved her hand, as if resigned to her loss. But not a minute later she was talking about her again:

- Shall I go and look for it? After all, it's daddy's gift!

- Go, my daughter, go, - suddenly purred Malis happy, - otherwise, God forbid, someone will steal your treasure.

With these words Malis almost forced her out of the house. Moline looked at her questioningly.

- What are you doing, my friend? Spit it out!

- What is there to talk about, do not you see that she has to sneak out of the house? Nain spent half a day in front of the mirror, and then he wanted to take a walk.

- Oh, really? - Said Moline, with a splash of her hand, - I see she's not herself this afternoon. She comes running in, eyes gleaming, purring. Well, like a cat in spring.

Then women automatically began to look around, looking for a cat, and then in one voice began to call: - Kitty, kitty.

It did not take long and appeared on the doorstep, looked at them expectantly, they said, why did you call?

- Pour milk, let her drink it, - said Malis in a tender voice.

- I'll cut off some fresh fish for her, too, - answered Moline in a tone of voice.

...Watching the cat eat, both women began to pray to the goddess Bastet[1], asking her to help them and their children.

- Why are you all fussing over the cat? - Serbai asked them, entering the house, - is this the first time you've seen it? Without waiting for an answer he asked Malis:

- When did Bahan promise to be here?

- Tomorrow, if God allows.

- I think so, too: my nose itches too much. He can smell it beforehand," said Serbai, hinting at the drink.

- He'd better smell something else, - Moline grumbled.

- I'd better get home, - said Malice, calling up, - I've got a headache.

- You dragged me here, - Moline continued to grumble at Serbai as she walked Malis home, - didn't give me much time to talk.

- What do I care, - Serbai was surprised, - even if you talk all night, as long as tongues wouldn't fall off. That would be great!

No sooner had Malice arrived home than Boby came running in.

- Mama, - he shouted from the doorway, - I'm hungry.

- Wash your face first, and I'll give you some beans and fried fish.

- Oh, Mammy, - Boby mumbled with his mouth full, - I've caught so many fish with a Nain rod, a lot of them.

- Where's your fish?

- I gave it to the boys who didn't catch anything. Let them take it home. And the next time I don't catch any, they'll give me some. Right, Mom?

- That's right, that's right, son. Have you seen Nain?

Boby sniffed his nose and smiled shyly.

- I have. He's down there on the shore with Fooige.

- Well, thank goodness, - Malice was pleased, and as she touched her son's hair, which was sticking out in all directions, she sent him off to bed.

- It's time for me, too, - she thought, - Nain will probably not be home soon.

She lay down. But whether it was because she was waiting for Nain to return, or because she was worried about Bahan, sleep did not come. Various thoughts swirled in her head.

- If this keeps up, I'll soon be a grandmother, - she thought of Nain and Fooige. How quickly he had grown...

It seemed like only yesterday she was a young girl, and she was still running around on a date with Bachan herself. - I'm not old yet, - one inner voice protested, and the other contradicted her:

- Old, look at yourself - before you were beautiful and slim, and now?

- What about now, - argued another voice, - well, you got a little rounder, just a little bit, and your breasts got bigger. The men are still looking around, and Bahan says I am the prettiest girl in the world.

- It's a dog's job, - she thought to Bahan. Being a tax collector is not as easy as it sounds. It's honorable, of course, but it's a lot of trouble and enemies. Especially with a character like Bahan has. But people respect him for his fairness and honesty. Not everyone, of course. There are people, especially the rich, who seek to pay as little as possible. They sleep and see in Bahan's office another collector, who for a bribe can reduce the tax. They are at war with Bahan. And now, on the complaint of some rich man, he has been summoned to the capital. They say, to Pharaoh himself. Rumor has it that along with the complaint went to the capital a large bribe with a request to remove Bahan.

- Just so he doesn't ruffle there, - Malis worried.

She was well aware of her husband's character and was confident that he would not silently bend his back to his superiors. How many times it had failed him. He would lick and he would bark. ...And his crazy idea about tax redistribution, or, as he said, the introduction of a progressive tax?!

Then Malis heard the slight creaking of a door and her eyes, accustomed to the darkness, discerned Nain, who, trying to be silent crept to his bed and fell asleep.

- How happy he is now - she was glad for her son, and, unnoticed by herself, fell fast asleep.

She dreamt of a goat that had allegedly crept into their house and shat in all the rooms.

1. Women of Egypt worshipped the goddess Bastet, a cat who was the patroness of women and beauty.

CHAPTER 6:

Fooige

On her way to Neal's, Fooige met her neighbors, who, having washed their laundry, were returning home with their baskets full of wet rags.

- What's your hurry, red maiden? - Verna asked her, in a sweet voice, - Did you lose something?

- Yes, I dropped my hairpin today, - answered Fooige, embarrassed by her lie, - so I thought I might have left it on the shore. Have you seen it? The red one was made in the shape of a cat.

The women nodded their heads and smiled. Yes, go and look for it. But Verna couldn't stand it.

- Yes, we did, - your hairpin's hiding in the reeds, - she shouted merrily and Fooige could hear the women laughing.

- Well, now the whole town will know, - thought Fooige, and then suddenly decided, - Never mind! She had hidden her love for Nain, even from herself, for too long. Trying not to let anyone notice her feelings for Nain, and especially him, she always, in spite of herself, spoke to him in a mocking tone and even with a sneer. She liked him, very much, and Fooige could not understand herself why she had chosen such tactics and why her caustic tongue spoke only nastiness to him.

So today she, rejoicing in the soul of the lilies he had brought, unexpectedly for himself, advised him to give them to Verna.

This surprise made him blush, and he must have been very offended. Frightened, Fooige decided to make a date with him.

The closer she got to Neil, the harder her heart pounded. If her heart beat just a little harder, it seemed that it would jump out of her chest and fly to the sun god Ra.

...There was no one on the beach!

- Was he so offended that he decided to punish me and did not come? - Fooige was taken aback.

- So I should! I was making fun of the lad, so he got his revenge!

But at that moment the papyrus began to stir, and Nain burst out of the crowd. He was embarrassed and began to shake off the grasses to hide it, and then muttered that he was glad of this chance encounter. Nain must have been so overwhelmed by his happiness that he forgot that their meeting was not accidental. When Fooige and Nain realized this, they laughed merrily, and this laughter took away the tension with which they had been waiting for this meeting. They felt that they were the only ones in the world that the stars shimmered only for them, that the Holy Nile carried its waters only to their feet, and that it would always be so.

CHAPTER 7:

Pharaoh

Pharaoh was clearly in a bad mood. This was always the case with him when he was unhappy with himself. For so many years he had dreamed and contemplated a grandiose project, and now today he realized that he should not dream, but do. Time had passed, he had grown old, and things were still not moving forward.

Pharaoh Cheops built the Great Pyramid and glorified himself forever, but what will he leave behind?

- No, it's time to begin, - Pharaoh decided, - and if I don't have time, my son will finish what he has planned. Thank the gods; his son has grown into him, just as he had dreamed. He is also not sitting still and is spending all his time and energy on the improvement of his native Egypt.

And Pharaoh planned to build a great dam across the Nile!

The Nile is the treasure of Egypt! The Nile is bread and a strong army! The Nile is the life, strength, and power of the Egyptian people! Praise be to all the Egyptian gods that for many years the Nile has been flowing at its proper time and feeding Egypt faithfully. But how many times has the Nile not flowed! The whole land was groaning with hunger, and the world seemed to be coming to an end.

Egypt can no longer rely on the blind chance of nature; we must build a dam and control the flood. This would make Egypt a paradise on earth, it would make it the mightiest and richest state in the world and everyone would dream of living in this beautiful country!

There have already been attempts to control the Great Nile. Many years ago, the Great Pharaohs dug up the lake of Merida by draining a huge swampy area, the Oasis of Fayoum, and the water flowed through a channel into the lake for six months during the flood and six months back when the Nile was lowered. It was an enormous reservoir - 200 kilometers in circumference! What labor it cost!

It seemed that the Nile was tamed, and to commemorate this great event, a huge palace-temple to all the gods of Egypt at once was built on the banks of this miracle[1]. But Nile did not give up, and year after year it dragged a huge amount of silt into the lake like a rebellious God, and no matter how much people cared for its miracle, no matter how they cleaned it every year, the forces were unequal. The Nile won, and there was nothing left of the lake.

- No, I will still tame you, Great Nile, - thought Pharaoh, - you will still submit to the people. It's time, it's time to do business, and the people will understand and support you. The people will not be frightened by work!

Then Pharaoh remembered the yesterday's conversation with one of the tax collectors of the Upper Nile Bahan. The chief tax collector of Egypt, Mat, had decided to conduct a show trial against Bahan the bribe-taker and punish him. Pharaoh ordered Ochos to get involved in the case and check whether Bahan really reduced the tax for a bribe, and how to expose the other criminals. Ochos checked - it was a lie. Of course it was a lie. As soon as Pharaoh listened to Bahan, he realized that this man cared about his business, did it honestly, and most importantly, thought about how to make it better. His idea of a progressive tax is marvelous in its simplicity and its effect on farming. As he accurately said:

- A rich peasant is a rich state!
  You could not have said it better.
- But if he is right, why didn't I do anything yesterday? - I hesitated, and I should have let him do the experiment and compare the results in a year. Am I getting old?
- Ochos!
- I'm listening.

- Do you happen to know if Bahan sailed home?
- Is that the tax collector from yesterday? I saw him at Mata's this morning, maybe he's still in the capital.
- I need him still.

  Ochos bowed and went out.

1. The temple that was built was so huge and had so many exits that it was easy to get lost. The ancient Greek name for this temple was Labyrinth.

CHAPTER 8:

Bahan

Bahan was pleased, and his heart rejoiced as it had been many years before, when he hurried to see his future wife Malis. He, a petty official, had the honor not only of seeing Pharaoh himself, but also of speaking to him! Who in their city could boast of that?!

Frankly speaking, Bahan was really frightened when Mat - the chief tax collector - started stomping his feet and demanding to confess to extorting bribes for lowering taxes. Only then Bahan understood the serious turn that he had taken in the forgotten case, when he had reduced the tax of one peasant, because the Nile had washed away his garden and the size of his plot of land had decreased. Apparently, in his irreconcilable struggle with the rich, he had crossed the point where they could no longer tolerate him and where no one could save him. No one but Pharaoh is. And (oh, the miracle!) he was summoned to him. Pharaoh spoke to him and protected him. And not only protected him, but listened carefully and approved of his idea!

Having finished the last business in the head office, Bahan was going home, and leisurely walked through the capital market, choosing a gift for Malis. Suddenly, as if from under the ground, two warriors armed with short spears from the Pharaoh's personal guard grew in front of him.

- Follow us, - one briefly ordered, and they headed toward the palace.

- Eh, perhaps I rejoiced too soon, - thought an anxious Bahan as he followed the soldiers, and the closer they approached the palace, the more anxious Bahan's soul became. And when he saw Pharaoh again, who was wrathfully reprimanding Mat, Bahan's heart sank, and he knelt down before the god who lived on earth.

- Listen, Bahan, to my command. I, the Great Pharaoh, appoint you chief tax collector of your city and allow you to determine the amount of the income tax yourself. Stand up, Bahan, - Pharaoh said to him in a different tone, as if he were talking to a friend. It's hard to define the benefit of your plan in one year, the harvest is different from the harvest, but in two years I'm waiting for you with a detailed report on the results of your work. If your idea shows good results, and I think you are right, I will appoint you assistant to Mat.

...And another thing, from a good tree - good fruit, so I command you to send your son to the Main Temple. If he has gone to you, Bahan, then Egypt will get a good scholarly husband and priest. Go home with God.

As he was already leaving the hall, Bahan heard Pharaoh order Mat:

- Find the one who framed Bahan. If you don't find him, I'll ask Ochos to do it. But then beware!!!

Bahan expected everything from this meeting with Pharaoh, but not this. He had been given great power! Of course, he was happy, but it wasn't about power, it was about the fact that at last he could carry out his idea and, most importantly, that no one would be able to stop him. No one! Pharaoh would not allow it.

One thing that saddened Bahan was the upcoming separation from his son. But, on the other hand, it was the greatest honor - to be a priest in Egypt, not everyone could get it, and one had to be crazy to refuse it. Give it up? What are we talking about? Who would dare disobey Pharaoh's orders?

Forgetting everything in the world, Bahan jumped into his boat, and ordered to steer home. Hurry, hurry!

CHAPTER 9:

The High Priests

The chief priest was strict and stern, which is why discipline in the Main Temple of the Sun God Ra was always at its best: rise at sunrise, breakfast and classes until sunset. Only after that could the priests rest and attend to personal matters.

The Chief Priest was preparing a surprise for Pharaoh. As his first counselor he knew of his dream to build the Great Dam and tame the Nile. For the past three years the chief priest had been designing its construction and had almost completed the work, except for the details. Tomorrow Pharaoh will visit the Main Temple and see the finished model of his dream. Pharaoh's idea to block the Nile, which seemed crazy at first, had seized him so much that contrary to his habit to control all Egyptian temples personally, he put his deputy Beran in charge and, as it turned out, for nothing. In the morning, after a break of three years, he finally sat down to the reports of the abbots of the temples, and to his astonished eyes a sad picture was revealed. He had long known Beran and respected him for the vast knowledge he possessed. According to the Chief Priest, Beran was a genius and only one defect, in his opinion, separated Beran from perfection: he did not like the people and did not hesitate to call them flock.

- It will pass in time," the Chief Priest reassured himself, but time passed and Beran remained the same. Even now, on his way to Beran, he still hoped that all these reports were some kind of misunderstanding.

Beran was talking to the archivist, Mow, who, upon seeing the Head Priest, bowed and left without a second's hesitation. Beran was 40 years old and very tall, so he had to look down from above when talking to people.

Being in the temple since his early childhood, when he, an orphan, was assigned to the temple, by the age of 25 he had studied everything that was stored in the archives, surpassed the other priests in complex calculations, astronomy and, especially, in architecture. His designs were astonishing in their perfection, beauty and grandeur. Paying tribute to his talent, the Chief Priest promoted him in every way, and at the age of 30 Beran reached an unprecedented position - he became the second priest of the Main Temple. But after that he became arrogant, did not tolerate the opinion of others, and all his opponents in scientific disputes, thanks to his position exposed as worthless and talentless people.

Some, not wishing to associate with him, stopped communicating with him and enter into discussions, others, on the contrary, flattered him in every way and sought his friendship.

All this fiddling of the Chief Priest with the dam project was like a gift from fate and Beran decided to act. He had corrupted some of the priests by idleness, exiled others who were disobedient to distant temples, and now his plan had entered its final stage. He had little else to do - remove the High Priest, the Pharaoh and his son, and seize power in Egypt!

Of course, he can't take the throne himself. According to the laws of Egypt, only a member of the royal family can become a pharaoh, but putting his own man, a puppet pharaoh, on the throne is possible, and then all the power will pass into his hands.

At first he, like the chief priest, was seized by the pharaoh's idea of taming the Nile. With his analytical mind he at once saw the enormous advantages that the state would gain and, succumbing to some boyish fervor, he made the necessary calculations and even produced a small model in eight weeks.

For eight weeks he worked like a slave being whipped incessantly. He took great pleasure in the simple solution he had found. He felt like a god! But when the project was finished, his eyes, which had been radiating a kind of mad brilliance the whole time, suddenly went out. The feeling of creative insight was replaced by dejection and anger.

Why my project? Pharaoh will build my dam, and all the glory will go to him. Pharaoh's name will be on everyone's lips, and I, the great scholar, will be forgotten, and not a single dog will remember the brilliant priest Beran. In a fit of blind rage he burned all his blueprints and calculations, destroyed the layout, and, sickened for a while by the feeling that he had killed his own child, Beran hated the world around him even more, and devised an ingenious plan to seize power. The trump card in his puzzle was Moses.

In his time, Beran had to teach Pharaoh's son Ram and grandson Moses calculus. In the time he spent with them, he noticed that Moses had the qualities of a leader, was jealous and incurably ill with an ambition for power. Beran knew this disease for himself, and as soon as he learned from his tame Mow that Moses was not Pharaoh's own grandson, he devised a coup plan in a heartbeat.

The calculation was, like all geniuses, simple: remove Pharaoh, heir to the throne of Ram, and on the grounds that Pharaoh had no brothers, power should automatically pass to Moses' grandson. But Moses is the adopted grandson and has no right to the throne. With this information, it would be possible to blackmail him and hold him as a puppet. Yesterday was the start of this exciting and dangerous race for power. Lolling back in his chair, Beran listened to Mow, who reported to him the results of yesterday's conversation with Moses. If all goes well and Moses shows up here, the hour of action has passed, but if not and Moses reported everything to Ochos, then he, Beran is a complete idiot and does not understand people. Then we will have to invent another plan, wasting time. Beran had no fear of Ochos, for tonight the foolish Maw will die and by his death cut off all paths leading to him.

The face of the High Priest who entered Beran expressed all his feelings.

- Now he's going to start teaching me, - Beran thought with annoyance. The beginning of the actions gave him such a sense of confidence and permissiveness that the whole pathetic look of the old priest made him feel like a man who had a fly attached to him that could do him no harm - only a temporary inconvenience.

-Why didn't you start building the temple in Upper Egypt as we planned with you? Why did you close the eight schools to the common people? What is going on?! - With a voice that grew almost shouting, the chief priest did not ask, but exclaimed.

Beran felt like a misbehaved boy. It made him lose his equilibrium; he blushed, jumped up like a lion ready to jump and yelled, which he had never allowed himself before in conversations with the Chief Priest:

-We have no money! We get crumbs from the Pharaoh, on which not only to build, we cannot exist. Yes, I spent the money to improve the existing temples! Why should the priests, that blue blood of the Egyptian people, have to live in poor conditions? We, who are above all, we, who determine the life of everyone on this earth, exist as mere peasants! And your schools are for the common people!? I can't even find the words to express how I feel about them! We teach the people, we impart to this herd our knowledge of numeracy, architecture, cultural values. For what purpose? So that tomorrow the people, having mastered them, will say that they don't need us anymore? We should not open schools, but, on the contrary, close them and keep everyone in total darkness. This is the only way we can control everyone.

- How wrong I was about you," thought the Chief Priest bitterly, listening to Beran's tirade.

-Answer me Beran, - the Chief Priest asked him quietly, - what is the purpose of religion and we, the priests, as its guides? Are we for the people and the country, or the country and the people for us? Don't you think you have forgotten that you are a priest and not a miserable official who cares only for himself? You have forgotten the great purpose of religion in enlightening and educating the people, and you want to make religion closed to all. Do you want to put it above the interests of the state and the people? You are deeply mistaken! I will consider what to do with you, and I regret that I raised you.

Beran, grinning, looked at the High Priest.

-You may do what you want, - he said and as if wishing to spite him he added, - but your dam cannot stand the pressure of water of maximal flood: its height does not correspond to the area of its foundation.

It was as if the Chief Priest was struck by lightning. For three years he had been trying to solve this difficult problem and no matter how hard he fought, he could not find the optimal ratio of the base to the height of the dam.

- How did Beran determine that, since he had only seen my model once? - thought the Chief Priest and turned sharply and hurried to his room.

Perhaps it's still too early to show the project to Pharaoh. He would have to double-check it. And then a good idea occurred to him: what if he built a model of the area, where the stream will flow imitating the Nile, and on this stream build a dam? Then they would experimentally obtain all the necessary proportions and parameters of the dam!

CHAPTER 10:

Hosea

Hosea never knew his parents, or rather, did not remember them, since he was raised by his grandmother. They lived in Gesem[1], where traditionally almost only Jews lived. The people did what they did, although there were basically, as it were, three communities here: one produced building materials and conducted the construction itself, another was engaged in growing bread and livestock, and the third was a reseller of both. Due to the good harvests, the Egyptian economy had been doing quite well in recent years, and in Gesem there was just an economic boom and so it was flourishing. The wealth of the people was growing, and every Egyptian suddenly wanted to live in a brick house. Wasting no time, the business-minded Jews quickly set up the production of good bricks, and this kind of business began to bring in a good income.

Hosea, a guy in the prime of his life and with fists hardened in fights, was engaged in trade. He did not even think about getting married: there were enough broads in the taverns, and from their visits Hosea's purse was always as thin as a cow that had not been fed for a month. He resold bricks, grain, cane, fish, and everything else that could be resold. Frequent binge-watching prevented him from getting a decent business, but that did not bother him, for his main income came from another trade: Hosea was a professional assassin.

When there was work to be done, the old Jew Abram, who kept a fish stall at the port, would send his grandson to him, and Hosea would abandon his trade and sometimes race to the other end of Egypt, causing his trading clients to go to other middlemen. But Abram paid well, and Hosea could afford to celebrate every business with a good drinking spree without worrying about his commerce. He was conscientious about his main job and made only one slip-up during the whole time, when he got drunk on arrival at the place and broke his leg falling down on the wharf. The case was made by someone and Hosea, after lying with the beautiful widow for almost three weeks, returned home. Old Abram did not show his displeasure, but three days later, when Hosea was in his favorite tavern, the Fat Goose, missing his girls, two strange big guys beat him up so badly that Hosea got back in bed, where he licked his wounds for a couple of weeks. I see, it was Abram who taught him to respect the rules of the game.

All right," he thought of Abram, - as long as you, old nag, give me a job, I won't touch you, but then watch out.

It's easier with the big guys. Without delay, Hosea found the executors of Abram's punishment in Memphis, and they gave their souls to God.

Gosha was about to leave when old Abram's grandson knocked on his window and then came in. Giving him a small coin, Hosea cursed. This was all very unfortunate. Today he had to buy bricks from David and take them to the wharf for loading.

- Well, - thought Hosea, - the bricks can wait. Let's see what Abram has to offer.

Abram, the old fox, greeted him as if he were his own son. After his two young men from Memphis were found murdered, he understood what was going on and began to treat Hosea with respect.

Leaving his son behind the counter, Abram took him into the back room and silently put the money on the table. Gosha got worried: there was as much money as he usually got for three people.

-So, - said Abram, - as usual, that's half, and you'll get the other half tomorrow. But it's a serious business, and if you can't do it, you'd better not take it and tell me at once, because if you fail, neither you nor I will be in trouble.

Hosea was neither afraid of God nor of the devil, but the tone with which Abram uttered this warning made Gosha nervous nor his inner voice told him to refuse. Hosea looked at the money, instantly calculated that's enough money for almost a whole year of partying and said: - A job is a job. Who, when and where?

- This night. A priest of the Main Temple named Mow. Tonight, as usual on this day of the week, he will go to his sister's as darkness falls. Memorize the address and be on your way. Hurry up, Memphis is far away.

1. Gesem is an area of the Nile delta. According to the Bible, Pharaoh gave this prime fertile land of Egypt to the Jews for the merits of Joseph the Jew for private use. The Bible, Genesis 47:6. Chapter11. He knew too much...

After his conversation with Moses, Mow hurried to the Main Temple. So far, everything was going well, if not good. Moses, judging by his words and reactions, seems to agree, and that fool Beran has no idea that he, Mow, has introduced himself to Moses as the Head organizer of the coup. If it all works out, Moses will make him Chief Priest and then he will take out that arrogant Beran in one day.

The next morning Mow hurried to Beran for a report, but before they had even had time to exchange views, the Chief Priest showed up. The conversation had to be interrupted and, bowing, Mow bowed.

-You won't have long to live," Mow thought gloatingly of the Chief Priest, "and neither will you, Beran.

To pass the time, Mow shifted the papyrus in his archives from place to place and could not wait for the evening to come. Finally, his assistant Sokh called him in for supper and, after a quick meal with all the priests, Mow hurried to his sister's, as he always did on this day of the week, anticipating a lavish feast, wine and the laughter of his sister's widowed neighbor, for whom he loved to go to his rich brother-in-law's house.

Walking through the hushed streets of evening Memphis, Mow thought that soon he would no longer have to walk in the dark and beat his feet on the goddamn bumps. He would be carried on a luxurious stretcher with all the honors due to his new rank. In his daydreaming, he didn't notice how he reached his sister's house. Mow had already reached out his hand to open the gate, when at that moment someone stepped behind him and a sharp knife, glinting coldly in the darkness, pierced his heart.

CHAPTER 12:

Love

No sooner had Bahan returned than the news that he had been appointed Chief Tax Collector of the city had spread all over the city. No sooner had he washed his face and had a snack, than the house was filled with friends who came to congratulate him on his new appointment. Passers-by, who did not know it, but who saw the festive excitement in Bahan's yard, wrinkled their foreheads, trying to remember what holiday it was, and, failing to recall, shrugged their shoulders. From the noise made by the guests, it seemed as if the whole town had gathered in Bahan's courtyard. Enos, the former chief tax collector, had already arrived. The old man, who had grown rich in that position, warmly and sincerely congratulated his successor. He did not hold a grudge against Bahan, but was glad to be sent to a well-deserved retirement. Having held that difficult job for many years, the old man was tired of the fear of being exposed for the bribes he took from time to time. His sons were all well settled, his daughters were married off profitably, and now the long-awaited peace fell upon him as a gift of fate. Of course, he would like to place his relative on the breadwinner and had already discussed the details with local governor, but he could not argue with the orders of the Pharaoh himself. He had never seen a Pharaoh himself appointed to such a petty position by the standards of the capital.

-Now everyone will fawn over him, - knowing the established mores, Enos thought of Bahan and was not mistaken, seeing how those who had always considered below their dignity to say hello to Bahan entered the courtyard.

Malis was torn apart. So many guests, she had to cook, serve, and clean up. Her head was spinning, and if it weren't for Moline, she wouldn't know what to do. They quickly fried pieces of fish and vegetables, while Fooige served the food to the guests. A second barrel of wine was opened. Musicians from the local tavern, perched in a corner of the courtyard, played old-timey tunes. There had not been such a feast in the city for a long time.

When the guests, drunk and full, began kissing, swearing eternal friendship, Nain pointed his eyes in Neal's direction. She understood and, ducking inconspicuously into the darkness, went toward the river. A few minutes later Nain caught up with her and, embracing, they walked to the bank of the Nile.

The Nile carried its waters calmly and confidently to the sea, as always. In the reeds, startled by something, a duck quacked noisily, and the moon, shining dazzlingly bright in the clear sky, made a path from their feet to the other shore. It made them feel as if the gods themselves were inviting them to follow this luminous path of love, promising them their protection and protection.

Only yesterday they had kissed for the first time on this very spot, but it seemed to them that more than a thousand years had passed since then, and that it had been, and would always be. It seemed to them that no matter what happened to this good world, no matter what cataclysms happened, nothing could stop them from loving each other, and that no one would ever be able to separate them.

A large fish feeding in the reeds, apparently a crucian carp, slapped its tail on the water, and that sound made Nain and Fooige return from their reverie.

-Will you love me always? - Nain asked Fooige cheerfully, and though she knew he would answer, her heart beat excitedly, waiting for his answer.

-Always, - Nain affirmed, and, kissing Fooige, added uncertainly, - though I can't imagine how one can love at forty. All people after thirty seem old to me, and what kind of love can old people have? All they can do is nag at each other, or worse, quarrel with each other. My father accidentally knocked a cauldron of whey off the stove just before he left, and she went on the rampage and called him a clumsy sheep, and he called her a cluck in return. Is that any way to be loved? But today, when my father came home from the capital, I saw the first thing he did was press my mother against him and they kissed hard. You should have seen, Fooige, my mother at that moment! She was like a young girl clinging to him, and she was glowing with happiness, and my father didn't even notice that Bobby was hanging on his leg like a tick. What is it, Fooige, love, or are they just used to each other?

-I don't know, - she answered, - but I promise you, Nain, I won't call you a clumsy sheep. Clumsy cat maybe, if you deserve it, of course, and, laughing, she ran along the shore, terrified of his fury.

-Ah, so, - Nain exclaimed with feigned anger, catching up with her, - pray, wretch, now you will die in my arms.

CHAPTER 13:

Goodbye Love

Nain woke up in a great mood. He felt like the happiest man on earth, and this feeling overwhelmed him, looking for an outlet. After a quick wash, he sat down at the table with everyone else, as was the custom in their house. Winking cheerfully at his parents, he began to bully his brother, telling him that he had seen Boby wooing the fisherman Rabsak's daughter, and that he had even fought with the boys defending her cat.

-They're probably kissing already, too, - he concluded cheerfully.

-Not yet, - protested twelve-year-old Bobby. - I don't like those girls; they don't even know how to fish, all they do is play with their dolls. But Bobby's flushed ears gave him away.

Everyone laughed, but Nain noticed that the parents were very serious today and were laughing unnaturally. They seemed to be laughing, but there was sadness in their eyes. Not only that, they lowered their eyes when they talked to him, and if they did, they looked somehow guilty, as if pitying or sympathizing with him.

To get rid of this strange feeling, Nain asked his father where his office would be now and if he was going to promote Nain.

It must be said that his father had taught him counting and literacy since he was a boy, (as he was now doing with Boby) and for over a year Nain had been officially a clerk in his father's office, helping him to collect taxes.

His father suddenly choked and lowered his eyes to his plate. After hesitating for a moment, he raised his face decisively and said: - Pharaoh commands you to become a priest. You must go to Memphis. These are his orders.

-Я... I cannot, - whispered the stricken Nain, - I do not want to be a priest, I..." he uttered, and tears came from his eyes, - I love Fooige, and I want her to be my wife. Bobby shrank back frightened as Nain stood up abruptly and held out his hands to his mother and said: - Mother, priests have no right to marry and have a family. You will never babysit my children! Mother, don't let me go!

Malis rushed to Nain and, holding him close to her, sobbed, as one sobs for an irretrievable loss.

Her father grew even darker, and slapped Bobby on the back of the head in annoyance: - What is it that your sandals are tattered; I do not have time to buy.

Bahan pushed away the plate, stood up, looked guiltily at Boby's sniffling nose, and said firmly: - There's nothing you can do, you're going to the temple in two hours.

CHAPTER 14:

Moses' Choice

The night seemed so long to Moses that he could not believe it would ever end. He woke up many times, twisted from side to side and fell asleep again, only to wake up a short time later. Then he dreamed that he was Pharaoh, then that he was a slave and worked in a quarry, then as if rats in unprecedented numbers attacked the palace, then the muddy and dirty water in which he was drowning.

-Shall I go to Ochos after all? - Moses, getting up after a long night, thought. - Well, what am I missing? I have everything I want, and if I don't have something, all I have to wish for is that everyone will hurry to fulfill my wish and deliver anything I want. Everything, but the throne of Pharaoh. And that's exactly what I want. In this way Moses answered his own question. The decision was made.

He got dressed and went to Pharaoh. As he walked through the corridors of the palace, Moses passed armed guards who froze like statues and looked him over with unmoving eyes. Any man not of Pharaoh's family and servants would be instantly killed by them if he entered the palace. Only at the entrance to Pharaoh's room did the four guards block Moses' way, while the fifth, the steward, bowed to him and slipped out the door. After a few seconds, he came out and gave the command to let Moses pass.

Pharaoh was talking to his daughter Adith, Moses' adopted mother, about something. As Moses entered, they cheered and Pharaoh gave him a hand to kiss him. Moses bowed and kissed her and leaned over his mother and kissed her hair.

- You must be looking for Ram, - said Pharaoh, - but he has gone early to the banks of the Nile to choose a place for the dam.

- I know, - answered Moses, - he came to see me and offered to go together, but I have decided to go with you to the Main Temple. I need to look in the archives; I want to know what happened in Egypt and on the earth many, many years ago.

- That's right, Moses! - Pharaoh exclaimed. - History teaches us how to avoid past mistakes, and I believe that one day your knowledge will help you to make the right choice that will affect not only your destiny, but also the destiny of our great nation.

Pharaoh had no brothers and sisters, only a son, Ram, and a daughter, Adith. He loved them both, but if he regarded Ram as a man and the future Pharaoh, in Adith he saw, above all, a woman, namely, his wife, who had died in childbirth of Ram. She died long ago, but a part of her, her continuation, Adith, lives on. She had long since grown to adulthood, and he continued to treat her as a little girl - with the tenderness and love that fathers love their daughters.

Long ago his daughter fell in love with the general Mahud, and the delighted Pharaoh was already dreaming of a grandson when Mahud died saving Pharaoh in one of his campaigns. Since then, Adith has lost her taste for life and has turned from a jolly giggler into a melancholy woman. In vain did Pharaoh and his wife think that time and youth would take its toll. Time passed and she did not change. The turning point came when Pharaoh had already lost hope. One day while walking, Adith found a baby on the bank of the Nile, and all her unspent love suddenly splashed out on him. She came alive and, hearing her joyful laughter in the morning, Pharaoh's father's heart melted. Maybe because of this, or maybe because Ram was born at the time and the two tomboys were brought up together, Pharaoh loved them both, and if they fought he punished them as his two sons, giving no preference to either.

Moses looked at his mother and suddenly thought; - I might have to kill her, too.

But somehow he was not moved by this monstrous thought, as if he were talking about a stranger.

An hour later the procession was on its way. From the Pharaoh's palace to the Main Temple, it was only a 30 minute walk, but what a hassle it was for the guards. Despite the fact that Pharaoh was guarded by a hundred best soldiers who formed a quadrangle inside which Pharaoh was carried on a stretcher, every 20 meters along the way there was a soldier dressed as a citizen with a concealed weapon under his clothes, and if there was the slightest threat to Pharaoh's life two more squads of personal guards would encircle the area in an instant.

Upon arrival at the Main Temple, Pharaoh was met by the High Priest and Moses went into the archives. Leaving the guards outside, he ordered that no one be allowed in. The old priest, Sokh, led him to the shelves where the papyri Moses was interested in were kept, and put the ones that the Pharaoh's grandson pointed out in a basket.

-Where is the keeper of the archives? - Moses asked him. - Why doesn't he meet Pharaoh's grandson?

Sokh was confused for a short time, and then he reported that because the priest Mow had been robbed and killed last night, he, the priest Sokh, was now the temporary keeper of the archives, and he was ready to fulfill any wish Moses had.

-Nothing, nothing, don't worry, - Moses replied, - I don't care who the keeper is.

And he himself became frightened. Was it an accident? Not of course. Moses suddenly had an epiphany and realized that someone very powerful and experienced was behind all this that someone, just like him, wanted to gain power and this someone wanted to use him, Pharaoh's illegitimate grandson, as a cover to achieve his goal. He realized that the game was on, and that he should expect a surprise any minute now.

-Well, - Moses thought, - when I come to power, then we'll see who will put whom into the grave.

CHAPTER 15:

Ram. Son of Pharaoh.

Sorry that Moses should not have come with me, - thought Ram, - his advice would always have been useful.
Ram loved Moses, and when he was away for a long time he missed him. Though Moses was the son of Ram's beloved aunt Adith and was considered his nephew, Ram thought of Moses as his brother. Oh, they had done some mischief in their childhood! Somehow he was reminded of an occasion when, driven by curiosity about the opposite sex, they decided to spy on the palace maids bathing in the pool after work at nightfall. Sneaking in, they hid behind flowerpots and watched the women with gleaming eyes. The sight of the naked women's bodies fascinated them so much that they did not notice Pfi the cook who came up behind them. They were seized by her scruffy neck and were too ashamed and horrified to utter a word.

-You rascals, - cried the naked Pfi, - you have come to spy on women. Well, I'll teach you! Now you will not only see but feel a woman's body. She began to poke their noses one by one into the stiff, hairy spot below her belly button, muttering softly: - Now you'll know where babies come from. After that she gave them freedom, and they rushed to Moses' room, where they thought at length how they could escape punishment in case Pfi told everything to Pharaoh.

He drove the unpleasant memory away and Ram admired the majesty of the glittering pyramids in the distance. The Pharaohs who had built them had glorified themselves forever, but his father had built himself a humble tomb. Ram was there with his father when the workmen, guided by the priests, finished its construction. Nothing great! How could one compare this deep down cave with the great pyramids, with these cascades of stone blocks arranged in a beautiful shape!

Suddenly a brilliant but frightening idea came into Ram's mind. He twisted his head, as if he feared that someone might read his sinful thoughts. The alarmed guards began to look around for the object that had frightened the Pharaoh's son, but there was no one around. - I must discuss it with my father, - thought Ram, - and however wild and immoral my suggestion may seem, he must understand me.

CHAPTER 15:

The Death of Egypt

For some months now there had been excitement in the Main Temple: Pharaoh had decided to begin the construction of the dam, and almost all the priests were busy working on the project. Necessary calculations were made, the terrain was surveyed, drawings were made, models of such complex units were made, and locks were designed. Maybe that's why students weren't given enough of a learning curve and studied only until lunchtime, spending the rest of the time wherever they were assigned to serve.

Nain was assigned to work in the archives in place of the murdered Mow. The old priest Sokh had to teach Nain all the intricacies of record-keeping and papyrus preservation, and if Nain will pass the exam in due time and received the title of priest; he would probably stay in the archives for the rest of his life.

The first days Nain spent in the temple was the most painful for him and he almost went crazy from the separation from Fooige. He dreamt about her almost every night. Gradually, he began to get used to life without her, his parents and friends. Thanks to his earlier education and his work as a scribe in his father's office, science was relatively easy for him. Of course, there was a completely different level of knowledge and sciences that he had never heard of before: astronomy, and anatomy and more. But Nain especially liked the history of Egypt. When he read the papyri, which were thousands of years old, he was in awe. He imagined people in those distant times and it seemed incredible to Nain that people were the same as they are today: working, fighting, loving. It turned out that time doesn't change people and more than a thousand years would pass and people would remain the same.

Today, as he read the old papyrus, Nain was seized with terror. It was as if he could hear the hoarse voice of the priest who had written this terrible story.

Egypt, Great Egypt was dead.
There were only a handful of people left alive.
It's been 40 years since the Nile spill out last time.
Where is this great river? Nile is gone.
This is a pitiful stream instead of the Nile.
The gods have turned their backs on us.
There is nothing to feed the children and the people have killed
Them. People eat people.

The papyrus was very old, and part of it had been torn off. The torn part was not preserved, and it was not known what had happened in those distant days.

- Did it really happen? - Nain asked the old Sokh.

- Yes, Nain, there have been several such tragedies in the history of Egypt.

- What if it happens again?

Sokh shrugged his shoulders and answered: "I am sure of it, for history teaches us that everything in our lives repeats itself. Life moves in a circle, repeating and repeating itself with more tragic consequences.

- So this is why Pharaoh decided to build his dam. He doesn't want the people of Egypt to suffer, - Nain said, and immediately asked the question, ah - why didn't the gods help Egypt and the people, but Sokh? After all, they can do everything, they are so great and nothing is impossible for them. How could they let people die, and it's as if they didn't see their suffering? Did they not shed a single tear as they watched the death of children?

- You will know and understand later," Sokh answered him thoughtfully. - You have much to learn, Nain. You will read that not only

Egypt was dying of hunger and disease. Other countries suffered just as much and the gods never helped them. Never, Nain!

- Why?

- Study, son, and you'll understand. And first, do you know how God formed the world? Come, I'll show you the shelf where the very old papyri are kept.

With these words, Sokh led Nain through a long room of archives, whose walls were lined with shelves with compartments.

- How do you know where the papyrus you want is kept? - Nain asked. - After all, there are thousands of them here.

- You'll soon find out, - Sokh answered, - that they are arranged in a certain order. For example, if you wanted a papyrus from the time of Pharaoh Cheops you would find the sign for Pharaoh and then the sign for CH. Then Nain noticed that all the shelves were signed with different signs and by reading them you could easily find your way through the great number of papyri.

Leading Nain to the shelf with the sign *Earth*, Sokh handed Nain a decent-sized papyrus:

- Moses, the grandson of Pharaoh, ordered himself a copy of this document. Apparently he is also interested in the history of the formation of our world. This is a very important document. Do you see this badge? - All the papyrus with that mark has no value and must not be taken out of this room. Nain took the papyrus handed to him and thought that being a priest wasn't so bad. At least there were things he could learn here that he never would have known if he had worked in his father's office.

After fixing the candle, Nain began to read, and the more he read, the more he was amazed at the story told on the old papyrus!

CHAPTER 17:

The Beginning of Everything[1]

In the beginning God created the Universe and the Earth, but the Earth was a cloud of smoke, and God flew around it until the smoke turned into a shell of stone.

And God said, "Let there be light," and he turned into the sun, into God Ra, and the Earth swirled around him, and day began to change into night. And God spent one day on it.

-Only one day! - Nain exclaimed, astonished, but Sokh smiled and said, "Keep reading son, and you'll see that God took only six days to form all that is on the Earth now.

-Only six days?

-Yes, but no one knows how much time one day held: 24 hours, like now, a thousand hours, a million millions. God didn't tell us that. Keep reading.

Then God said: - Let Earthly firmament be in the midst of the waters: and let her separate the waters from the waters. And he created Earthly firmament; and he divided the waters that are Earthly firmament from the waters that are under Earthly firmament. And God called Earthly firmament the sky.

Day two.

- Nothing makes sense, - said Nain, and looked questioningly at Sokh.

- Oh, how nimble Nain is, - he laughed, - you want to understand from the first time what the priests have been arguing about for centuries. Well, look, I'll try to explain it to you.

- After God formed the earth from the smoke, it was very hot, and steam began to come out of it, like from a cauldron when water boils in it. This steam rose above the earth and formed the sky above our heads. Another part of the steam turned into water and covered the whole earth.

- How simple and clear you make it sound, - Nain said in a satisfied voice and began to read more.

Then God said: - Let the waters under the heavens gather into one place and let the dry land appear, and so it was. And God called the dry land, and called the assembly of waters the sea.

And God said, Let the earth grow green herbs and trees, and so it became.

The third day.

And God created a small light to guide the night, and the stars.

Day four.

Then God said: - Let the waters give birth to reptiles, the souls of the living: and let the birds fly over the earth in the sky.

Day five.

- So life on earth originated in the sea-ocean of Sokh?

- You're not such a foolish pupil of the priest, - he smiled, - go on.

And God said, 'Let the Earth produce animals according to their kind, cattle and let us make man in our image, after our likeness: and let them have dominion over all the earth. And God created man, male and female, and blessed them, and said unto them, be fruitful and multiply, and fill up the whole earth.

Day Six.

-Was the first man an Egyptian? - Nain asked?

-I don't know. It was so long ago that no one remembers. Though an old papyrus claims, that life for the first people on earth began on the banks of the great rivers Tigris and Euphrates. Now let's go to bed, for tomorrow we will continue reading the old papyri.

1. The author gives his interpretation of the Genesis chapter of the Bible.

CHAPTER 18:

Father and Son

Pharaoh's son Ram, the successor in power and tradition of Egypt, was confused. He, the future Pharaoh conceived of a cause that outlawed him.

Pharaoh's entire power was based on the army, officials, and priests. The power of the priests, in turn, rested on faith in the gods and adherence to the religious traditions of the ancestors. These traditions prescribed that the tombs of the dead pharaohs be guarded like the apple of their eyes, and that anyone who trespassed on the peace of the dead pharaohs be punished by death. The tombs were sacred and inviolable! At the slightest hint of sacrilege any person would be put to death.

Once Ram was present at the execution of three tomb robbers who were not only hanged but their bodies were cut into little pieces and thrown into the fire. No one had the right to touch these relics, no one ever!

And he, Pharaoh's son, was determined to break this eternal and inviolable law of Egypt! And he decided not just to touch the shrines; he decided to destroy the pyramids to the ground!

Oh, gods! What his father would tell him, what the priests would tell him, what the people would say!

This crazy thought came to him when he went to choose a place for the dam, and it had been haunting him ever since. Then, looking at the great number of stone blocks stacked in the pyramids, he thought,

"What if the stone blocks of the pyramids were used as building material to build a dam across the Nile? It was a monstrous idea, destructive for religion and traditions, and no matter he was a son of Pharaoh, he would have been beheaded for it. But, it is a genius idea, and only divine providence can explain its realization in his head. How should it be?

Ram, speaking to his father, began from afar.

- Father, he said, "I have found a solution which will help us reduce the time needed to build the dam from forty to twenty years. This solution will help us to make the country truly great without much effort.

At his son's words Pharaoh stood stunned and looked intently at Ram as if he was seeing him for the first time. He was silent, and his eyes changed from amazement to pride and love. What he had dreamed of had happened! His son had grown to the point where he could assume power and serve the country for the benefit of the people.

But Ram's next words struck him just as much and shocked him.

-You know, father, that the chief problem in construction is the problem of quarrying and delivery of the stone blocks. I propose, - he paused, and Pharaoh waited impatiently for what he would say. - I propose that we dismantle the three great pyramids and use their stone blocks to build the dam!

Pharaoh was smitten! He had not expected such blasphemy from his own son. His face was frozen and in a voice full of anger and frustration he said, - Today we destroy the tombs of our ancestors, tomorrow our descendants will destroy our tombs, and the day after tomorrow there will be chaos and the country will perish from barbarism and ignorance.

Ram was prepared for such a turn of events and his father's ominous tone did not shake him.

-I know this, entire father, and a week ago I would have answered the same way as you did to any man, but let's reason as people responsible for life of all people in our country. First, the dam will serve Egypt and make it invincible. Right? Right! Second consideration. We, through the priests, will explain to the people that the Gods and our great ancestors, foreseeing the construction of the dam, specially prepared this building material for us. And this means that the titanic work of all Egyptian people on building of pyramids was not lost in vain and will serve for the glory of Egypt. Thirdly, we rebury three pharaohs with the great honors, and people will see that traditions, culture and religion of Egypt live, and nobody is going to destroy them. Fourth, I propose that we give your already completed tomb to these great pharaohs. We will expand it, make three burial chambers in it and move the remains of the pharaohs there. And we will build another tomb for you, you are not old yet. I very much hope that you will have time to finish this construction. And lastly, what if we built your tomb right in the dam? We will save money and time again. Well, that's all for now, - Ram finished with a contented expression, - I am ready to hear your objections, Father.

Pharaoh was astonished! He realized that Ram was right, a thousand times right. How well he had thought of everything, how good he was!

- I am proud to have such a son," he said excitedly and clapped his hands together.

Pharaoh ordered to the servant who appeared: - Bring the Chief priest to me immediately.

CHAPTER 19:

The Capital

Moses, frightened by the death of the priest Mow, could not calm down for a long time. But gradually he began to regard what had happened as an insignificant episode, and it was only the anticipation of the death of the Chief Priest that kept him from complete peace of mind.

He saw the chief priest coming to Pharaoh at such a late hour and thought: - They must be busy with their dam again, they had better think how to arrange the capital[1], otherwise you can break your legs at night on its streets, wherever you step, there are pits and ditches everywhere.

Memphis was situated on the bank of the Nile, only a few miles from where the Nile divided into several streams and stood on the border of Upper and Lower Egypt, and thus was in the center of events. From the west, it was securely sheltered by the desert, and from the east, the Nile itself protected it with its broad chest. The city prospered thanks to this convenient location. The working-class quarters of Memphis grew especially large. Shipyards were built, weapons, furniture, glass, textiles were produced, and the loan business and resale of goods produced flourished. The wealthy capital attracted people from all over Egypt like a magnet, and it was growing right before our eyes. It was almost 30 kilometers[2] from the southern and northern outskirts of Memphis, and provincials who first arrived in the capital wandered through the unfamiliar city, frightened by the maze of dirty streets. The shabby, mud-brick houses of the suburbs could not be compared with the center of the city, where the majestic palaces of the nobility amazed people with their luxury and architecture. Colossal statues of the various gods and deceased pharaohs were visible at every turn, and it seemed to the people that they were little bugs.

Throughout Egypt, only Ililol[3] city could argue with the greatness of Memphis, and among the administration of the two cities always reigned silent competition, Memphis defended its right to be the capital, and Ililol tried to take it away.

Ililol was indeed beautiful and with its majestic temples striking the imagination, but in industrial respect it was far from Memphis and the pharaohs understood it very well.

- I will build here such a palace; - thought Moses, - that it will outshine not only the great pyramids, but all the palaces of the world, and the damned dam shall remain in the drawings.

1. The Bible does not tell us the name of the capital of Egypt at the time of Moses, but by implication we can conclude that it was Memphis and not the other famous capital of ancient Egypt, Thebes.
2. According to French scientists at the time of Napoleon, the city was washed over 150 stadia. 1 stadia = 200 meters.
3. The Greek name for the city of Ilipolis. On the site of the city now is the village of EL-Matariyyah, near Cairo, where an obelisk 20 meters high, carved from red granite, is still preserved. Since ancient times, the temple of the Sun of Ililol was famous for its school which prepared a large galaxy of scientists. The famous Greek scientist Plato was a graduate of this school.

CHAPTER 20:

Mack and Buck

As soon as Nain found himself in the temple, he decided to fail the upcoming exam, for a temple novice who fails the exam cannot be a priest.

- I will fail this damned exam, and the priests will kick me out of the temple in disgrace, - Nain planned. It may be unpleasant, my father may scold me, but I will go home and marry my little Fooige. Mother will be glad to have me back!

Sokh knew of Nain's love and hoped that gradually his pupil would forget Fooige and by the time of the examination his state of mind would be back to normal. Love comes and goes, but you always want to eat, - was a popular wisdom that had ruined better men than that. But the exam was coming up, and Nain disregard to prepare at all. Sokh had become attached to Nain as to his son, and his sense of responsibility for this young rascal forced him to take action, because things could turn out quite differently than Nain had imagined. One evening, when Nain was again dreaming of a future life with Fooige, Sokh sighed sadly and said in an angry tone, - Shut up and listen to me! It is a secret and I cannot tell it to you, but I, will break my oath for your sake. I may take a great sin upon my soul, but what else can I do? You leave me no other way to convince you to take the exam seriously. The truth, Nain, is that a well-functioning religious system will never allow the knowledge and secrets acquired by the students to escape from the temple. You learned something while you were here, didn't you? It's enough to keep you here for the rest of your life, or you'll be silenced forever. Well, you have no choice, son, either you pass the exam, and you are proclaimed a priest, or, if you don't solve the task offered to you, you will be led through a secret corridor of the temple, and one of the slabs made in the floor will suddenly overturn under your feet, opening the way to a deep well, where there is no exit. It's always been that way - either you're a priest, or you die at the bottom of that well. There already lie the bones of many disobedient or insufficiently intelligent young men. It's an old temple tradition, and no one's going to break it. Not even for some young man in love. Come to your senses, Nain, and begin your preparations. The price of the exam is life or death.

- So be it, - exclaimed Nain, - it is better to die than to lose Fooige and live in that stone sack!

He had always called the temple a stone sack, which was built as a huge rectangle with an inner courtyard and was essentially a fortress. It was a fortress of power and religion. Along the outside walls, every 20 meters there were huge figures of pharaohs who had lived once, and it seemed that they propped and held the walls and it was impossible to destroy them.

The inner courtyard of the temple was used by the priests for solemn ceremonies on great feasts, and in ordinary times, when the evening chill descended on the temple, they liked to walk along its alleys, enjoying the fresh air...

Today, as he strolled between the flowerbeds, Nain curiously watched the priests, who were in groups discussing their problems animatedly.

Only two of the priests stayed out of the way. They were Mack and Buck. Not that anyone liked them, they were feared and avoided. They evidently got used to it a long time ago, and they were not eager to discuss anything with other priests. Mack and Buck were busy making mummies, and this proximity to death instilled a subconscious fear in the other priests.

Nain remembered visiting their creepy rooms. Once, while repairing a shelf, he had cut his arm so deeply that blood flowed from the wound like a small stream. Sokh tried to bandage the wound, but the blood wouldn't stop and kept pouring onto the floor around Nain. Then he took Nain to Mack and Buck. They often assisted the other priests in cases of various injuries and illnesses. It was rumored that the brothers reached unprecedented heights in their craft and once attempted to reattach the arm of a high ranking nobleman who had been cut off in a drunken argument. According to these rumors, they succeeded, and the nobleman left the temple with two working hands.

The brothers' room was a long room with a huge window overlooking the courtyard. All the walls were lined with an incredible number of jars and vessels of various calibers. There were three tables in the middle of the room, and on one of them was the body of a recently dead priest, and the brothers were trying to remove his liver through a small incision in his abdomen. Nain was quite frightened, and one of the brothers curiously examined Nain's wound and tied a leather cord around his arm. Meanwhile, Buck mixed some powders in a bowl, added some liquid and, having received a poisonous green mixture, began to irrigate the wound of the apprentice. It seemed to Nain that Buck had poured fire, not liquid, on his arm, but the pain and fierce burning quickly subsided. After waiting for Nain to stop blowing on the wound, Buck took a copper needle and began to sew up the wound like an ordinary rag. As he did so, he hummed a tune to himself. When he had finished sewing, Buck proudly looked at his work. Apparently he liked the work, and he untied the leather cord that was pulling the arm. There was no blood coming out of the wound. Buck grinned contentedly and, losing interest in Nain went to continue gutting the dead man. Mack wrapped a clean rag around the stitch and ordered Nain to come see them in a week, and immediately if he felt fever or chills.

As frightened as Nain was, curiosity won out, and as he was leaving the room, he turned around and asked: - Tell me please; is it true that you sewed the arm of a nobleman and he has two hands?

- They lie, - answered Buck, without turning round, - the hand is blackened and rotten, and had to be cut off. Unfortunately, we have no tools for such delicate work. But that's all right, we'll do it. If you cut your hand off, we sew it back on, won't we, Mack?

- Sure, - Mack smiled as he looked at Nain's frightened face.

...The wound healed quickly, and Nain bowed respectfully to the brothers as he walked past them, chatting excitedly.

CHAPTER 21:

The World Flood

A woe happened in Egypt, the bull Apis died. Each temple contained a sacred animal that was the temple's guardian god. It could be a lion, a cobra, a hare, a cat, a crocodile, but the main sacred animal for all Egyptians was a black bull with a white star on his forehead, Apis. He lived of course in the main temple and was cared for like a pharaoh. And then yesterday, suddenly, without being sick, Apis the bull passes away. All Egypt shuddered; the death of Apis, according to the deep conviction of all, foreshadowed great misfortune for the whole state. Throughout Egypt the priests began to choose a black calf to be the chief sacred animal, and Mac and Buck proceeded to mummify the dead bull, whom Nain and a group of priests could barely lift onto the table in their room.

After supper, Nain hurried to the archives. Sokh had promised to show him an interesting document about a great tragedy that had played out in a distant overseas country many years before. In the archives he found Sokh laughing merrily across the room.

- You're out of your mind, - Nain snapped at him, - everybody's grieving for Apis, and you're having fun!

-Oh, ha-ha -ha- the priest wouldn't let up, - Nain, read anecdotes from the time the Cheops pyramid was built, and they'll make you laugh. Listen to one of them:

Workers building the pyramid are talking.

- What's up? Why all the pomp and circumstance about?

- The servants brought Pharaoh to see how the work on his tomb was progressing

- Are they rehearsing a funeral?

Nain rolled with laughter, and Sokh, with a gurgle in his throat, howled from laugh.

- Where did you get that, - said Nain, looking cautiously at the door, - the jokes like that can get you in trouble, don't they?

- Anecdotes are folk wisdom and clever pharaohs ordered them to be collected all over Egypt. They read them, they laughed, and maybe, of course, they were outraged. But after thinking about the folk wisdom, they drew conclusions.

- Is it true that now, after the death of Apis, Egypt is in for misfortune, - asked Nain, who had calmed down, - the bull did wrap his horns. Everybody is talking about God's punishment for our country.

- Don't mind him, - Sokh answered, - a bull is a bull, and misfortunes don't depend on him. It's a big country, and a lot of tragic things happen every year: sometimes the dike bursts and a lot of people drown, sometimes there's a big fire, or some other misfortune. Take the famous palace soothsayers. Everyone is surprised, and Pharaoh is among them: how could they predict a big disaster a year or two before it happened. Pharaoh listens to them and rewards them, but in fact they are charlatans, but clever charlatans. They speak their predictions in such incomprehensible language, so convoluted, that almost any tragic event can be attributed to this prediction, and there are always more than enough tragic events. It is even possible to predict historical events, and with great accuracy. For instance, I can predict that the glorious city of Memphis will be gone in many years.

- How so? - Nain wondered, - where will it go? Fall into the underground?

Sokh stood up and like a magician, making a smart and mysterious face with sorrow in his voice howled: - woe to thee, glorious city, and woe. I see you dying, I see you no longer on this earth.

After the howling, the soothsayer became Sokh again and said: - Nain, in many years in the world surely, any city will die, and everyone will think that I am a great soothsayer. If it happens to Memphis, everyone will think I told about Memphis, and if trouble happens to another city, they will think I told about it. Although, about our capital city, Memphis, I can definitely say that it will disappear from the face of the earth. You want to ask why? It's simple, Nain, you know the former capital of Egypt, the city of Thebes, which many years ago flourished as Memphis now flourishes. But today Thebes is dying, and soon there will be nothing left of this city. There was a city, but it's gone! And trade was to blame. Merchant ships would come to Egypt from other countries and moor in the port of Memphis because it was closer to the sea. But, in time, people will build another port closer to the sea, and then it will be Memphis' turn to die. Simple, isn't it?

The astonished Nain was silent, while Sokh unfolded an old papyrus and spoke, - Here is a document where a priest sent to see other countries has written down a terrible story that happened many years ago. You do not know the old Egyptian language, so I will read to you, and you listen and think.

In the beginning of the narration, the priest tells that at the request of Pharaoh he sailed with his merchants across the Great Sea[1] to the countries situated on the shores of another sea, which people call the Black Sea, where he heard this amazing story. And God created a beautiful valley north of the Great Sea. There never was such a valley on earth, nor will there ever be again. It stretched for hundreds of kilometers from north to south and hundreds of kilometers from west to east, and in the center of it was a huge freshwater lake. And the climate of that wonderful valley was ideal for human habitation. It was warm, but not hot and not dry. Plant a dry branch here and it would sprout! People built beautiful palaces there, created astounding works of art, and it seemed a little more time, and people would reach perfection. But the god, dissatisfied with the merry clamor of the people who kept him awake, decided to punish them, and created a great earthquake that destroyed the natural dam that separates the valley from the Great Sea, and the water from the Great Sea fell on the people who lived in that wonderful valley, sweeping away everything in its path. No one survived, and only one man named Noah[2] saved himself and his family with a raft made of Gofer wood[3]. So a new sea was formed, and in memory of this black period of history, people called it the Black Sea.

Nain became frightened. He imagined the people scrambling to escape the rising waters, their terror, and helplessness and despair as they climbed onto the roofs of buildings with children in their arms in the hope that the water would stop its ascent. They begged God to save them, but he only watched indifferently as the people and their children drowned.

Nain wanted to ask Sokh why God had not helped the people, but, frightened by his hunch, he wished him good night and wandered off to sleep.

1. The Great Sea is the biblical name for the Mediterranean Sea.
2. Noah is a biblical hero. The Bible. Genesis. Chapters 5-10.
3. Gofer is the name of the tree from which Noah built his ark. The Bible. Gen.6.14

From the author. Gofer, this is an old Armenian word and means poplar. According to the Bible, Noah's ark at the end of the flood docked on Mount Ararat. The Bible.Gen.8:4, but the Bible does not tell us where Noah began his year-long voyage. If the tree Gofer is an Armenian word, then obviously Noah began his journey from the shores of Armenia, i.e., we can determine with certainty the place of the tragedy - it is the area of the Black Sea coast of Georgia, Armenia and Turkey. The Bible as a source of human history has many places where the events described do not stand up to any criticism and the biblical account of the Flood is not only plagiarism but the weakest point of the Bible. As a historical event, the Flood did occur, but not on the same worldwide scale as the Bible describes. Here is why:

a. It is hard to imagine that Noah›s family of eight could have built such an ark: 150 meters long, 25 meters wide, and 15 meters high. That›s the size of a modern aircraft carrier!
б. Even assuming that, according to the Bible, Noah took all the animals aboard a couple at a time, what about the food for them, where did Noah store it and especially the meat for the predators?
в. How could 8 men service such a ship and in addition feed and clean up after the animals?
г. According to the Bible, the ark was tarred on the outside and inside and had only one window that was not opened for a year. The Bible. Gen.6:16, 8:6. How could such a ship be served in the

dark? Any oil lamps would have inevitably led to a fire. And the problem with ark ventilation? Manure gives off a flammable gas, methane, and that gas explodes with the slightest spark.

There are other serious problems, but the most devastating blow not only to this chapter but to the entire The Bible was struck in 1872 by archaeologist Georg Schmitt. He found a clay slab, written in Assyrian cuneiform, containing the story of the flood with striking accuracy and detail repeating the biblical account of the flood, but with different names of the main characters in the narrative. Instead of Noah, we find the name Hizizadra. But, this story was written several hundred years before the Bible was written. This is the problem and the downfall of the claim that the Bible (the Pentateuch) was written by Moses from the words of God and is, in fact, the word of God. It turns out that Moses was the first plagiarist in the history of literature! Even Eric Nyström's *Bible Dictionary* had to admit this scientific fact! Priests don't like to talk about Georg Schmitt's discovery, but a fact is the fact and readers can see his famous clay tile in the British Museum.

CHAPTER 22:

Poison for Pharaoh

Evening had not yet come, and the palace was stuffy.
- Ram has forgotten all about me, - thought Moses, - instead of relaxing with beautiful women as before, it's as if he's gone mad, helping his father with his crazy project...

Well, the hell with it. I'll go for a ride on Pharaoh's yacht, - Moses decided, and without putting it off, he went to the wharf.

He was lying on the soft cushions and looking lazily about. Here and there fishing boats were scurrying about, but as soon as the fishermen saw that their course might cross Pharaoh's boat, they darted away from it. Heaven forbid that they should come nearer; there would be trouble from the guards!

Suddenly the guards became alarmed as one of the boats got too close to Pharaoh's boat. The owner of the boat gave the impression that he was either mad or intentionally looking for a meeting with Pharaoh's boat. This little boat was carrying a priest, who was on deck praying to God. Moses realized that there was a reason for this and with a wave of his hand ordered the priest to moor and board. The priest was from Ililol, where he served in the temple of the god Osiris[1]. He bowed low to Moses and, invited to have a conversation, lay down beside Moses. The priest was evidently nervous of such proximity to a member of Pharaoh's family, and after quickly recounting the latest news of the city and the temple, hastened to take his leave, citing the need to continue his prayer.

- There's a second bottom, - he said in a low whisper, so that only Moses could hear it. Moses was surprised but expecting something similar. Before he set sail the priest praised Pharaoh and his grandson and gave Moses a beautifully crafted box as a gift from the priests in the temple of Osiris. The box was empty, but now Moses understood what the priest was talking about.

A wave of feelings came over Moses. He became agitated, though nobody could tell from his appearance. The first feeling was that of approaching power. That sweet feeling lifted him to the seventh heaven, but the next feeling made Moses tremble to the tips of his toes. It was a feeling of fear! It even seemed to Moses that fear had the invisible form of a real person and that person was touching his heart with his sticky fingers.

- Go to Ochos, - his heart, shrinking with fear, advised him; - it's not too late and it's not too late yet.
- Well, isn't what you have enough? - whispered the inner voice.
- Not enough! - Protested the inflamed brain of Moses, and in his head echoed, - Not enough, not enough, not enough!
- Not enough, - Moses decided firmly, and ordered to rule to the palace, where, taking refuge in his room, he found two small glass bottles in a double-bottomed chest.

1. Osiris - the god of earth and fertility of ancient Egypt. According to mythology, Osiris was the first pharaoh and taught people agriculture. Osiris had a brother, Seth, the god of the desert, who was jealous of him and passionately wanted to seize power. According to legend, one day he brought a beautifully crafted coffin to his palace and wished to give it to whomever it matched his size. As Osiris lay in the coffin, Seth closed the lid and drowned the coffin with Osiris in the Nile. Osiris died. Isis, Osiris' wife Isis, protector of wives and mothers, hid for a long time in the reeds from Seth and raised her son Horus, who, when he grew up, fought the treacherous Seth and defeated him. Isis found Osiris' body and revived him, but, having risen from the dead, he did not wish to live on earth, but became a judge in the realm of the dead. When, after death, a man comes to the realm of the dead, Osiris, according to his

deeds on sinful earth, either sends him to heaven or, if he was a bad man, to hell. Isn't he a prototype of Jesus Christ, who was similarly put to death and resurrected to judge people?

CHAPTER 23:

An Assassination Order for the Head Priest

Abram, the old and cunning fox, prayed to God. Yesterday, when he received the order to kill the Chief Priest and a huge sum of money he realized that the logical end of his professional activities had come. After such high-profile cases no one is left alive and most likely they will kill not only him but his whole family, disguising the murder as an accident. There is practically no chance of surviving. Knowing the sad end of all hired killers, Abram had long been prepared for this turn of events. He invested all his hard-earned money in the cattle and farm of his eldest son, who lived in the Median lands. There, in the middle of nowhere, no one will find Abram.

Having talked to his youngest son, who was aware of all the dirty business, Abram ordered him to start packing and to leave the city with the whole family at dawn, unnoticed, i.e. without attracting attention.

- Take nothing with you, leave everything, - he told his son and at his surprised exclamation simply asked: - Do you want to live?

- On the outskirts of the city you will buy donkeys, provisions and everything you need for the road. In the city of Tahranes do not linger, and in Elaf[1] you will wait for me one week in the tavern of Bahmut. If by the end of the scheduled period I do not appear, then I have been killed. You would buy cattle and move to the brother. With these words he took out a leather sack full of gold from under the bed and threw it on the table.

- Take care of the money from the thieves. Don't let your woman scream, or she'll raise a howl in the whole street. The slightest noise and they'll kill us in a jiffy.

Then Abram sent his grandson after Hosea, ordering him to find him, no matter what pub he was in. In less than an hour Hosea showed up at the shop, delighted at his timely earnings. Hosea, after all, had run out of money, and he was eager to work.

So, Hosea, - old Abram murmured; - as always here is half the money due to you, the rest after the case, - and he laid out a huge sum in front of the murderer.

Hosea whistled, and his eyes gleamed greedily.

- Is it the priest again, - he guessed and, seeing that Abram nodded accordingly, began to bargain. - Then give us all the money at once, - he said, - the risk is too great, and who knows how it will all turn out and how it will end.

- A camel's tail, not the other half, - thought Abram, - you won't need the money anyway; you'll be killed on the spot. When pushing the money to Hosea, Abram didn't show that he knew about Hosea's sad end and firmly said, - I know, Hosea, we got a dangerous order, and that's why I pay so much, and that if I were younger I would undertake it. Here's half, the other half after the case. You know the rules.

- Priest again, I'm lucky to have them. And who do they bother, - thought Hosea, taking the money, - but it doesn't matter to me, as long as it's not a pharaoh.

- In three days, at night you will knock at the Main Temple. They'll ask you what you want. You'll say you've come to pray to God and that you're from the city of Ililol. That's the password. And then you do as you're told. - That's all, and don't forget to pick up the other half after the case, - Abram joked.

A feeling of unease did not leave Hosea all the way home. He had been paid too much money and if he well to invest, he could give up this dangerous business. Hosea knew that he was deceiving himself, and that he could not quit his trade, however much he wanted to. He, like old

Abram, will drag this strap as long as he was healthy enough, or until he was killed as an undesirable witness.

- What if I were offered to take out Pharaoh? - He wondered, - would I do it? Too dangerous! Too damn dangerous! But maybe that's the beauty of this case? Not everybody can do it, and you can earn enough money to go to the pubs for ten years. Perhaps I would have taken on such a case, - he thought confidently. If Pharaoh is mortal, he could kill him.

Obeying his instinct, Hosea decided to bury the money in a safe place away from home. Just in case.

1. Elaf is a city on the Red Sea coast, the modern city of Eilat, a major Israeli port.

CHAPTER 24:

Exam

Sokh was very worried. Nain has an exam tomorrow. Could he cope with the task? Grumpy Sokh moved through the archives and looked anxiously at Nain, who did not seem the least bit worried about the result of tomorrow's test. Finally scolding himself that he was only depressing Nain with his gloomy appearance, Sokh sat down at the table, looked at him affectionately, and began to instruct him. Nain had heard all this instruction from Sokh more than once, but seeing that the old man was very worried, he did not interrupt him.

- The main thing is not to panic! I know, the task can be very difficult, but remember, students are only given tasks that can be solved. It may seem absurd, wild and unsolvable to you, but don't lose your spirits and pay attention to everything in the room. The priests for sure to bring to your cell something that will be the key to the solution. It may be a rope, a stick, a rag, so remember my words and look for the key. If you find the key, you will find the solution.

Nain was silent, he had long ago decided that he would not solve any problems, and that in three days he would find himself at the bottom of a deep well, where he would die, thinking of his beloved Fooige.

- He will die, and she will suffer for the rest of her life, remembering me, - thought Nain, - and why do the gods punish poor Fooige? Or maybe the gods, on the contrary, wish her well and protect her from such a sinner I?

Nain remembered how, when he was a child, he had stolen fish from the nets the fishermen had set up with kids like him. Back then, roasting it over the fire and arguing about how people in the stars lived, they didn't think they were doing anything wrong. Eh, he should not have stolen fish, it is a sin, and perhaps for this transgression the gods will punish him in three days with death. For what else? Maybe for torturing the neighbor's goat when he tried to ride it like a war horse? But his neighbor had beaten him with a whip so severely that the gods were bound to forgive the sin of the reckless rider. These recollections made Nain feel very bad. It was so bad and painful that, feeling sorry for himself, for Fooige, for his parents, for his brother Bobby and the neighbor's goat, he snorted his nose and blinked his eyelashes. To hide his feelings, Nain got up, wished Sokh good night, and crawled off to bed.

- Come, come, you need a good night's sleep, - the old priest nodded.

Strangely enough, Nain fell asleep quickly and woke up only when Sokh touched him on the shoulder.

- It's time, son, - he whispered, and Nain saw the three priests come for his soul. They silently shaved his head, fed him with wheat gruel, and led him through the corridors to the problem-solving room. All the priests that they met on their way were looking at Nain with affection, bowed to him and tried to encourage him with smiles as if to say: - Don't be afraid, you can do it. They had been through this ordeal long ago, and now looking at Nain, each priest remembered the day when he had been led to this room just as Nain is now, and the other priests were also bowing and praying to the gods.

In front of the door of the room Nain waited the Chief Priest himself. Nain bowed, and the Chief Priest said: - You have exactly three days to solve the problem. Even if you solve it before that, don't knock or shout, no one will open the door before the deadline. With these words he took a boulder from the assistant's hands and said: - We ask you to find the volume of this stone, - and handed it to Nain. Nain reached out, took the stone, and stepped into the room. The door, with a heavy creak, slammed shut behind him.

Nain looked around. The room was very small, with one narrow window that only a cat could fit through. The room was half-dark. There was a pile of straw in the corner, a pile of pitas, a piece of cheese, two jugs of water, a basin, a mug, and a ruler.

The first thing Nain noted was that the priests were laughing at him. How could you measure an irregularly shaped stone with a ruler! He was taught to calculate the volumes of regular geometric shapes such as: a cube, a cylinder, a parallelepiped. If you know the width, length and height of a stone, it is easy to find the answer there. But how to measure these dimensions if the stone is irregularly shaped! He looked carefully at the piece of granite. It was a piece of granite the size of a fist and was shaped like a heart, which people draw as a symbol of love. Nain remembered Sokh's instructions and decided to examine every object in the room. - The straw in the corner couldn't be the key to the solution, Nain decided; it had been sketched to make him sleep softer. Pita and a piece of soft cheese so he wouldn't starve to death. Jugs of water and a basin - to drink and wash. A mug to drink water. That leaves a ruler, which is most likely the key to the solution, but it is unclear how to measure the dimensions of a stone with such a strange shape.

- Ah, let all the priests leave me alone, - thought Nain, - let them solve their own problem. He lay down on a pile of straw and lay staring at the ceiling for two hours. Then he took a piece of cheese and began to mold a hippopotamus. He succeeded in making the hippopotamus's body but the head did look like a head of cabbage. Nain took a bite the head of hippopotamus and ate it, and then ate the hippo's legs and tail. Nain stared at one point on the wall, trying not to think about anything. He felt uneasy and caught himself thinking that he wanted to solve this tricky task and prove to everyone that his head was worth something too. He really wanted to!

What if you first find the volume of the mug, then grind the stone into powder and pour the powder into the mug? - Nain began to reason; - by the height of the powder in the mug I can easily calculate the volume of the stone!

Yes! - Nain rejoiced, - I must be very clever.

Turning the stone in his hands Nain realized that he had been too hasty, for the priests were not so foolish and had given him granite that he would not be able to crush without a hammer, so the ruler was most likely the key, but how would he use it in this case?

Nain tried other ways to measure the stone, but found that none of them were good enough.

- Think Nain, think, - he forced himself, but fatigue and apathy forced him to lie down on the straw.

- Ah, the hell, - he thought again and began to remember everything that had happened to him in the past year, but there were not many pleasant memories, and then he began to think about the question that had been bothering him all the time - why the gods are so unfair and cruel to people? It is a strange contradiction, because if the gods created people and are our fathers, then why do they always try to destroy their children, sending all sorts of disasters on their heads? Why do they punish newborn babies with death? What did newborn babies do wrong in the minutes they lived after they were born? Why do the gods punish entire nations by subjecting them to destruction? Could it be because humans aspire to acquire knowledge and become equal to the gods? But can a father destroy his child because he wants to be his equal? Where is the praised justice of the gods that the priests are so fond of talking about? Where is the mercy that, by virtue of the high development of the gods, must be inherent in them? Where is the parental care and affection? People receive everything from their parent gods: famine, disease, natural disasters, death and destruction, everything but the good! Then Nain remembered a story from an old papyrus that told how God had destroyed four cities in the valley of Siddim[1]. The cities were Sodom, Gomorrah, Admah, and Zaboim[2]. The people of these cities had sinned so badly that God decided to kill all their inhabitants without mercy. The valley of Siddim was rich in bitumen, which was mined from deep wells[3] and sold around the world. And God made the flammable gas come out through these wells and fill the whole valley with it. In vain the people cried out to God for mercy, but He provided a spark, and there was such an explosion that a huge crater was formed in the valley. The inhabitants of all four cities died in a monstrous fire. Now there is the Dead Sea in its place.

- And what about the people of these four cities, thought Nain, why did God not spare them!

Nain fell asleep while he thought this over, and when he awoke, it was dark and it was nighttime. All that night and the next day Nain tried unsuccessfully to find a solution to the damn problem. He remembered everything the priests had taught him, he went through dozens of variations, but the problem could not be solved in any way.

How could he avoid the shame? Death did not worry him as much as the sense of humiliation he would feel if he did not solve the problem. This feeling overshadowed for him even his feeling of love for Fooige, and he had completely forgotten that as recently as yesterday he had not wanted to solve any problem at all, but to die at the bottom of a deep well.

Nain fell into a panic. His thoughts ran feverishly through his head, interfering with each other, making him unable to concentrate and think them through. He was almost running around the room with glowing eyes, or sitting on a pile of straw with his head on his chest. And he dreamed of his Fooige! They were walking along the bank of the Nile, and he Nain held her hands in his and said he would never give it to anyone. Suddenly a group of priests emerged from the reeds and surrounded them in a tight ring.

- Can you Nain measure the extent of your love for this girl? - The priest with the face of Sokh asked him angrily: - Give us your answer at once, or you will die a dishonorable death at the bottom of the well.

Even in his sleep a feeling of dislike for the priests burned Nain.

- What do you know about love? - He exclaimed, - You priests who have never experienced the feeling. I love Fooige with all my heart, and you cannot understand me! I love her with every cell of my body, with every drop of blood, and as much as my heart can hold those drops is the amount of my love for her!

It was as if the priests disappeared into thin air, and Nain became free and easy. A light Nile breeze picked him and Fooige up and carried them to the stars. Nain awoke from this feeling of lightness and freedom. Remembering his answer to the priests, he jumped up cheerfully. Why hadn't he thought of that before! Apparently his inflamed brain did not stop working even in his sleep and finally came up with a solution. If the volume of my blood in my heart is equal to the volume of my love, then the volume of water displaced by this beautiful stone from the jug will be equal to its volume. How simple it is! Nain looked around. So not only the ruler was the key to the problem, but also the slice of cheese, the jugs, the basin, the mug, and the ruler!

- What a cunning priests, - thought Nain, - they wanted to trick me like a boy. No way!

He put one jug in the empty basin and began to fill it with water from the second jug until the jug was filled to the top. Holding his breath Nain dropped a piece of granite into the jug filled with water, and the water displaced by the granite flowed down the walls of the jug into the basin. Nain removed the jug from the basin and poured the displaced water into a mug. The rest was quite simple; Nain measured the diameter of the mug and the height of the liquid in it, did some simple calculations and got the answer to the problem offered to him.

One thing Nain did not know was that the key to the problem was a piece of cheese, and when the priests, who were watching him through a secret window, saw that he ate the key to the problem, it became clear to them that the fate of Nain was sealed and death awaited him at the bottom of the well. Fortunately for Nain, the priests could not guess that Nain was a genius who was far ahead of his time and had found a way to determine the volumes of irregular bodies, through the volumes of fluid displaced.

All day long Nain felt elated, and only when it got dark did he lie down on the straw and fall fast asleep unnoticed.

1. Siddim is the biblical name for a place near the Dead Sea. The Bible. Gen.14:3
2. The Bible. Genesis 19:25, Deuteronomy29:23
3. The Bible. Gen.14:10

From the author. In this famous biblical story, God promised Abraham that he would not destroy these cities if he could find 10 people living righteous lives in them. He didn't find. I guess He wasn't looking hard enough. According to the Bible, God decided to destroy those cities for homosexuality, because, as the Bible stated and still states, all the inhabitants of those cities from infants to old men were homosexuals. Don't believe it? Check it out: The Bible. Genesis 19:4, 5. Unbelievable! Even more incredible is something else, namely that Eric Nyström's *Bible Dictionary*, agrees that the cities of Sodom, Gomorrah, Admah, and Zaboim were destroyed by an explosion of gas released by Earth crust shifts in that seismically dangerous place on the planet! So it was just a natural disaster and not a punishment from God! Sadly, the Bible has deceived people for thousands of years. A question arises to the ministers of the church: Is it not time to clear the names of those who perished in this terrible catastrophe of undeserved accusations of homosexuality?

CHAPTER 24:

Fire

Old Abram was preparing for his last night in Gesem. He was sorry to leave the comfortable Gesem, but he had no other choice. To remain here to live after the assassination attempt on the High Priest meant certain death. Only now did Abram realize how dear to him this corner of the earth was, and how attached to it with all his heart. Though Abram had foreseen it all beforehand, he did not think it would be so hard. Truly they say that if you don't lose you can't appreciate it. Otherwise, Abram was calm and calculating. Feelings have always gotten in the way of business. Can you imagine a hired killer feeling sorry for his victim? Or a loan shark forgiving a debtor out of pity for him? If you follow your feelings, what would there be on earth, heaven or hell? Abram thought hell, and by following his principles he felt no guilt for his dirty work. No remorse, nothing. All he cared about was two words - family and money. Money is that was his conscience and his god. Maybe it was money that got him into this business, for mercenaries were always well paid. Yes! it was definitely money. Abram began his career in the beginning as a simple performer, and then set up his own business. The business flourished, there are always people around us who want their neighbors dead, and demand creates supply.

Having prepared everything he needed, Abram went to the market. Slowly, moving among the rows and pretending to choose a purchase, Abram was actually looking for the right person. After trying several candidates, he chose an old beggar whom he had seen for the first time. Apparently he's new here, and he's my height," Abram thought to himself and gave him a small coin. He was glad and began to thank a goodman. Abram began to sympathize with the tramp by talking about the hard life of the homeless. Abram even shed a tear and offered the tramp dinner in his shop, to which the homeless man was unspeakably happy.

In an hour the old beggar, not ceasing to be amazed at the courtesy of the glorious Abram, was hastily swallowing pieces of fried fish, trying to eat enough to spare, while Abram poured and poured him strong wine from the jug. Anamim, as the beggar's name was called, was full and quite intoxicated. Apologizing for his present situation, he began to tell Abram the story of his life.

- And I was a famous glassblower. My vases are worth a pharaoh himself, yes. And those overseas merchants were the first to ask for my blowing vases. Fatima, my wife, bore me three daughters and a son, and we lived happily ever after. My daughters got married, and my son got married.

- He is also a glassblower, like me, - the old man said proudly, - and he works there in the workshop of venerable Kishi. Hesy is his name. Perhaps you have heard my son's name? My health was beginning to fail. All the years I've been working, I've burned out my lungs, so I can't blow anymore. But that's all right; we'll all grow old someday. I was sad when my swallow died. Oh, I loved her! I used to run to work in the morning, as soon as possible to blow something special, and when it was almost lunchtime, I wanted to go home and see Fatima, to hear her voice. She was strict. If something was wrong, not according to her, she would come on like a hurricane! And I got my ass kicked, though I'm a serious man. But she was also fair, and she loved me! God forbid she should notice some woman looking at me, and then she'd be gnawing at me for a year. She was always on my side. In three days she burned down. She left me alone, and my son, he listens to his wife. And his wife's a bitch, everything's wrong with her. Of course, I had his grandchildren and I wanted to teach them how to blow glass. But a week ago, he couldn't tolerate it anymore. The grandchildren were played and overturned the pot of chowder.

- Grandpa? - They said, - our mother would come to beat us. Could you protect us, please? So I told her that I accidentally dropped it and she hit me in the face with a dirty rag. And all this in front of my son, who just looked away and kept quiet! Yes. I left them. I'll better ask for food on the street, and the gods will help me. You said to go to my daughters? What will they do? They have their own lives, husbands, and children. They are not mistresses in the house. Although the middle daughter was looking for me at the market. Limp Idai, who sits with me at the market, he said she was in tears. She's kind, like my mother, who was the same way, she takes pity on everyone.

Abram poured more wine, and that sip of wine knocked Anamim out. He fell silent, and not a minute later he fell asleep.

Abram lit a specially prepared candle, closed the door, and sat down on a donkey and disappeared into the darkness.

An hour later the neighbors were awakened by a fire, old Abram's shop was on fire. No one had time to do anything about it, and from the shop was left a pile of ashes.

In the morning, among the soot people found the body of old Abram, who had apparently fallen asleep without putting out the candle.

Without waiting for their son, who, as the late Abram said, was visiting relatives, the neighbors buried him according to Jewish rites.

CHAPTER 25:

The Bow and the Arrow

Following Abram's instructions, late in the evening Hosea knocked at the Main Temple. After an exchange of passwords, the young priest led him for a long time through the corridors of the temple until he led him into a small windowless room. Here Hosea found a bed and a table with scones and a bowl of soup on it. After locking him, the priest disappeared, and Hosea set about his supper. Half an hour later the door opened and the priest he knew entered the room.

- Let's go, - he ordered briefly and led Hosea to the roof of the temple.

Tomorrow morning, said the priest, there will be an examination ceremony for the apprentice priest in the temple courtyard, and it will be presided over by the Chief Priest. You must kill him in one shot. Here he led Hosea to the inner edge of the roof, beyond which the courtyard began. After the shot, you run this way, and he led Hosea to the west side of the wall.

- You see the rope, - he showed me a coil of hemp rope attached to a ledge on a stone block, - you will throw the rope down and use it to get down to the horse, which will be waiting for you downstairs, well, it's not our business where you will go. Do you have any questions?

- Let me look around, - Hosea answered and walked around the perimeter of the roof. Then he had a long time at the place where he was supposed to shoot from and the place where he was supposed to go down. After that he was taken again to a room where a heavy bow and one arrow were on the table. Hosea was good with various weapons, and when he took the bow in his hands he knew at once that this thing was good. Having drawn the bowstring, he sort of took aim and, having released it, was satisfied.

- That's it, Hosea, - he thought grimly when he was alone, - and tomorrow you'll be killed like a trapped wild boar. Even there, on the roof, Hosea realized that the horse would not be ready after the shot, and he would be killed as soon as his foot touched the ground. There were no options. Try to run? But these guys must have foreseen such a move, which means that there is practically no chance to escape.

- I'll fight, - thought Hosea, - I won't give up so easily.

He possessed an iron sangfroid, which had more than once saved him from various troubles. A natural gift to find the right solution in critical situations sharpened his sense of self-preservation, and Hosea's brain worked with all the power it could. Inspecting the roof of the temple, Gosha noted a pile of sand at the eastern side of the wall. The walls were at least fifteen meters high. It is pretty high. The chance of breaking his legs and neck was very high. It turns out that jumping from the roof onto the pile of sand is the only chance to save the hide.

CHAPTER 26:

The Assassination of the High Priest of Egypt

The priest who took Hosea to the roof wished him good luck and left. He was left alone on the roof. Sneaking to the spot where Hosea had seen the pile of sand, he made sure the sand was there. Hosea ran around several times, as if trying for a jump, trying to correctly calculate the speed of the run so that he could jump to the center of the pile of sand. Sitting on the edge of the roof in the shadow of a rocky ledge, Hosea thought: - Why don't I jump now without making the fatal shot? And then how would I get home? Those who ordered the murder would find me anyway, they would know where to look, and Abram would also tell them. If that old fox is still alive.

Hosea watched the yard filling with priests for the rest of the time before the shot was fired, trying not to miss the moment when his target appeared. Here, at last, this apprentice was being led, and the Chief Priest came out to the center of the square with a palm branch in his hand. Taking the bow in his hands, Hosea began to take aim. Here the Chief Priest dropped the palm branch, here he bent down, and he picked it up and straightened up. It's time! Hosea let go of the bowstring and tossed the bow aside.

Hosea was sure that he hit the target and did not watch the flight of the arrow. Without a second's hesitation, he ran across the roof in huge leaps and jumped down without stopping. As Hosea had expected, he landed on the slope of the pile and, sliding across it, somersaulted a few meters. He jumped up quickly. No pain, so he was in one piece.

- So help me my legs, - he thought, and he ran as fast as he could along the bank of the Nile and disappeared into the papyrus bushes. After wandering through the bushes for a few hundred meters, Hosea came out into the city buildings and headed in the direction of the workers' quarters. In a few minutes he was lost among the artisans hurrying to their workshops.

An hour later Hosea was sitting in a small tavern, where, despite the early hour, there was a buzz of activity. The night-time thieves had already sold their loot and wished to squander the proceeds merrily.

- I can't stay here, - he thought, - a raid will start at any moment. Hosea tossed a coin to the fat owner and asked him to introduce him to some local beauty. The owner smiled comprehensibly and gave him his son to guide him to a merry widow who lived not far from the tavern. Ten minutes later, Hosea was sitting at the pretty widow's house drinking wine. His legs were still trembling from the excitement, but he realized that even this time he had luck.

****
****

********** As soon as the door creaked open, Nain immediately woke up. He looked at the priests cheerfully, jumped up from the pile of straw and bowed low to them. One of the priests who entered poured water from a jug over his bent back and handed him a towel. As he wiped himself off, Nain suddenly remembered that he would give up his priestly title and that he would have to die at the bottom of the well. The mood was pretty bad. He did not want to die at the age of twenty. Maybe a miracle would happen, and the priests would pardon me, because I had solved the problem? This little hope flickered in Nain's soul.

Coming out into the corridor, the four priests formed a square and put Nain in the center of it. The procession moved into the temple courtyard. Suddenly the priests began to sing an old prayer in such a pitiful voice as if it were a funeral. Nain was troubled and sad and wanted to cry. He did not understand the words of the old language and thought: - What are they singing about? Maybe about the fact that by becoming a priest one lost the right to love and to have a family? Or were they mourning in advance for a man, which will to die soon at the bottom of a well?

The entire courtyard was filled with priests who, according to custom, were dressed in white festive clothing. Each took his assigned seat. Soch's seat was far from the path that led Nain, and he could not see his face, by whose expression he wanted to determine whether Nain had solved the problem or not. Soch had not slept all that night, nor had he slept the previous two nights. His whole spirit protested against the cruel law of either priest or death.

- I will throw myself on my knees before all the priests, I will beg the Chief Priest to let him go in peace," he decided, "and the task is too difficult for such a young man. When the Chief Priest announced the task to Nain, its condition quickly spread throughout the temple. Two evenings priests discussed the problem and tried to find a solution. To the surprise of all the priests the problem was too difficult, and everyone just shook their heads. It seemed to everyone that it was impossible to solve the problem. Finally one of the priests explained that the key to the problem was a piece of soft bryndza. He said that Nain had to mould an exact copy of the piece of granite from the cheese. Then he would form a cube from the made copy, measure it and calculate its volume. The priests could not understand why the apprentice was offered such an insidious task. No one said it aloud, but almost everyone thought that Nain could not cope with it, and in their hearts every priest prayed for his soul. As the disciple approached the high priest, the tension in the crowd increased. Everyone waited impatiently to see whether the Head Priest would raise the palm branch, which meant the correct answer, or whether he would throw it at the pupil's feet, which meant failure and death for the test taker.

When Nain was finally led to the Head Priest, he suddenly became agitated. His head was buzzing, his hands were shaking, and he wished only one thing - which it would be over as soon as possible.

At the Chief Priest's request to announce the result of the calculation, Nain held out the stone to him and, hesitating, said the answer.

The Chief Priest knew from the report that Nain had eaten all the cheese and therefore could not solve the problem in any way. When he heard the right answer, he was so amazed that he dropped the palm branch at Nain's feet.

There was a mournful silence.

Sokh was petrified when he saw the Chief Priest drop the branch at Nain's feet.

-How come, my son? - He whispered, realizing that Nain's fate was sealed and that he was going to die.

The Chief Priest, having come to his senses, quickly bent down and grabbed a branch and raised it high above his head.

And then the whole courtyard rumbled like an awakened beehive. The priests, always sober, cheered as if they were boys. It was as if everyone had gone mad, and Sokh was crying unashamedly.

In the midst of everyone's jubilation, no one noticed how the Chief Priest swayed and began to fall, pierced by an arrow from some unknown direction. The people who were closest to the High Priest were taken aback and just turned their heads in perplexity looking for the person who was shooting from the bow, and only Nain didn't understand anything, mechanically rushed forward and picked up the falling priest.

There was confusion. Suddenly, as if from the ground, guards started pushing everyone to the center of the courtyard. Mack and Buck ran up and began to examine the head wound that was resting on Nain's lap. The poor man was still alive, though the arrow had struck him squarely in the heart. It shuddered, repeating the beats of the priest's heart, and the red stain of blood was rapidly increasing on the priest's robe.

Mack and Buck ordered body of priest to be placed on a stretcher and carried to their room.

-You help us, - Mack ordered Nain, and began shouting at the men carrying the stretcher on which they had placed the priest: - Faster, cripples, faster!

CHAPTER 27:

Heart Surgery

The porters carried the priest into Mack and Buck's room and paused in indecision. Mack ordered them to put the body on the table, but all three tables were occupied and the confused men did not know what to do. Realizing the porters' confusion, Buck swept the dead dog lying on one of the tables to the floor and, covering the table with a clean coverlet with a gesture, he ordered them - put it here.

The Chief Priest did not regain consciousness and Nain watched in shudder as the arrow that had pierced his heart is swaying and fluttering like a lilac bush in a strong wind.

- What are you standing there for? Get out of here! - Mac shouted at the porters, and they staggered away and disappeared through the door. Buck, meanwhile, cut and removed the priest's clothes.

- Nain, - Mack called to him, - your job is to keep an eye on the lamps. We need a bright light and the lamps should not smoke, but burn brightly and, reflected in the mirrors, fall where we need, - he said and began to prepare the tools. Meanwhile Buck had prepared a potion of different powders and poured it down the priest's throat through a funnel. All the while the brothers were talking, but Nain had absolutely no idea what they were talking about. It was a collection of words and terms that were only familiar to them. They were not fussing, but they were certainly in a hurry, and the fact that they were getting ready to pull out an arrow without fear suggested that they had done it more than once. They tied the priest's hands and feet to the table, and the looked at each other and said, - Godspeed, - and set to work. Mack brought the knife to the priest's chest, and after hesitating a little, as if making up his mind; he made a long slash along the ribs where the arrow entered. At that moment one of the lamps flickered and Nain began to adjust the wick.

- If even one goes out, - Buck told him, - I'll make a mummy out of you. He took the huge tongs in his hands and pulled them apart the priest's ribs. Nain was stunned to see the heart beating in the priest's chest.

The brothers examined the heart and found that the arrow, fortunately for the priest, had pierced through the chest, but not through the heart, but lodged inside him. After a short consultation, Mack prepared a needle and thread, and as soon as Buck pulled the arrow out at his command, he began to stitch up the wound, from which blood gushed out. With a few stitches, Mac made the fountain subside, then dry up. Buck, having examined his brother's work, found it good and pleased with it, winked merrily at Nain. Suddenly the priest's heart stopped and Nain got goosebumps running down his back - had all the work been for nothing? - He thought. Mack, without thinking, took the heart in his palm and squeezed it several times. The heart twitched and beat rhythmically in the priest's chest!

Nain could not believe his eyes. It was a real miracle!

- How great men are, - he thought, - there are no limits and no limits to their abilities when they possess knowledge.

At that time Ochos entered the room, but the brothers did not pay any attention to him and continued their work in silence. Carefully releasing the forceps and making sure the heart was still working, they began to stitch up the priest's chest. Once this was done, they bandaged it with long strips of cloth. The priest was asleep, and if it weren't for the setting and his bandaged chest, one would think the old man was asleep and lay down to rest on this strange table, somewhat unconcerned with comforts.

No matter how hard Ochos tried to learn from Mack and Buck the prognosis of the Head Priest, they answered in one-liners that they had to wait and that they could not guarantee a positive result yet. Without getting anywhere, Ochos left, and Nain, after sitting on the bench for a while, waited for Mac to let him go.

- If you want, you can come to us, - he told Nain, - we'll teach you our business.

Nain nodded his appreciation and asked: - Will the priest live?

-I don't know, we've done something similar with dogs and only sometimes succeeded. But it was very, very rarely. But at least we have hope.

Stepping out into the courtyard, Nain was surprised; the day was drawing to a close. So he'd been with his brothers most of the day! It seemed to him like an hour, two at most. The courtyard was filled with priests, no one was doing anything, everyone was praying. A crowd immediately formed around Nain, all asking about the Head Priest.

-He is alive...So far so good. The brothers said we need to wait, - Nain answered them. At that time Sokh finally made his way to him and dragged him to his lair, the archive.

- Well done, Nain! - He repeated, - I never thought I would see you again.

Sitting down on a chair, and drinking a mug of milk, Nain felt weak and dizzy. Soch's voice came to him as if from another room, and grew quieter and quieter. Nain dropped his head on the table and fell into a deep sleep.

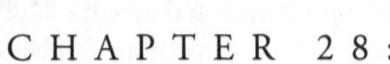

CHAPTER 28:

Moses the Chief Priest of Egypt?

Pharaoh had been feeling elated lately; all the trouble of preparing for the beginning of the dam construction brought him a feeling of fullness of life and satisfaction. He knew that the main thing was to start the construction, and then it would go his way and he would have a chance to live until that bright day, when the Nile would be submitted to people.

Pharaoh had two main associates. Like two hands, Ram was the right hand and the Chief Priest was the left hand, and these hands were clearly doing their job, bringing Egypt's triumph closer. The Chief Priest was not only a friend, but a guide in all his affairs. Even Ram's crazy idea to dismantle the great pyramids did not frighten him. Pharaoh had been thinking for a long time how to present this to the priest more cunningly, so that he would clearly understand the advantages of Ram's idea and wouldn't start protesting, but he underestimated his assistant, and everything turned out to be simpler, than he thought. The chief priest listened to him quietly and without any embarrassment of his quick reaction said: - I'm completely on Ram's side and I'm proud of your son.

The Pharaoh froze. He had not expected such a quick success and, without hiding it, was delighted. He was especially delighted when the chief priest called his son. Pharaoh was used to the fact that he was always and all around him unashamedly and insolently flattered, but the sincere praise of the chief priest gave him a great feeling of joy.

-Do you really think his idea is excellent? - He asked, as if he doubted, but really wanted to hear Ram's praise once more.

-He will be a good Pharaoh," the priest said and his words were honeyed on the contented father's heart.

Unlike Pharaoh who was concerned about economical and military might of Egypt, the Chief Priest was not less concerned about the problem of scientific and cultural enlightenment of people. He dreamed of opening schools, hospitals, libraries, even if small to begin with, even if not in all cities, but the main thing were to start this process, and it would be impossible to stop it. With his keen mind, the Grand Priest realized long ago that money invested in enlightenment and education of the people would bring huge dividends to the country in the future. Pharaoh knew about the priest's dream and agreed with him, but money as always was in short supply and he always got off with promises when he asked for money every year.

The chief priest was no flatterer or sycophant, but was a good negotiator, so, seeing how Pharaoh was moved by the praise of his son, the priest did not miss the opportunity to take advantage of it.

-Ram is well educated, and that helped him to find a good solution, - he began, - imagine how Egypt would rise if we had schools for the whole population all over the country. Yes, we... - But Pharaoh didn't let him finish.

-I know, buddy. Believe me, I want to see schools in Egypt too, but wait a couple more years, soon we'll start building a dam and I'll break down, but I'll find you the money you need. That can wait, the dam can't. Maybe tomorrow the Nile won't spill its waters on Egypt's land, and then the schools won't help us feed the people.

And then today, some bastard shot such a beautiful man! Pharaoh's rage was unrelenting. Even Ochos, who had seen Pharaoh's rage more than once, could not recall such a reaction.

Find him, Ochos, - cried Pharaoh, his face twisted with rage, - but not only the one who shot, but the one who organized it. This man has attacked my closest friend, the High Priest, my dam, and all of Egypt. He is my personal enemy and I want him dead. I'll give you three days, if you don't find him, blame yourself. Ochos was offended by Pharaoh's words, but he understood that as head of security he was responsible for the tragedy that had occurred. He had been informed of Beran's suspicious activities, and he had made a fatal mistake. He took too long to obtain evidence against him and delayed in arresting him.

- I will arrest him today, - he replied, - may I go?
- Do you know him? Who is he?
- Beran.
- What? Beran? Take him alive, I will torture him myself!

Ochos left, and Pharaoh began to consider his candidacy for the position of Chief Priest. There was no hope that he would survive such an injury. Not a chance at all! What he needed today was someone he could trust. He went through all the high priests in his mind, but none caught his attention. How could he trust them if the Deputy High Priest turned out to be a bandit and organized a conspiracy against Egypt? Who was helping him? Of course it was the priests in high places. Appoint such a priest from this vile place; coups would be a regular occurrence in Egypt. No, there must be a man of his own in that stratum of society, and God knows he was not of the priestly caste.

And then Pharaoh had an unexpected idea - Moses.

Oh-oh, how the high priests will be displeased, - thought Pharaoh, - they sleep and see themselves at the top of power pyramid, but I will break horns for you bandits in priests' tunics, I will show you how to make plots against me. Of course, Moses is inexperienced, but the grandson will take his assertiveness and energy, of which he has plenty. He's not Egyptian, but who knows? And what if he is Jewish? It's not a question of nationality, either. Do Jews love their homeland less, and are there no scoundrels among the Egyptians? Beran, for instance. And how many Jews in the army are? Take any one - eagles! One chariot commander, Ace, of all things. And Joseph[1]? Wasn't he the pillar of Pharaoh?

Ram returned. He had gone to the main temple to see for himself the state of the chief priest.

- What news, my son?

- No change so far. The two brothers who stitched up his wound don't talk much, as if they had swallowed their tongues. It's amazing, Dad, the arrow went through his heart, but he's alive, though very weak.

- I must consult you, Ram. If the priest should die, I should like to see my own man take his place, and a young one at that. When I am dead, he will have gained experience and will help you rule Egypt. Think what great things we can do forming a triangle, I – You - Moses!

Ram, as if expecting this, without thinking, agreed.

- You're right as always and it's a good idea, although I see one flaw in it. Maybe Moses doesn't want to live his whole life without his family? Maybe he's in love.

- I've been living alone since your mother died, - Pharaoh replied incomprehensibly.

- But you have me and Aunt Adith and Moses. And who's stopping you from getting married? I'd be happy to. She'd shake you up a bit. When was the last time you went sailing at night?

- Maybe you're right, - said Pharaoh decisively, - time, time is running out, and there's no time for foolishness. There's a lot of work to do and not much life left. I'm afraid I shall die without doing anything for the country. And let Moses choose for himself. Whatever it is, it's time he got to work. You go see him. He's been a bit lost lately. He's walking around like he's dipped into the water. Yes, one more thing, I'm gathering the officials for the Pharaohs' dinner tonight, I want to hear what the others think in connection with the assassination attempt.

1. Joseph is a biblical figure. He was Jew by nationality. He was sold into slavery by his brothers. In Egypt, due to his mental and organizational skills, he was promoted to the position of Egypt's chief governor. He especially distinguished himself during seven years of famine. According to the Bible, from 70 Jew people who came to live in Egypt, over 430 years Jewish communities grew to several million. Gen.46:27

CHAPTER 29:

Dinner at Pharaoh's

The news of the attempt on the High Priest's life made Moses very happy. He was so tired of waiting for the right moment to poison the Pharaoh and his son, that he had almost lost hope that it would ever happen. The fact that the Chief Priest was still alive did not worry him - he would die any minute, he thought, - with such wounds no one could survive and an arrow in the heart, that was a verdict and that was death. Well, and then, one lucky day, when he will slip poison into the king's food, two poisoned corpses will be found in the palace, everything he had dreamed of will come true.

Hovav entered the chamber and reported that Pharaoh was expecting him for dinner. This news sent a chill down Moses' spine.

- It's providence, - he decided, - it's today or never.

Preparing for supper, Moses took a long time to choose a cloak so that its folds would conceal the movement of his hands as best as possible. When he took out the two vessels of poison, he put them in his pocket, and he felt an extraordinary rush of strength. It was as if not two small bottles were in his pocket, but at least two powerful armies were standing behind him. Tomorrow he would be Pharaoh!

According to tradition, dinner at Pharaoh's house was quite democratic. Those assembled, after the meal, broke into groups and engaged in courtly conversation. Pharaoh, passing from one group to another, discussed matters of state with each group and listened to the opinions of the participants. As usual, there were as many groups as there were opinions. At the end of the dinner the democracy ended and Pharaoh announced his decision. Sometimes he took the groups' opinions into account, and sometimes he didn't, but everyone silently accepted his decision, bowing low to Pharaoh.

Just now, the governor of the capital was desperately proving something to Pharaoh's son Ram and waving his hands in fervor. Apparently Ram disagreed and appealed to the participants in the conversation with vigorous gestures, as if asking for their help in the dispute. At the other end of the room the top of Pharaoh's army was assembled. The commanders were far removed from religion and were clearly unwilling to discuss the attempted assassination of the High Priest and possible candidates for the seat that had been vacated. They were discussing the action of the Philistine tribes on the frontier. The group of high priests, on the contrary, was anxiously discussing the assassination attempt and possible candidates for the post of Chief Priest. The fact that there was no Deputy Chief Priest at the dinner, everyone noticed and speculated what this would mean. Everyone waited for the end of the evening, some with trepidation, and others completely indifferent.

Moses, flitting from one group to another, pretended to listen with interest to the talking dignitaries, while actually waiting for the right opportunity. Finally deciding, he went to his seat and, pretending to pour himself some wine, poured the poison into Pharaoh's goblet. He drank the wine from his cup in a gulp, as if he was thirsty, he began to pour himself more wine, and at the same time he emptied the second bottle into Ram's cup. He felt as if his heart was going to jump out of his chest with fear, and his hands were shaking like a malarial fever. After about five minutes, Moses calmed down, when Ram waved a hand at him, urging him to come up. He took him aside so that no one would hear what they were saying, and Ram looked cheerfully at Moses, and said, - You've gone quite sour, haven't you? Are you sick or something? Well, nothing, my friend, I'm going to tell you something that will make you strain your mind.

Moses didn't understand and looked at Ram anxiously.

-Yeah, you're already tense, so brother, your father wants to ask you to take over as Chief Priest. Of course, if you accept. You know, the vow of celibacy and all that temple discipline, so he doesn't want to force you. But Moses, it would be damn good, you'd be great to help us build the dam, and you'd gain a lot of experience in running the country. When the time comes, I'll be Pharaoh, and then you and I will move mountains! I'm the pharaoh and you're the chief priest. Yes, we'll build such an Egypt that the whole world will be aghast!

- Are you kidding, Ram?

- Not at all. He told me today, after the assassination attempt. He asked to talk to you. Moses walks around like he's drowning in water. Maybe you have a pain in your heart? Why didn't you tell me anything about the girl? Who is she?

- There's no one. You forgot me. I don't remember when we had fun.

- Life's long and we still have a lot to do. And what about your father's decision, you should think it over, it's too serious to decide so rashly.

Ram patted him on the shoulder and went to the table. Moses was astonished. He was talking to Ram as if nothing had happened, while a thousand thoughts were swirling in his head. The power he had longed for was coming to him. The chief priest is the second face of the state! No poison, just his desire to be the head of the temples. What is to be done? Should he rush to the table and, as if unwittingly, turn the cups over? But, who is behind the whole conspiracy and how will he react? What should I do?

While Moses was thinking, time passed, and Ram came to the table and drank his wine. Moses became frightened. He imagined the wine mixed with poison slowly flowing into the stomach of Pharaoh's son and beginning its deleterious effects. He felt pity for Ram, and Moses felt like screaming and howling in a wild voice and wanted to run away, so he wouldn't have to see his friend's face and feel like a villain.

Pharaoh went up to Ram and took his goblet, saying something to him. He was about to drink it, but the noise at the door stopped him. He froze, holding the goblet in his hand, and looked disgruntled in that direction. Bowing low to the room, Ochos' deputy Horum entered.

- Great Pharaoh, - he began, - the priest Beran has fled.

With these words, Pharaoh hurled his cup at him, but Horum didn't even blink as it flew by his head.

- Pardon me the Great Pharaoh, - he continued, - but Ochos has caught up with the dog and will soon deliver him to the eloquence room.

Everyone knew that the chamber of eloquence is the underground chambers where state criminals are tortured.

Pharaoh made a sign to end the audience and everyone began to leave in silence.

Moses: - Pharaoh said to him, - tomorrow you are to come with me to the main temple; I have an important state matter to discuss with you. I hope Ram has brought you up to speed?

CHAPTER 30:

That Sweet Word Freedom

When Nain woke up, he saw that the room was dark. Apparently, it was nighttime. In the light of a burning candle, Sokh was poring over papyrus.

- You're thinking of feeding me, - Nain asked Sokh in a cheerful voice.

Soch discarded the papyri and, delighted by Nain's awakening, began to set the table with the dinner he had brought into the archives. Because of the possibility of breeding mice, it was strictly forbidden to bring any food into the archive, but for the sake of Nain, he broke this strict taboo.

- How is the High Priest? - Nain asked.

- He's fine for now, he's awake, but he's still very weak and they won't let anyone see him. There are guards everywhere, checking all the rooms. Pharaoh's son came, but the brothers did not allow him to disturb the priest.

- Sokh! I saw the brothers stitching up his heart! Is that possible?

- Well, if you saw it yourself, then it is possible. Tell me how you solved the problem," he asked, apparently reluctant to speak of the assassination, "I was very nervous when the Master dropped the branch at your feet, it made my heart skip a beat.

Nain briefly told him of the solution and Sokh shook his head respectfully.

- You are a very clever boy and I am proud of you. You managed to invent a simple and reliable way to measure the volume of irregular bodies.

- And now people will use my method, - interrupted Sokh and a delighted Nain finished.

- You are wrong, my son, - Sokh answered with a sad grin, - the people will never know about it and also about the heart operation performed by two priests today in Egypt. All this will be a secret of the priests and it is the great misfortune of Egypt.

Nain looked questioningly at Soch, not understanding what he was talking about.

-The power of the priests, Nain, is based on the illiteracy of the people, the more ignorant people are, the easier it is to rule them, and the easier it is to keep the people in check. This is a law of every religion regardless of the country and the gods they believe in.

I have thought about this for a long time, all my life and I want to share my thoughts with you. May be in future the fruit of my thoughts will help you to understand the meaning of our life and, if necessary, will influence you to make right decision.

So, religion is an idea of the meaning of life and any nation which does not have this idea has no future. It will be wiped off the face of the earth. Religion, as an idea, unites people and establishes the laws of existence. Religion is morality; it is the spirit of the people and the dictates of the times. Times change, religion changes, gods change! But! Religion as an idea to unite society contains in itself a huge in its destructive power the law of total submission to the god. Humble yourself as to who you are and who God is! Take the blows of fate as punishment for your sins, do not think, God thinks for you, and do not even try to change your fate, for it is foreordained by God.

Here Sokh paused to catch his breath and finished his thought firmly:

- But there are no gods! God is the world around us! This world develops according to its own laws, and it makes no difference that you are, a tiny speck of dust on the face of the earth, a plant, animal or human. To God, as represented by nature, everything is one and there is no exception to anything and everything. The world changes and makes everything around it change and woe to those who can do nothing against these changes. There is only one law, either you have adapted to the changes of the world, or others will take your place.

Here Sokh finished his passionate speech, and Nain looked at him with amazed eyes and whispered softly: - Now I know why the gods never help people, they just don't exist!

- That's right, son! - Sokh exclaimed, and after a little hesitation he added: - Now, Nain, it is time for us to part. You have the right to leave the temple as you passed the exam, and until you take the oath of a priest, you are free to do as you please. Hurry, son, before you are missed. Run Nain home and get married. You must do so, and then no one will be able to force you to be a priest. No one!

Nain was stunned by Sokh's words; he rushed to him and started hugging the old man.

- Thank you, Sokh! Thank you for everything, I will never forget you.

- That's enough, that's enough, - the priest said, blinking back tears, - Here's money for you, hire a boat, and don't hesitate on your way. If I get a chance, I'll come and see you. The old man wants to see the girl for whom you were ready to die. She seems to be not only beautiful, but she has a good soul.

CHAPTER 31:

Escape from the Palace

Back in the hall, when Pharaoh threw the poison goblet at Horum, Moses was horrified. Everything was gone! He imagined what would happen tomorrow when they found that Ram was dead. The guards who ignored his actions at the table today would remember everything tomorrow and then! Then it is frightening to imagine.

Throwing himself on his bed, Moses howled softly. What was to be done? His head would be cut off instead of his throne. It seemed to Moses that the whole world had turned against him, and that it was a great injustice of fate to him.

At last he got out of bed, his face blackened and twisted.

- Hovav, - Moses called out.

Hovav, the son of a Median priest, was captured as a teenager and sold into slavery by one of the criminal gangs who traded in human commodities. He was bought by the administrator of the palace and placed in the servant's quarters of Moses. He was quite bright and had even learned to read and write by being present at Moses' lessons with the priests. Moses seemed to have felt all his life that Hovav would be useful to him in the future, often encouraging his servant and even promising to let him go free, though he was in no hurry to do so. Be that as it may, Hovav was as loyal to Moses as a dog and was ready to die for his master. He appeared at the call and froze in anticipation of the order.

Moses decided not to play hide-and-seek; right now it did not matter.

- I have poisoned Ram[1] and tomorrow my head will be cut off.

Hovav knew from Moses' voice that something unusual had happened. When he heard Moses' story, his chest felt cold.

- You too will have your head cut off, - -Moses said, - for no one will believe that you did not know about my plans.

- Let's run to my father in the desert, - suggested Hovav, - there, among the sands can hide not only a man, but the whole army.

1. From the author. According to the Bible. Exodus 2:12, Moses killed a simple Egyptian, and Pharaoh, learning of this, ordered Moses to be executed. Bible. Exodus 2:15.

It was these two verses that alerted me and gave me the impetus to write this novel.

Incredibly, Pharaoh orders the execution of his grandson for the death of a mere Egyptian! This could not have happened, for Moses, as a member of Pharaoh's family, could have killed a thousand people and gotten away with it. Instead, he fled from Pharaoh's wrath; all the way to the Median lands (present-day Saudi Arabia). The Bible goes on to tell us that God killed Pharaoh's son. So who did Moses really kill?

Be that as it may, Moses was originally a murderer, and a despicable and cowardly one at that! (Moses looked this way and that way, and seeing that there was no one there, he killed the Egyptian, and hid him in the sand). The Bible. Exodus 2:12.

And this is a prophet who is equated with Jesus Christ!? Furthermore, believers justify Moses in every way possible, citing that he killed the Egyptian justly for beating the Jew according to the Bible!? The Bible. Exodus 2:11. So everyone can kill another person without trial if they find that person is not fair?! Other believers justify Moses on the grounds that he killed at God's own command. These people are ignorant of the Bible, for God did not reveal Himself to Moses until forty years after his murder!

CHAPTER 32:

Ram's Death

Ochos received word that Beran had left a week ago for the Pta temple on the outskirts of the capital. Ochos did not know that this temple had an underground passage, but he knew his business and foresaw that Beran would try to escape from the temple as soon as he was informed of the arrival of Pharaoh's guards. Not finding him in the temple, Ochos simply waited, knowing that the men stationed in key places would not let Beran out of their hands. And so it happened. Beran was soon apprehended as he attempted to sail away in a waiting boat at the exit of the underground passage.

Ochos, who arrived, did not hurry to interrogate him, but ordered to bring him to go to dungeon - to the eloquence room.

As those in the know joked: -even the dumb from birth begin to speak once they are in it. Ochos had a number of excellent masters capable of unleashing the tongue of anyone who fell into their capable hands.

Beran looked with contempt on this uneducated, stupid man, as he imagined Ochos to be. He had covered the tracks of his criminal activity and calculated all possible options. Now, he decided, not a living soul in Egypt could prove his involvement in the assassination of the High Priest. But the closer they got to the household of Ochos, the more anxious Beran's soul became.

- What if something didn't work, what if Ochos did obtain something against me, - Beran thought, and gradually the fear filled his heart. His sticky fingers first ran down his back, then moved the hair on his head, and then tightly clutched his throat. At the end of the way, Beran, that arrogant and inwardly cowardly man, was horrified, and when he saw the rack and the master of the room, the huge, black-headed Nubian, he was hysterical. He fell at Ochos' feet, trying to kiss them, and, sobbing, began to tell him about the priest Maw, about old Abram, about Gosha. Ochos squeamishly pulled away and listened intently to the suddenly eloquent Beran. The scribe wrote down everything Beran said, and Ochos immediately gave orders for the arrests of the persons named by Beran.

-Moses, it's his entire fault, - the priest suddenly wailed, - he's the one who organized the assassination attempt on the High Priest. He is the one who dragged me into this affair, and he is the one who wants to poison Pharaoh and his son.

At these words, Ochos jumped up as if stung by a snake and rushed to the exit. He jumped on his horse and galloped at full gallop towards the palace, sparing no expense for the lash. The rare morning passers-by darted away from the galloping Ochos. His personal guards, not realizing anything, unsuccessfully tried to catch up with their boss and from a distance it seemed that they were desperately trying to catch up with the fugitive. This made some passers-by tries to help them catch the criminal and try to block the way for Ochos.

- I'll kill you, - Ochos shouted, and they, seeing his distorted face, took him at his word and darted away.

- Hurry, hurry, - he kept repeating to himself and his horse as he flew into the palace, but when he heard the heartbreaking screams in the palace interior, he realized that he was too late.

CHAPTER 33:

The Wedding

As Nain sprang out of the temple, like a clear falcon set free, he rushed home. It seemed to him that the rowers were in no hurry and that at this speed he would never make it home. But, the rowers, whom he had paid well, knew their business, and the Nile breeze was playfully blowing the sail. At last the familiar fracture of his native shore is showed in the distance. Nain's heart fluttered. For the first time in his life Nain was returning home after a long separation, and a thrill of excitement gripped him to the very last cell of his young body. He got up and, without waiting for the boat to dock, jumped into the water and swam.

A flock of boys fishing from the wharf squealed with indignation when they saw how some madman had scared away all the fish with his strange swim. And then Boby, Nain's younger brother, recognized the madman as his brother, raised a splash, jumped off the wharf and hung on his neck with a squeal.

As they hurried home, Boby had time to lay out that their house had been remodeled and had a separate room. That they had servants in the house in the person of aunt Zelfa, that his father now had two bodyguards, and that one of them, a huge man like an ox, Boby had put him down without any muscle strain as they wrestled. But the most important thing was that he now had a puppy and that dog was the smartest dog known around, or maybe even in Egypt. As much as Nain tried to ask him about Fooige, Boby only brushed him off, for he didn't think it was important, well, his neighbor lived and lived, what was interesting about she and went on gabbing that he had recently caught such a huge fish, here he spread his arms widely, that Nain couldn't even dream of it and that now every boy considered it an honor to talk to him about fishing.

Nain burst into the house in a whirlwind and startled his mother, who was sitting at the table talking to Bahan about something. She froze in mid-sentence, not believing her eyes, and then slowly, slowly rose from the table and rushed to Nain. She pressed herself against his chest and all she could say was, - son.

The father, coughing, came up to them, put his arm around both of them, and muttered: - Well, here's the mother, and here's our son at home.

The bewildered mother, whose eyes reflected all the warmth of the home, did not know where to put Nain and, fidgeting, decided to feed him first.

-Mamma, how is Fooige?

-Yes, she's long since fallen out of love with you, - said Father cheerfully, and pleased with his joke.

-What are you talking about, you old devil, -Malis shouted at him. - She is waiting for you, waiting, though there was no hope.

-You're a little hen yourself, - his father retorted cheerfully.

Nain knew that the word little hen could mean different things depending on his father's mood. Said in a cheerful tone showed his good mood and love for his wife, and said in an angry tone could mean his displeasure or bad mood.

Nain's heart jumped like a sparrow at his mother's words, and the blood chasing it stained his cheeks and ears bright crimson. Ordering Bobby out, Nain began to tell them his story of return.

- Daddy he spoke at the end, - if you want to go fishing with your grandchildren, if you want me to be with you, marry me to Fooige, and today. Let them kill me, but I am not going back to the temple alive.

- Why are you sitting around like a birthday party girl, -suddenly shouted angrily at Malis Bahan, - let's go to the neighbors.

At this time Fooige appeared in the doorway. She entered the room timidly and, forgetting to say hello, looked questioningly at Nain.

God alone knows what Fooige had endured during that long, long year. A sense of hopelessness was replaced by a sense of hope, a premonition of happiness by a premonition of disaster, and only faith in love, in that sacred and high feeling helped her to survive. And also, she discovered her talent to draw, apparently the feeling of separation from Nain sharpened her perception of the world, and she began to draw her vision of love like a true professional.

As a child she discovered her talent for creating, first with papyrus dolls that her girlfriends were crazy about. Then there were timid attempts to depict the world with a piece of charcoal on a freshly whitewashed wall of the house, for which she was punished by her mother. And this year it was her turn to draw with paints, looking at which her father reprimanded her mother: - As far as I know, we have never had painters in our family, neither have you, as far as I know, so tell me, my dear, from whom did our daughter receive this gift?

He was alluding to the proverb; neither her mother nor her father, but a passing young man.

- I don't know, answered Moline slyly, and, coquettishly, as if confessing her sin, but Serbai could see by her favorite eyes that she loved only him and no one else.

And so today, Fooige saw in her dream Nain, who, embracing her, said: - that he loved only her, and that they would always be together. Waking up with this feeling, Fooige fussed merrily around the house all day, and then went to water the flowers. At this time, Boby ran past their fence and shouted: - Hey, Fooige, Nain's back, - and without stopping he ran toward the wharf.

Fooige froze, then, dropping her watering can, went to the porch, but before she reached it, she turned back. Her mother, who had heard the news and was as surprised as her daughter, only shook her head as Fooige ran toward Nain's house.

-Why is he home, and has he not fallen out of love with me? - With these thoughts she entered Nain's house without knocking.

Nain's parents, cheerfully nodded at her, and left the house. At that moment, some kind of whirlwind swept Fooige up. Nain took her in his arms and whirled her around the room, and it seemed as if they were flying to God, and her heart was beating with joy: - Nain, Nain.

How many tears Fooige had shed for this love?

- Where does it come from, this love? No one knows. Or do people who've lived through it just not want to talk about it? Why does it happen that a normal person (not in love) today becomes insane tomorrow and can do things that he would never do if he were not infected with the disease? Why, life seems utterly useless without a loved one, and a man sick with love is willing to stick his head in a noose for this love no one understands?

Fooige did not know the answer to these questions, and even now it did not matter, what was important was that she loved and was loved and could certainly easily stick her head into the noose, submitting to this insidious disease called love. Oh, how Fooige had dreamed of this moment! Particularly often she imagined their wedding. She would be dressed in a white chiton and adorned with the family's hereditary jewelry. Her father and mother would lead her out onto the porch of her ancestral home, where invited guests would be waiting in the courtyard of the house. Here comes the groom's procession and this procession with noise, songs and jokes, merrily piles into the bride's yard. Nain's father and mother lead him to the porch and ask Fooige to answer the main question: whether she loves the groom with all her heart. Without this question no wedding can take place, for there have been times when the bride has been forced into marriage, and then those who do not want to submit to force, not love, shouted in the groom's face: No. Then the wedding was upset. That had happened more than once. But it wasn't about her, she would quietly say yes.

Then the newlyweds must kneel before their parents and ask them to bless their union, and they must sprinkle them with wheat according to established custom, and the priest of the temple solemnly concludes: - May the gods preserve your union. After which everyone rushes to congratulate them, and the merry procession moves through the narrow streets to the pier. This is the moment to look forward to for those who have not been invited to the wedding, because everyone will be poured wine and asked to drink to love. The thirstiest for wine, will make several laps to meet the procession again unintentionally. At the wharf, the newlyweds will be placed in a dressed up boat, and the rowers will carry them to the very middle of the beautiful Nile, where the newlyweds must throw two wreaths of flowers into the water. There is an omen that if the waves or current will blow the wreaths to the sides, the young couple will not be happy. But then why are there friends in the boat with the newlyweds? They do not count on chance and before throwing the wreaths into the water, will secretly tie them with a linen thread and everyone will rejoice watching how two wreaths, like doves, will swim side by side on the waves, promising the bride and groom a happy life.

Well, then, the whole procession got party at the groom's house for two or even three days.

In the meantime, the fate of the wedding was being decided at Fooige' house. Because of the unusual state of affairs, this meeting of the parents was like a council of war. Of course, Bahan and Serbai were warlords, and their wives, Malis and Molin, were mere procurers. The difficult, and seemingly unsolvable, task of putting together a wedding in a few hours was being tackled. The problem of supplying the party with wine and provisions was not easy, but it was solved, but how to gather all the relatives, friends and acquaintances on a weekday, it seemed, had no solution.

Out of despair, the commanders asked for reinforcements in the form of a bottle of good wine, but this offer was indignantly rejected, and on top of that they were accused of sabotage and disrupting the wedding.

In the midst of the planning, Bahan's bodyguard cautiously peeked into the room and began to make signals to him, asking him to leave. Bahan waved him off, but he kept making signs in spite of that. Whether he wanted to or not, Bahan had to get up and go out into the courtyard with him. A minute later he returned and was unusually gloomy. Walking over to the table, from behind which three pairs of questioning eyes were looking at him, he muttered: - There will be no wedding, mourning has been declared, Pharaoh's son has been killed in the capital.

CHAPTER 34:

The Funeral of Pharaoh's Son

Passions went out in Pharaoh's soul. Today even his dam seemed like an unnecessary fuss. He felt like a racehorse that had had its legs broken and had been left to die on the side of the road without finishing it. Left to die him in pain and with the feeling that the best things in his life were behind him, that there was nothing ahead, only loneliness and emptiness. From the time of Ram's death it was as if a candle went out in Pharaoh's soul and all the 40 days[1] that were allowed for the mummification of his son's body, he was in a kind of stupor. He could not believe that his Ram was dead, that he would never again enter this hall, or embrace him, or make him happy with some idea. All these forty days he had been afraid, afraid and in pain that it was impossible to bring his son back, no matter how much he cried, how much he prayed. Sometimes it seemed to Pharaoh that this was a nightmare and that he would wake up and everything would be the same, but the awakening did not come and the chilling consciousness of irreparable misfortune told him: - This is not a dream, this is reality.

Pharaoh had experienced all this once before, when his beloved wife had died in childbirth. He knew from sad experience that relief would only come after the funeral and that only in time would the pain subside and life would continue as it was, only without his son.

Forty long days had passed. Now all of Egypt will say goodbye to the body of Ram for another 30 days and only after that, he will be buried in his Pharaoh's tomb, because he didn't have time to build his own.

Today at the Main Temple, the coffin with Ram's body was placed in the courtyard to say goodbye, and every Egyptian felt it was his duty to come and say goodbye to the Pharaoh's son. The whole courtyard was covered with flowers, and they were carried, and carried, and it seemed as if Ram's coffin were floating on a river, where the flowers replaced the water.

After the thirty days of farewell, all the dignitaries would gather here in the capital, and the funeral procession would depart on its sad journey.

A hundred mourners will go ahead, and their cries will tear at the hearts of the assembled people along the way. Behind them, funeral cartage will carry the coffin containing Ram's body, Pharaoh will follow the coffin in a war chariot, and behind him the troops and anyone else who wants to walk to the burial site. There, at Ram's tomb, they will mourn for seven more days and only then lay him to rest for eternity until the gods resurrect his soul.

- How to survive all this, - thought Pharaoh, how not to go mad from this feeling of irretrievable loss.

Trouble does not come alone, his comrade-in-arms, his friend and like-minded Chief Priest died after all. It seemed that everything was behind him and his stitched up heart would work for a long time, but a week ago he had a fever and died the next day.

Pharaoh felt sorry for his old friend, but he was ready for his death, but Ram...

Pharaoh lost sleep from this shock. The sleepless nights seemed so long and so difficult that, at times, it seemed to him that the night would never end and he would not be able to wait for the dawn.

But the most painful thing for Pharaoh was thinking about Moses. No matter how hard he tried, he could not understand why Moses killed Ram. This question, why, had been on his mind for a long time until he realized that there was a special category of people, defective in mind and heart, who would do anything for their cause and for them there was no crime they would not commit.

All Pharaoh wanted these days was to catch the scoundrel. To catch him and execute him to a slow death with sadistic pleasure as he watched, how he suffered. He put a big bounty on his head, but Moses vanished into thin air. - Why I ordered the execution of Ochos, - thought Pharaoh, - he would have found.

1. According to Egyptian custom, the embalming lasted 40 days, 30 days to say goodbye to the body and 7 days to mourn at the tomb. Bible. Gen.50:3, 10.

CHAPTER 35:

Execution of Ochos

When Ochos woke up, he took a long time to figure out what was wrong with him and where he was. It was dark and his head hurt a lot. The last thing he remembered was the wild face of Pharaoh, who looked at him fiercely in the room of the murdered Ram, and his order to execute Ochos immediately.

- Eh, Pharaoh, did you really think I would want to live after your son's death! He, the chief of state security had failed in his duties and wished only that he had been allowed to stab himself in the chest with a dagger.

His deputy Horum, slowly, as if pondering, approached him, stripping his sword as he went, and stabbed the unresisting Ochos from above ti down.

So he's dead, and judging by the darkness around him, he's somewhere in the afterlife, and his soul is in a dark hell instead of a bright and blooming paradise. - It serves me right, - thought Ochos, - a blind man, not a head of security.

- But why does my head hurt so much, can the dead have a headache?

At that moment, they heard footsteps somewhere in the distance, and after a few minutes, the bright light of the torch illuminated Horum's figure walking toward Ochos. Ochos guessed that he was in his underground dungeons, that he was somehow alive. That is why his head hurts.

Horum placed a torch on the wall and began silently arranging the food he had brought on the table. Pouring wine into mugs, he finally said: - Let's drink to your coming back from the dead, Ochos, - and he laughed as only he knew how.

Ochos had spent many years with Horum, and knew his assistant very well. If he disobeyed Pharaoh's orders and let him live, then he was up to something serious.

-What a fright you gave me, - said Ochos to him, - I thought I was in hell and that the devil himself was coming to me to roast me on a red-hot frying pan.

Laughing as he did in the old days, Horum drank his wine, and in a moment he became serious, he said: - I acted unlawfully, Ochos, not by killing you, but only by stunning you. Unbeknownst to Pharaoh, I struck you not with the point of my sword, but with the flat of my sword. Your bodyguards noticed it, but I blinked at them, and they quickly dragged your supposedly dead body into the courtyard, where they chopped it up into pieces, as I reported to Pharaoh later. Ochos, I went against Pharaoh's will with good reason. Know that you no longer exist; you are executed, hacked to pieces, and buried like the last dog in the desert. Your new name is Hamat, you're a lonely man, and you live wherever you can. Why did I do that? I know that your soul, even up there in the stars, will never rest, and will flounder with a sense of unfulfilled duty. Go, Ochos, and do your duty, you know what you must do. Find him, get him from under the earth, get him from the bottom of the sea, and soothe your soul. I know you will do it.

PART TWO.

CHAPTER 1:

Exodus

Historically, there were three major landowners in Egypt. The first and largest was Pharaoh. More than 400 years ago, during the great seven-year famine, the common people sold their land to Pharaoh for a piece of bread, so that they and their families could survive. After the famine, they continued to live on what was now Pharaoh's land and had to pay Pharaoh 20 percent of the harvest, in addition to the general income tax[1].

The second major landowner was the temples. Not only did they pay no tax to the treasury, but they also received subsidies from Pharaoh to build more and more temples[2].

The third major landowner in Egypt was the Jewish community, who lived compactly in the Nile Delta and owned this fertile land as private property[3].

The Jews paid only income tax, and this advantage over the Egyptians made them quite wealthy, and contributed to the rapid growth of the Jewish population[4]. Coming into Egypt with 70 people, after 430 years there were over 5 million Jews in Egypt[5].

Of course, the Egyptians envied the elite position of the Jews, but by and large, the great Egyptian and the Jewish nations first formed on Egyptian soil lived amicably. They lived like two good neighbors who visited each other, did things together, had children, and helped each other if trouble came knocking at the door. The Egyptians, being more advanced and cultured, passed on their knowledge with an open mind to the Jews, and the Jews, absorbing them, were rising higher and higher in development. It seemed that in a few hundred years these two great nations would merge into one to form one great nation.

Unfortunately, as the course of world development shows, the two peoples living in friendship and harmony in one territory become sworn enemies as soon as difficult economic times come. These two formerly good neighbors suddenly begin to accuse each other of their bad life, draw borders and share common material and cultural values. And in the course of this division, any possible means can be used: open robbery, murder, military action and even genocide.

The murder of the Pharaoh's son, Moses, coincided with the start of the economic crisis, which led the Egyptians to blame the Jews for their plight. Discontent was growing and all that was missing was that little economic spark that would blow up the old way of life. But, until there was one, life continued in the same direction. It was unknown how long it would last, and the most far-sighted Jews, either anticipating or reinsuring, began to leave Egypt. Some moved to Cyprus, some to another island, some to somewhere else. But who is happy to see strangers on their own land? And they were not welcomed with bread and salt, but as potential rivals in the struggle for a piece of bread, so the main wave of Jews moved to wild and sparsely populated places such as the Sinai and Arabian Desert. Everything happened in a chain, first one Jewish family settled somewhere, and then another of their relatives moved there, a third and a hundredth.

Of course, the well-to-do Jews did not think of leaving the so cozy Egypt and the thin stream of immigrants flowing out of Egypt consisted of people who had somehow lost their land, people of an adventurous disposition and those people who at all times feel an awl in one place.

And the wagons started pulling away from Gesem, taking away their most precious possession - their children and leaving behind no less precious possession - their homeland. The EXODUS has begun!

1. The Bible. Genesis 47:20, 24
2. The Bible. Gen.47:22
3. The Bible. Gen.47:6, 11
4. The Bible. Exodus 1:7
5. According to the Bible, there were 603550 Jews over 20 years old who left Egypt during the Exodus alone. The Bible. Numbers 2:32

From the author. The history of human development repeats inexorably, over and over again, this lesson, from which we can draw no conclusions. The events of the last century in Germany, in the former republics of the Soviet Union, and in Yugoslavia show how easy it is to break down wood and kindle an infernal fire of national enmity. Of course, the economic situation serves as the primary ignition, but religion plays a second important factor in its unflattering role. Instead of bringing goodness and uniting the nation, religion acts as a brutal pogromer of human values, focusing not on the value of human life, but on fanatical belief in the right god.

I can imagine the anger with which faith zealots and clergymen will begin to sling mud at me for this statement. Do not hurry, take the famous biblical reference book of G. Helley, which has stood more than a dozen editions and is intended to enlighten people. Open p. 174 (the year of reprinting1989) and see what the book teaches. The dictionary states, that a people of low culture have no right to exist our planet. They must be destroyed! Said bluntly and clearly! And of course, it is up to God to decide which nation is worthy to live and which nation is worthy to live and to conduct that decision through his prophets. Isn't Hitler studied this the dictionary when he divided nations according to their right to exist? Wasn't it on the advice of the religion obscurantist's that he ordered the extermination of millions of people?

CHAPTER 2:

The Shepherd of the Sheep

Having miraculously escaped from Egypt, Moses and his servant, after a long and arduous journey, came to Hovav's father Jethro[1], the priest of Midian. Jethro had long lost hope of ever seeing his son again, and thanked God unspeakably for the mercy shown to his family. After hearing the story of the escape, false from beginning to end and presenting Moses as a victim of intrigue, he became frightened. At any moment one of Pharaoh's flying squads could show up here looking for Moses' soul, and who could guarantee anything in such a situation. But, as time went on, all was quiet, and gradually Jethro calmed down. He calmed down to the point where he began to look at Moses as a good match for his daughter, of whom he had seven, and finding a groom in the desert was not an easy task. Besides, Moses, though disgraced, was the grandson of Pharaoh. This is both an honor and a small, small hope that Moses, God willing, might one day become Pharaoh. To put this plan into action, he made his daughters go every day to the well where Moses was appointed by Jethro to be the shepherd and drink the sheep.

Moses, on the other hand, could not recover for weeks. Frightened to death by the failed attempt to get power, and then by his escape and the possibility of being captured at any moment, he had no feelings except a sense of animal fear. Only gradually, following these foolish sheep, did Moses begin to come to his senses, and when he finally did, he could not believe what was happening.

Surely he is not Pharaoh's grandson Moses herding sheep in the desert, but some complete stranger, because the grandson of Pharaoh cannot exist in this godforsaken place. Moses, who lived in a palace, bathed in luxury and had everything his soul desired could not be a shepherd and eat only unleavened flatbread.

But time passed, and this terrible nightmare did not pass, and one day, sitting at the well, waiting for the sheep to drink, he thought: - And it is I, Moses, the grandson of Pharaoh, who am far away from Egypt, and this flock of my dirty sheep, and I will now be a shepherd for the rest of my life.

Having fallen into the deepest depression, Moses, in order not to go crazy, decided to get married. He had long since noticed that Jethro would not mind marrying him off to one of his daughters, of whom he had seven[2]: - You wretched dolls, what are you compared to the daughters of the Egyptian nobles, - Moses grinned contemptuously to himself, watching as they went to and fro trying to please him, and having no feelings for any of them, he chose the elder, Zipporah[3].She was not ugly, but not beautiful either, neither slender nor fat.

- What difference does it make to me, - Moses thought, - do I have a choice in this goddamn desert?

And the days flew on like two peas in a pod, as if someone had stopped time in this part of the world, and so life became one long, long, never-ending day. Even the birth of Gershom and Eliezer's son[4] did not touch his heart, as if his wife had not given birth to them, but someone else's, and for him it was no more significant than the birth of the two lambs in his flock. It was as if he had fallen into a deep sleep, like a Siberian bear in winter and was waiting for the coming of spring, which was obliged to wake him up with warm rays and call to leave his den in search of the continuation of stopped life. The only thing is, when this spring will come, and will it come at all!

1. Jethro is a biblical figure. Moses' father-in-law. The Bible. Exodus 3:1
2. The Bible. Exodus 2:16
3. Zipporah is a biblical person, the wife of Moses. The Bible. Ex.2:21; 18:2.
4. Gershom and Eliezer are biblical figures, the sons of Moses. The Bible. Exodus 2:22;18:3;18:4.

CHAPTER 3:

Aaron and His Family

Mariam, Aaron's older sister, lived in her brother's house. She had no luck in her personal life, and in her forties Mariam never married. Expecting from love some miracle, something unusual and super natural, and of course, that love would necessarily be brought to her heart by a prince, she looked sternly at all who tried to court her, and not feeling for any of them what she expected, gave them all resignation.

The time for weddings had passed, and now no one tried to pay any attention to her except old widowers, who was ready themselves had to go to their dead wives. Not unlike other old maidens, she had not become grouchy and irritable, and only her heightened sense of justice, which had been noticed in her since childhood, had grown stronger and broader. From this she was not afraid to tell the truth in the eyes of anyone whom her life confronted her, and people believed that if our Mariam happened to meet the Pharaoh, he would not pass by her truth either. For this she was respected, loved and... ...and feared.

Not unlike his sister, Aaron married his princess Elizabeth[1] early, and his swan quickly bore him four sons. In order to cope with these tomboys, Aaron invited Mariam to help his wife and live with them. Since she had no children of her own, Mariam gave her nephews all of her unspent motherly love, and they thought they had two mothers until they grew up and loved her just as much as they loved their mother Elisabeth.

And so their life went on quietly and measuredly, like the water in the Nile, until it overflowed and carried its waters into the sea at the speed of a rabid mare. Aaron was a man of good peasant breeding, his lands were not bad, and with the help of his sons, who had grown up, he brought his farm to a level that others could only dream of. But as it often happens in our life, one day everything is turned upside down and the familiar life begins to change rapidly. And so fast that you just have time to turn around!

As it turns out, Aaron has a younger brother, Moses, who he didn't even know he had! He hadn't known this until he had made an attempt on Pharaoh's son. And this brother of his, the adopted grandson of the living deity of Egypt! In principle, this news would not have been bad if the brother had not killed Pharaoh's son Ram and Pharaoh's guards suddenly appeared in the house and turned the whole house upside down in search of the fugitive. Then they went off to his parents' house to look for him, while a surprised and frightened Aaron sat for a long time gathering his thoughts. It took him a long time to understand why his parents never told him about his brother, and the frowning Mariam only shrugged her shoulders in answer to all his questions. Having made up his mind and waited until his neighbors, agitated by the appearance of the guards, had cleared the street, Aaron went to his parents who lived across the street, having bought the house immediately after his son's marriage.

His father sat at the table and watched his wife.

- Hey, Dad, where are your pitchforks, I'm trying to gather manure, and mine are broken," Aaron asked the first thing that came into his head, trying to hide the reason for his appearance.

- Don't you know the pitchfork is in the barn? And when have you ever asked me that? - His father suddenly shouted at him, but stopped and, with a sigh, said, - Sit down.

Aaron was not happy to be here, but he obeyed his father and sat down on the edge of his chair.

- There, son, I didn't know I had three children. All my life I had two, and now in my old age I find out that I have one more. How exciting!

He could find no more words to express his feelings, flailing his arms, getting up and sitting down again. Aaron was well aware of his father's condition and didn't say a word or he would explode. Even his mother, who was never afraid of the husband and never went into his pocket for a word, moved silently through the house, cleaning up the belongings and household utensils scattered by the guards. Having witnessed his parents' many quarrels, Aaron knew in advance what would happen next. The first thing his mother will do was to pour his father some strong wine and, after he had drunk too much wine, tell him such a story that by nightfall his father would be blaming himself for his anger, and his mother would listen graciously to his apology.

Not wanting to be present, Aaron got up and left. Having understood nothing, he went home. It happened just as Aaron had foreseen. When Jochebed got her husband drunk, she told him the invented story that Moses was his son, but forcibly taken to the palace by Pharaoh's daughter. And they took a terrible oath from her to keep everything a secret. Otherwise Pharaoh's servants threatened to kill her whole family.

Amram, in his mind, knew that he had been deceived all his life, but in his heart he always believed in Jochebed. He believed and forgave all her adventures. But this story was too much even for his soft heart, and for the first time he held a grudge against his wife.

1. Elizabeth is a biblical figure, the wife of Aaron. The Bible. Exodus 6:23.

CHAPTER 4:

Nature's Blow

There was a dormant problem in Egypt that no one had been able to solve for centuries. This problem passed from generation to generation and the pharaohs of different times avoided making a decision on it and passed its solution to other pharaohs, i.e. better times. The problem was too delicate and it was very easy to get into trouble. It all came down to the taxation of the Jews. Historically, the Jews were paying 20% less than the Egyptians, and while Egypt was prospering, it was not so conspicuous, and the Pharaohs and the Egyptians accepted it, but it could not go on like this forever. Pharaoh thought for a long time about a long-standing problem and could not make a decision. Pharaoh knew the history of his homeland[1]. Whenever there was a famine[2] in the land[3] where Jews had lived before Egypt, the crowds of Jews migrated to the banks of the Nile and were always welcomed by the Egyptians. But as soon as their interests were diminished or the economic situation in Egypt changed for the worse, they left Egypt for places where they thought life was better and more comfortable.

The injustice had to end, Pharaoh decided, and decided to raise the tax on the Jews. The murder of Ram by a Jew had no effect on this decision. Pharaoh was well aware that it was about the criminals, not their nationalities. It soon became clear that this encouraged people to flee the country, and the stream of Jews leaving Egypt increased. All that was needed was a push to turn this little stream into a mighty and flowing river.

And this push came! And it was so strong that the sky over Egypt literally and figuratively darkened. No one knew what happened in the world, but at the beginning of February the sky was covered with heavy smoke, and in the daytime there was half-darkness, and then for three days it was so dark that people burned lamps 1. Soot was falling from the sky, as if somewhere there was a huge bonfire that threatened to burn the whole earth. The council of priests urgently assembled by Pharaoh could not tell him exactly what had happened. A papyrus was found in the archives, which tells of a huge fire-breathing mountain that exploded many years ago, and then it was dark by day as well, and soot was falling from the sky.

Be that as it may, the sun came back again, and the people thanked the sun god Ra, though the sun shone less brightly and the weather in Egypt was unusually cool. The assembled council of priests again expressed the opinion that small particles of soot and dust remained flying in the atmosphere and was reflecting the sun's rays, preventing them from warming the earth and they spoke of the punishment of the gods. People, who were always preoccupied with their cares and did not hurry to visit the temples, suddenly turned into pious people and flocked to the temples to atone for their many sins. The priests rubbed their hands in satisfaction over the generous sacrifices. But they rejoiced too soon! The Nile did not overflow in July! In vain did the people kneel on its banks, waiting for its overflow, in vain did the priests standing on their knees in water, asking the gods to have pity on people, in vain did the women weep - Nile the Provider didn't overflow. And not only didn't it flood, but its water dropped to a level that no one had ever remembered. Instead of a majestic river there was a huge swamp with dead fish and a huge number of frogs. Algae covered the Nile like a carpet, which made the water in the river, already red from the silt suspended in it, appear to be not water, but blood! In addition to this misfortune, the water in the Nile had gone stale. The people who had been using the beautiful and delicious water of the Nile for centuries had to dig wells to keep from dying of thirst

All of Egypt froze. It was like a man who was suddenly confronted with great danger, which paralyzed by fear. Everyone understood what lay ahead of them: - famine.

1. The Hebrew tribes of the Helephites and the Thelephians, under the common name of the Philistines, had left Egypt before Abraham and settled in Palestine, and another related tribe, Cattorim, moved to the island of Crete. The Bible. Genesis.10:14; 21:34; 13:1.
2. The frequent natural disasters and calamities of the Palestinian land were a cause of famine. For example, in 1522 in Palestine was found a stone with the inscription: - *Do not be surprised by the snow in April, we saw it in June.*
3. The forefather of all the Jews, Abraham, was born in Mesopotamia and made his way to Egypt from the shores of the Euphrates. The Bible. Gen.11:27, 28.

CHAPTER 5:

Eternal Immigrants

O h, Nain was frightened when they declared mourning for Pharaoh's son, which broke all his plans in an instant. For the first minutes he thought all was lost and there was no escape. The frowning father, said something to his mother and left, but half an hour later returned in a fine mood.

- The wedding will take start in an hour, - he announced, and everything spun into a frantic rhythm and unimaginable bustle. The wedding had to be done as in poor families, without solemn ceremonies and a large number of guests. Thanks to father's connections, he managed to persuade the priest of a nearby temple to sanctify the young couple's union in spite of the country's declared mourning period.

Nain did not know what his father had told him and how much he had paid, but after the wedding, the priest came to them for dinner for five days, and each time he got drunk to start feeling sorry for themselves. Weeping he repeated and repeated the story of his first and last love, and cursed the dog's life that he said had accompanied him ever since he had been taken from his beloved to serve in the temple. With tears and the accompanying snot on his cheeks, he would kiss everyone, and each time it cost a lot of trouble to escort him to bed.

Only after a while did Nain realize that his fear was in vain, and the attempt on the Chief Priest and the Pharaoh's son made such a commotion that no one cared about his person, and he was simply forgotten about, as if he never existed and was not an apprentice priest in the Main Temple of the sun god Ra.

Fooige had moved in with them, which made the matchmakers' house, as Monin said, quite deserted, and they spent almost every evening in Bahan's house.

Nain went back to being an accountant in his father's office and, to Bobby's dismay, he gave up fishing. Now he spent all his free time with Fooige, helping her water the vegetable garden, after which they would disappear without supper and reappear at home when everyone was long asleep. Then, because of Pharaoh's decree for an extra tax on Jews, there was more work in the office, and Nain and his father came home when it began to get dark, and after the Nile tragedy they came home at bedtime. Pharaoh, because of the threat of famine, ordered to count all the food reserves in the country and organized a special fund of grain to help the people and especially the poor segments of the population. Everyone wondered about the fate of Egypt in the future. Egypt would survive this year, the accumulated grain reserves would be enough till the next harvest, but what if the Nile did not break the next year?

The first to react to the death of the Nile was the grain market; grain prices rose sharply, and continued to rise every day. But even that didn't stop people from buying up all the grain thrown on the market. Then the fish market collapsed. All the fishing businesses went bankrupt in a matter of days. All the fish on the Nile died[1] and the people who had always bought cheap fish lost one of their staples[2]. A chain reaction began and the prices of everything, like being thrown up by a powerful spring, skyrocketed. This added to the work of the tax accountants and the chatter in the office. The question of raising the tax on Jews was a particularly frequent topic of discussion. Nain believed that Pharaoh's decree was just and would bring peace and consolidation to the community.

- The new law is just in time, - he said, - so it is right.

His main opponent was the old Jew Moha, who served as an accountant like Nain.

- Right is right, - he agreed with Nain, - but not at the right time.

- Why do you think we have to wait another 400 years to enact it, - Nain asked.

- Earlier it should have been introduced at least 10 years ago when the crops were good, - Moha answered him, - and not in one jump but in parts, one stage at a time, so that it would not greatly afflict the pockets of Jews, so that they would accept it year after year. And now what? I know these people, a Jew myself, will grieve and start packing for the road. And others have already gone wherever they want to go, just to get away.

- And where are they going, - he was either asking Nain or talking to himself, - who is waiting for them there? Do they really think that when they leave their native land they will find honey and milk in foreign places? Do they really expect to be welcomed there with open arms? Don't they realize that immigration means losing their culture, their friends, and everything they have gained over the years? Don't they know that immigrants have a lot of hard, thankless work that locals won't take? Poor Jews, - Mocha shook his head, - I guess that's our fate, to be eternal aliens in a foreign country.

- But why, if it's easy to understand, do they still leave, - Nain exclaimed, - why do people leave the graves of their ancestors and rush to foreign lands? - It's hard to say Nain, maybe it's in their blood or they're built that way. It's complicated. People know well the proverb - It is good where we are not, - so they strive to get to this good, hoping for a happy life, not understanding to the end the meaning of this proverb and the ghostliness of this distant paradise. Only later, when they get there, they begin to understand that man does not live by bread alone, and it is not the welfare of the family that determines his spiritual comfort. But, unfortunately, they do not understand it at once, and when they understand it, they start to deceive themselves, trying to prove that it's good here and they got what they dreamed of. And so they live this deception invented for themselves, and only once in a while, as if waking up from hypnosis, which is their own doing, do they think about it and ask themselves: - God, what am I doing here? Why am I here and not in my own sweet land, where every blade of grass pleases me. Where every bush and piece of the earth tell the heart that they are a part of your soul, and just the memory of familiar places and familiar faces, some kind of fairy-tale grace floods all over the body, and tears come to my eyes.

But life takes its toll, a man forgets in this vanity, he ceases to understand the state of his soul, his true desires, and he needs a reason to one day, in moments of rare calm, go back to his thoughts and ask himself: - God, what am I doing in this strange land?

1. The Bible. Gen.7:21
2. The Bible. Numbers 11:5

CHAPTER 6:

Hosea

After the assassination attempt on the High Priest, Hosea covered his tracks for a long time. Now, when he gave his name, he added that he was the son of Navin. The whole time he was in hiding in Egypt he had the feeling that the ring of persecution was closing in on him and that it was only a matter of time before the Pharaoh's guards would catch him. Hosea circled around Egypt, trying to sneak into Gesem, where he had money buried, but all his attempts were unsuccessful. When one day he sensed that he was already being targeted and should expect to be arrested by evening, he spat on his treasure, conned the spies, and successfully left Egypt with a group of Jewish settlers. Soon he was in Elath[1] on the border of the Median lands. Feeling at last free and wanting more of it, he freed his companions from their horse, or, more simply, stole it from them, and set out to seek adventure through the Jewish settlements of the Sinai desert.

Not long ago, one could ride here all day and not see a single living soul, but now there were Jewish settlements of immigrants from Egypt all around. But what settlements they were! Tents and shacks made from whatever was available, poverty and squalor. Hosea was heartbroken, there was nothing to steal. So he did not stay long in any of these settlements, and soon fate took him to the Median lands. No one knows how long his odyssey would have lasted if one day he had not met Moses, the grandson of Pharaoh, who was watering a flock of sheep at a well.

Although he had changed his appearance from a shaven Egyptian to a shaven and unshaven Jew, Hosea recognized him immediately, and he smelled money, women, and adventure.

-So this is where the culprit of my wanderings is hiding, - thought Hosea, and decided to go ahead, "The main thing is to find out where Moses keeps the money. After talking a little about life, business and health, as is customary between two strangers in the wilderness, Hosea suddenly asked: - How long are you going to hide here Moses?

At this point Moses almost had a stroke. Hosea counted on it, and watched with pleasure as Moses' eyes widened in terror, as he looked around in anticipation of the other Pharaoh's men, and as his lips turned white. After enjoying the spectacle, Hosea said as if nothing had happened: - Don't be afraid Moses, no one but me knows you're here yet, and I'm not going to give away the secret. Drink some cold water and take it easy, I'm your friend. Hosea wasn't lying, even though a big reward was promised for Moses' head, and in another situation Hosea wouldn't hesitate to give him up for much less, but the problem is that his head is wanted too, and he could still use it.

- I, Hosea son of Navin, and I saw you several times in Memphis. I have a professional memory and I recognized you without difficulty, Moses, but others may recognize you, so I asked you how long you were going to hide in this unreliable place.

Moses was so frightened that he couldn't think of what to answer or what to do in this situation. Invite him home and kill him when he fell asleep? Tell him he was mistaken and he wasn't Moses and he was just confusing him with Pharaoh's grandson?

It was as if Hosea had guessed his thoughts and continued: - You have nothing to fear from me, I know what you are thinking now and my death will not save you anyway. Sooner or later someone else will recognize you and then you're dead. To inspire confidence and dispel Moses' fears, Hosea decided to go all the way: -I am the man you hired to kill the High Priest. To your regret, I only wounded him, but you ordering to kill me after the deed.

Then Moses was surprised again.

-I didn't plan to kill him, - Moses lied to Hosea just in case, -it wasn't in my plans, and anyway all these rumors about me are obviously exaggerated, I'm just a victim of someone's intrigues and I had to run away. Well, I didn't know anything about you, and I've never seen you before.

- Of course you didn't know, because everything went through tenth hands," Hosea affirmed cheerfully, - and you have to run away, Moses. With your money you could make a good home on any of the islands in the Great Sea. I'm willing to help you, for a decent fee, of course.

This was Hosea's real plan, he believed that the Pharaoh's grandson must have money, and lots of it, and it would cost him nothing to fool such a sucker and get away with his money.

- But what kind of a sucker is he, - thought Hosea, - if he managed to kill Pharaoh's son. He's a man to watch out for.

- I don't have any money, - Moses said, and it was true. The escape from the palace was so fast that it did not occur to Moses to take anything of value with him.

- I do need a reliable assistant, - Moses suddenly said to him, - and your reward will be truly royal, but after the job is done.

- In our business it is customary to pay half in advance; - Hosea answered him without enthusiasm; for some reason believing Moses that he really has no money.

The stress of Hosea's sudden appearance broke through the shell that had enveloped Moses ever since he escaped from Pharaoh, and he realized his mistake. All this time he had been pitying himself and his unfulfilled destiny. Pitying that he was floundering in this hole, pitying that he didn't have a wife but a fool, pitying that things weren't going the way he wanted them to.

- He suddenly scolded himself, "You don't have to feel sorry for yourself, and you have to act. There is still nothing to lose, there is a famine in Egypt, the Jews are fleeing like cockroaches, and the worse it is, the better it is for him.

- It is time to go back," he suddenly decided, - to raise the population dissatisfied with Pharaoh and the Jews in the first place, to promise a sweet life to all those who will help him to take the throne and finally seize power. All He needs, to hit the two main targets - taxes and land. These are the two cornerstones of any state and they decide everything. All we have to do is promise to reduce taxes and give away land to whoever wants it. And promise to do it forever. Of course, he's not a fool to do it if he comes to power, no state can exist without taxes and land control, but that's for later, and right now, promise, promise and promise.

- One thing is wrong with my plan, - Moses thought wistfully, - I don't even know the Hebrew language[2] and how can I raise the people without knowing the language? We need fiery speeches, we need words that will make everyone listen with their mouths open and believe it. Then Moses had a good idea. Even before the assassination attempt, he had collected information about his relatives, just in case, and it turned out that his brother Aaron had a well-tongued tongue.

- So what was the problem? - He thought, - Let Aaron be my ideologist and my mouth[3].

All these thoughts raced through Moses' mind in one minute, as if some illumination had come over him with the appearance of this Hosea.

- I will still be Pharaoh, - Moses suddenly said to Hosea, - and if you will help me, I will appoint you..." Then Moses began to think what position to give Hosea to get him to agree.

- Just the chief commander," Hosea said before Moses could think, and imagined himself accepting the parade of troops in the main square of Memphis on Pharaoh's birthday, standing in a golden chariot before the troops lined up.

- Are you good at warfare? - Moses wondered.

- Yes, I do, - Hosea said, - As boys we often played war, and I was always in command.

Moses laughed. You won't get bored: - wiping away his tears, Moses said, - Look at him, he was playing with the boys. So did I, but it's not for you to wave a stick, it is to lead a battle.

- When fighting, Hosea took offense at him, -the main thing is to outwit the enemy, and then the victory will be for your army, but if you rush at him like an angry bull, then you and your army will be beaten. My army of boys always won, because I'm cunning.

He was about to add clever, but he changed his mind.

- If I was smart, I wouldn't be sitting here in this shit, I'd be rich as hell and have lots of women, - he chided himself.

- Tomorrow we're going to Gesem, - Moses announced, and it made him feel so good, as if something he had dreamed of all his life had come true. Moses felt a change in his boring life, a new excitement, and most importantly, that everything was finally moving forward, and this gave him hope.

- Maybe we should go somewhere else, - said Hosea, not wanting to go where the detectives might be waiting for him, but when he saw Moses' angry look, he stopped talking.

- At least Gesem, - he thought, - at least I'll dig up my money, wherever we went.

In spite of their passing acquaintance, the two men became at once soul mates, and felt a perfect trust in each other. It was as if they were molded of the same dough and thought exactly the same way, and most importantly they suddenly believed, one that he would be a pharaoh, and the other that he would be a military leader.

Instead of sneaking out of the house unnoticed, Moses blurted out to his father-in-law that he was going to Egypt for a few days.

His wife must have realized that he was not coming back, so she gave a frightful shout. Moses was sorry for his silly mistake, but waved her hand to get ready go with him.

- You won't get very far, old witch, - he thought sneeringly.

So they set out, he and Hosea on horses, and his wife and children on donkeys.

At the first night's rest, as soon as his wife fell asleep, Moses and Hosea quietly disappeared into the darkness.

1. Elaf according to ancient authors - Elana, was a port city near Ezion-Gaver on the Red Sea. E.laf stood on the site of modern Aqaba.
2. Bible. Exodus 4:10
3. Bible. Exodus 4:14. 4:16
4. Bible. Exodus 4:18
5. .Bible. Exodus 4:24

From the author. The overnight scene in Exodus 4:24 raises several questions; why did God suddenly decide to kill one son of Moses and not both, why did his wife's name change? The fact that she, not Moses, did the circumcision suggests that Moses left them. One gets the impression that one person wrote the Bible before Exodus 4:23, and after verse 23, another. Bible has two authors? How is it then to claim that Moses wrote this book (Exodus)?

CHAPTER 6:

The Army or the Jewish Community?

Pharaoh could not decide at any time on a reduction of the tax on the Jewish community and all the peasants in the country. Day after day he pondered the situation in the country, considered the various options, and could not decide on any of them. The question was the most difficult one, and the future of the country, his power and the life of the people depended on the right decision. Pharaoh was solving a puzzle: under the threat of famine that has arisen in Egypt, to cancel the tax on the population for this year or not.

On the one hand it seems simple; a strong peasant is a strong state. So we should cancel the tax and let the peasant survive the hard times. In the future he will pay off the treasury in full.

On the other hand, how to maintain the army? To lose it was to lose the independence of the country and his personal power.

Of course, the Pharaoh also considered the options available in any case, namely not to cancel the tax, but simply to reduce it by half. But, then the number of the army and the remuneration of soldiers would have to be reduced. In this variant both peasants and soldiers would be dissatisfied, and how to balance the scales in this case?

There were some more variants, but more complicated and also not solving the main contradiction between incomes and expenditures of the treasury.

After the death of his son, it was as if all misfortunes fell upon the country at once, and Pharaoh no longer dreamed of starting to build a dam across the Nile in the next few years. No, he had not abandoned the idea, and the famine in Egypt had proved once again to everyone that a dam was necessary and should be built, if not now. It seemed to Pharaoh that nature, sensing that it was going to be tamed, began to take revenge for it, and threw all its forces into the fight, trying to prevent the people who had become too insolent.

And what was the big problem with the Jewish community?!

Of course he was hasty in levying such a heavy tax on them, but he was looking for justice. Everyone had to pay an equal tax whether you were Jewish or Egyptian and everyone should have understood that. But only the Egyptians understood this, and the Jews reacted by increasing immigration and Pharaoh did not know how to stop the flow of minds and hands from the country. The Jews were a strange people, many times they came to live in Egypt and many times they left. The last time they came 430 years ago, and until recently they did not even think of leaving, and it seemed that now they had nowhere to go from the graves of their fathers. They seemed to have joined the Egyptian nation, and mingled with it, and would soon melt into one great nation. It seemed...

- And is it worth stopping them, - thought Pharaoh, - if a man flees his country in its time of trouble, can we trust him[1]? Such a man lives by the proverb, where good is good, there is homeland, and to hope in such a man is like hoping in a mercenary who is faithful as long as he is paid. Such people are like tumbleweed, here today and there tomorrow, the only difference being that they do not go where the wind blows, but where it comes from.

Pharaoh had not assembled a council since the death of Ram, and now it would be good to gather like in the good old days: to discuss problems, news, current affairs. He was about to order a council of officials, but the thought that it would be like before, only without his beloved son, made him change his mind. Instead, he ordered to call the chief advisor and as official stood in front of him waiting for his words, he said: - Do not abolish or reduce the tax.

- Whether I will preserve the Jewish community in the country is unknown, but I must preserve the army, - he firmly decided.

1. The Bible. Exodus 1:10

CHAPTER 7:

Headquarters of the Revolution

Moses was pleased with his new assistant. This rascal knew everything in the world and acted so quickly and deftly that there seemed to be no case he could not accomplish. Thanks to his quick thinking and ability to instantly navigate the situation, they easily avoided unwanted encounters and guard posts guarding the borders of Egypt and, after a long journey, found themselves in Gesem. Moses could not imagine what he would have done or where he would have gone if he had gone without the commander of his future army.

Without drawing attention to him, Hosea led Moses to an old acquaintance of Mosha, a lonely barber who had a shop in the marketplace.

Mosha was on a binge. The turmoil and the hungry times had replaced people, and the shop, which was always full now, was empty. No one wanted or had money to get a haircut, and thus Mosha's life mode, which had been developed over the years, was disrupted for he could not live without human contact. In the old days, from dawn Mosha would shave important officials rushing about on business and, conversing with them, would be up to date on all political news and events. After breakfast and the obligatory mug of good wine that constituted his morning routine, the common people piled into his salon. Merchants, artisans, and peasants, having done their business at the market, wanted to rest and clean up. Most of them, with the exception of the peasants who came from distant villages to sell their produce, Mosha knew him well. And they, in turn, loved him for his friendliness and ability to tell the latest news in a way that made everyone laugh. Mosha knew everything! For example, if you want to know why two Egyptians got into a fight yesterday at Isaac's butcher shop, go see Mosha. He has already discussed it with many of his customers and, shaving you, will recount all the details of this incident yesterday, right down to the deep roots of its origin.

When he saw two men enter his salon, one of whom he immediately recognized Hosea, who had disappeared into obscurity, he began to sweep the dusty chair. Mosha tried not to show his drunkenness while sweeping the chair. Who would want to shave with a drunken barber? Waving his brush, Mosha fussed and told the latest quips on the hottest topic of the day, locusts. After Hosea said something in his ear, he regretfully put his brush aside and escorted his guests into the back room, which was his break room, kitchen, and bedroom. Seeing the bottle of good wine that Hosea took out of his bag, Mosha immediately cheered up, but no matter how hard he tried, he couldn't find even a piece of scone to treat his guests who had fallen on his head. Waving his hand, what do you want from an old bachelor who had a mouse starving to death in his house, he put three mugs on the table and waited impatiently for Hosea to pour a red wine into his mug?

- Is this our life? - He said, drinking the wine in big gulps as if he were thirsty, - people don't go to get their hair cut, they get eaten by locusts! It's as if the whole world had gone mad. Ask me an old Jew what's going on, and I'll tell you, I don't know. Instead of Mosha making people look good, these people prefer to bypass my workshop as if someone else could do it better than me.

To interrupt Mosha, Hosea poured him another mug and nodded at Moses to see for himself, and left. Moses was sleep-deprived from the chronic lack of sleep he had had on the long journey. He listened to Moses, and gradually he became so sleepy that he didn't care about the whole mess with the conspiracy, the fears, and the willingness to run away at any second. Moses drank another cup and fell into a sound sleep, while Mosha, began to discuss the future of the country after the cursed famine.

CHAPTER 8:

The Ideologist of the Revolution

Aaron loved the land and hated the weeds growing out of it, as one can only hate an enemy. If nights had not fallen, he would have had more time, and then he would have freed the land from these bloodsuckers and let it breathe with its full chest. The land and imagined to him to be a living creature and Aaron secretly, so as not to be laughed at, even spoke to it as if it were a dear person to him. Walking from one plot to another, he promised to water it, then to weed it. Then he would apologize for the weeds that had not been knocked down at the right time. Elizabeth knew Aaron's habit of talking to the land, and it made him jealous of that sweat-watered piece of land. Especially when he found such affectionate words for it's as he did not say to her.

He was lucky in life after all. He was lucky to have an intelligent and beautiful wife, sons who had grown up one by one, and his plot of fertile land which he had inherited from his father. His breadwinner, the land, gave him the reputation of a good steward, which is always respected, and Aaron's word carried great weight in the Jewish community.

It was a good land, I tell you! It had never failed them, and what a sense of satisfaction you get when you work it! You work from sunrise to sunset, and you don't get tired, or even a little bit, and you want to do more, but when the evening comes, with regret you have to leave your work till morning and go home.

And at home there is a different feeling of satisfaction. When, after washing up body, everyone sits down to dinner and all the food seems so delicious that you can swallow a spoonful. And the boys, his hope and his pride, shoulder to shoulder, are eating the soup with both cheeks, and his wife Elizabeth is so beautiful that the world seems so well-ordered that you want to catch Elizabeth scurrying from oven to table and kiss her soundly, without waiting for night to come. Aaron had done so before, but lately he had stopped for fear of seeing a smirk on his sons' lips, for they thought there was no need to kiss at that age.

One worry, there's not enough land. He has enough, but what will he give to his sons? Aaron had saved up money to buy some land, but then Pharaoh's decree about a new tax came up. So he had to give money away with trembling hands.

- But nothing, - thought Aaron, - I will save up more and then I buy a piece of fat land from a lazy and lazy neighbor who was not tilling, but torturing the land. The neighbor had already given him his boot[1], and already Aaron had planned in his mind how he would arrange this plot, and what would grow on it, and on which side to start plowing.

But trouble came whence he was not to be expected, the Nile did not spill! He was not such a master that he would let the farm be ruined by a crop failure. He had grain and seeds in reserve for such an event, and he had something to feed the oxen. Of course, they did not starve like other families, they did not eat grass stew, but it was not sweet for them either.

Pharaoh was not willing to reduce the tax due to the poor harvest, so Aaron had to scramble like a beetle to get the damn tax due. They did everything they could think of and do with their sons to make money. In the beginning, Aaron set up a brick factory, but it went bust. There was never enough straw[2] to support livestock in Egypt after the threshing process, much less bricks. And who needed bricks when there was nothing to eat. They extracted seaweed from the Nile to feed the cattle, dug wells and tried many other things to get by in these harsh times.

Everyone waited for July what would happen to the Nile. To the great joy of all Egypt, in its due time, the Nile spilled over with water as full as it had been in good years.

Unfortunately for Egypt, a hailstorm fell. Where it came from is unknown; some people have never seen it in all their lives. So it beat winter barley and flax[3]. Fortunately for Aaron, their neighborhood was spared the hail.

- Now the neighbor's land is in my pocket, - Aaron thought.

Yay! Aaron rejoiced over someone else's grief, foreseeing that barley and flax prices would skyrocket and bring him fabulous profits. But apparently it is a great sin to rejoice in the sorrow of others, and God punished Aaron for it, as well as all Egypt. A second plague came upon the country - the locusts[4]. Within a few days, the voracious creatures had devoured everything that grew, including the grass. Because of the lack of food, the livestock was put to death[5]. It was a collapse. The people were terrified, a time of great trial was approaching, and they did not know how to survive, how not to descend into that bestial state when a hungry man turns into a beast capable of tearing apart anyone, including his fellow man.

Aaron almost had a stroke. As if he did not realize that there is no escape from so many locusts, he ran about his field trying to save his crops. In a kind of madness, Aaron crushed the locusts with his hands, trampled them with his feet and even used his teeth. It was all in vain. Now he could not look at his fields without crying, and he spent all day in the barn doing various trifles to keep him from going mad. The barn was empty; a few days ago, he had ordered his sons to slaughter the oxen. There was no fodder, and they were going to die out anyway. He couldn't lay his hands on the oxen, which he loved and cherished probably as much as he cherished his children.

Aaron's face turned black and he walked around angry, looking for a reason to nag him, but his household knew it and tried to keep out of his sight.

-We shall not die of hunger, - thought Aaron, rummaging in the barn like a beetle in dung, - we shall catch crocodiles, and eat them at the very least, but where shall we get the money for the tax? The thought of having to sell his land to Pharaoh to pay the tax made his life unbearable. To him, who knew every hillock of his land, abundantly watered with sweat, the thought meant death. He rose and fell asleep thinking only of this, and for him everything else ceased to exist. The night before yesterday, seeing how he was suffering, and to distract him for a moment from his damn care, Elisabeth tried to caress him, but he old fool sharply pushed her away and shouted to the whole house: - Have you lost your mind, have you found no other time to do this nonsense! His wife was offended, and he spent the next day thinking about it, cursing and chiding himself for his lack of restraint. Trying to make amends, he tried to embrace her, but Elisabeth threw a towel at him and gave him such a look that he backed away from her, and decided not to make the beast angry.

- Nothing, - he thought sadly, - I'll fix things, and then you'll suffocate in my arms again.

Obeying his habit of not sitting idle, Aaron hung a net in the barn and began to mend it. After last year's pestilence fish appeared, but they were still too few to feed in Egypt, and yesterday Aaron and his youngest son had great difficulty in catching three small crucian, and a crocodile that suddenly popped out of the reeds frightened Aaron so much that he looked around long before stepping into the river.

- Why are you so cowardly today, - said his son, laughing at him, - you are afraid of every frog.

- It is better to be frightened ten times than to get piss once in pants, - said Aaron, frowning at the reeds.

A stranger peeked in on Aaron in the barn, and seeing that he was alone, cheerfully greeted him.

-Another detective has come to visit, they have nothing better to do, - and Aaron thought angrily and got ready to listen to his stupid questions.

But he was mistaken and the stranger, whose face reminded Aaron of someone he had met before, looked at him in a friendly way and said that Brother Moses wanted to meet him.

-?!
-Will you come?
-I will!

But the thought occurred to him that Moses might have some money and his brother might be able to help him pay the tax.

-Then, when it gets dark, come to Moshe the barber.

- Can I really get away from trouble with help of my brother, - somehow believing that his brother would lend him money, Aaron rejoiced, and this hope gave birth to the certainty that it would happen that way. He had relaxed and that made him hum his favorite tune: "Turn the millstones faster. Grind my grain my little the oxen".

The wife, who had come out of the house to hang the washed rags and had not seen her husband like that for many many days, raised her eyebrows in surprise, and her heart rejoiced. She knew Aaron well, and if he was purring his oxen, it meant that things are going well, or at least something good had happened. As darkness fell, Aaron crept quietly out of the house and went to meet his unknown brother.

- He must be an outlaw, - thought Aaron, - for all Egypt is looking for him. The hell with him; he was not going to baptize children with Moses; let him only give him money till the next harvest. And Aaron will not allow himself to be dragged into any kind of murder. That's what Elizabeth says, too.

Aaron never had any secrets from his wife, and he told her about the stranger's visit and that he wanted to borrow money from Moses.

- Oh, look, Aaron, don't let yourself be deceived, - she whispered, so that her sons would not hear, - if you see that he is up to no good, run home at once, damn this money to hell, we will live honestly and die honestly. Already on the porch she snatched the silver ring off his finger, the only expensive thing Aaron had, and wished him well.

Hosea, who had spent the rest of the day watching Aaron's house in case he ran to the guards, waited for Aaron to enter the barbershop, and suddenly appearing from behind, locked the door with a bolt.

- Come into the back room, - he said suddenly to a bewildered Aaron and sat down in Mosha's chair, as if he were going to have him cut his hair.

Aaron had already regretted coming to this meeting ten times, but Hosea had locked the door, and it was too late to retreat.

- And why did I come here, - Aaron thought wistfully as he went into the back room, - there must be a conspiracy going on here, and I, a peasant, have no use for it; I have to plow the land, not deal with politics. Let others play with power, but I will reap my bread.

In the back room Aaron saw a black-tanned man of his age, and since there was no one else in the room, he assumed that it was his famous brother.

- Sit down, sit down, and tell me how you are doing.

- Yes, - said Aaron, taking a seat on the edge of his chair, - you know we're in trouble. All I care about is how to raise the money to pay the tax. At this Aaron's voice came to life and he said in a begrudging voice: - "Help me out, brother. Loan me some money, or I'll lose my land. I'll be your slave to the grave, I'll do anything you want, but help me out, for God's sake.

- Are there many poor men like you in Gesem, or are you the only one? - Moses asked him.

- Oh, come on, - Aaron answered with a frown, anxiously waiting what Moses was going to tell him about the money. - The whole nation is howling with despair and soon they will sell their children as slaves.

- Would it help you if I gave you money?

- Yes, - answered the excited Aaron, - I will repay you quickly. My land is wonderful! I will be your servant, - he began again to ask Moses, - for God's sake bail Moses out.

- And if locusts and drought and floods and God knows what else come, do I have to give you money every year," Moses interrupted him sternly. Aaron lowered his head.

- That's not why I came here, Aaron, risking my life every second. I came to solve the land problem forever and to free the peasantry from unjust taxation. I have come to remove all these Pharaonic fetters from the hands of the working people and give them long-awaited freedom and justice. I have come to bring them long-awaited prosperity and well-being! And I am ready to die for the happiness of my people, - Moses finished his speech with pathos, and his own throat tightened with pride in himself and a touching desire to die for his people.

Moses had been preparing this speech all the way to Egypt, and now he watched the impression it made on Aaron.

Aaron did not understand anything that Moses was telling him except one thing, that he would not be given any money, and all the other words of Moses only surprised him, and he could not understand in any way what freedom Moses was talking about. Aaron even looked at his hands as if trying to find the Pharaonic fetters from which his brother wanted to free him.

Seeing Aaron's surprised face, Moses decided to speak more simply.

- How would you live Aaron if there was no tax?

- All right. Only, how is that possible?

- Very simply Aaron, the Pharaonic system is obsolete, it's rotten to the core, and all that's left is to push it to make it fall. I have come to do that. I'm going to abolish all taxes, and I'm going to give the land away to people who want to farm. Everything in my system is simple - land to peasants and workshops to artisans. I just need help, that's why I came to you. We must raise the masses and throw off the unwanted Pharaoh, who has sucked on the body of the working people like a leech, and if we manage to do this with you, you will get as much land as you want.

When Moses spoke of land, Aaron was wary, the subject was close to him, and Moses' promise to give him as much land as he wanted was a honey on his heart. What peasant doesn't want more land? For a good farmer there can never be much land, there can only be little.

And a life without the soul-wrenching tax? Wouldn't that be great!

And Pharaoh, judging by the words of Moses, has become arrogant enough to reap where he did not sow.

- What a brother, - thought Aaron, completely stupefied with pride, - what a real Pharaoh!

- Tomorrow Aaron you will gather the elders[6] and talk to them. Explain to them my plans and the goals that you and I have set. Tell them what kind of life they will have after Pharaoh is overthrown. Just watch, everything must be quiet for now, don't attract the attention of Pharaoh's detectives. Well, now come on, brother; let's drink to the meeting and to victory.

Removing and handing over the shoes to the purchaser obligated him to assign his right to something. The Bible. Ruth.4:7

1. The Bible. Exodus 5:7
2. The Bible. Exodus 9:24,31
3. The Bible. Exodus 10:14,15
4. The Bible. Exodus 9:6
5. The Bible. Exodus 4:29-31

CHAPTER 8:

The Hut

Hosea was working feverishly in preparation for his seizure of power in the country. Moses never saw him sleeping. When he fell asleep, Hosea was still on his feet, and when Moses opened his eyes, Hosea was already giving orders to the early visitors. Mosha's empty workshop became a busy place in an instant, and Mosha, drunk from the early morning hours, had no time to cut the young men's hair, who, after cutting it, would receive instructions in the back room, which Hosea had turned into the headquarters of the revolution. To Moses' delight, things began to boil over, and he never ceased to marvel at his commander's organizational skills.

Pharaoh's spies, as it turned out, were not eating their bread for nothing and, sensing the danger, Hosea suggested that Moses urgently change his residence, which, as it turned out, was done in time. At night the soldiers cordoned off the neighborhood and stormed Moshe's house, where there was no one but the dead drunken barber.

The new headquarters of the revolution was organized on the outskirts of town in a dense thicket of reeds. They built a hut big enough to accommodate three or four people, and work began with renewed vigor. Every hour messengers from the various communities of Gesem arrived and, having received instructions, disappeared into the thicket of papyrus. In the space of a week Hosea had organized volunteer detachments in almost every town in Gesem, and pleased with his work, he reported to Moses that 12,000 men were ready to take up arms and die for the new Pharaoh.

- It's time, Moses, - he declared, - Everything is ready on my part.

On Aaron's side, too, everything Moses wanted was done. His brother visited him every day and reported the results of his meetings with the elders of the clans. He said that at first they had been skeptical of Aaron's suggestion for reorganizing the existing order. And that was understandable; a peasant could not be a dreamer. The preparation of the land, the sowing, the provision of fodder, the harvest and other peasant concerns are the reality of his life, and if the peasant launches into a demagogic discussion of rearranging the unjust world, who will feed the country? All this is the truth of life, but propaganda always wins over stupid minds, and this fool Aaron, at first, believed himself and then, with his passionate speeches, made others believe that such a fair arrangement of society is possible, where everyone will determine the amount of tax to the treasury himself and where no official can oppress him neither with bribes, nor with a set of confusing and contradictory laws, which make one dizzy. Yesterday Moses had a meeting of Aaron with the elders in secret, and he loved the words of his brother at the end of his speech: - Down with Pharaoh! Down with his insatiable officials! Long live the working people and their leader Moses!

Well, I guess it really is time to take power. Everything was working out just fine. Pharaoh's army was taming the rebellion in Ethiopia, the masses of Jews in Goshen were stirred up by misfortune, and all that was left was to bring a torch for Egypt to burst forth and blaze into one great conflagration.

Moses called for Hosea.

- Yesterday was too early, but tomorrow will be too late, - Moses said with a smart face, - it's today or never. It's time, Hosea, for your men to show what they can do. How are you going to start?

Hosea smiled slyly, he had worked out a plan to start the rebellion long ago and had been patiently waiting to show it to Moses.

- Tonight I will order to smash the pharaohs' wine cellars, and the soldiers inspired by the wine will do whatever we order: kill, pillage, and burn.

- Genius idea, - exclaimed Moses, - when the hops have passed, it will be too late to think.

- By the middle of the night I plan to seize all the key posts in the city and the prison. Unfortunately, we can't take the temples and they'll just have to be blocked, and by morning we'll march on the capital, - finished Hosea.

- All is well, with one exception; - said Moses; - give the order to loot all wealthy Egyptians and all rich people who are at hand. That's all right; the revolution will pay for everything. Let the fighters drink blood, leave no one alive, chop, chop and chop. The more they are soaked in blood, the better. They won't have a way back after that. But most important of all, Hosea is Pharaoh. Get this through your head, if we don't kill him, you and I will have to flee to my father-in-law's desert again, and even there we don't have even the slightest chance of staying alive. Only Pharaoh's death gives us hope that the army will submit to me as Pharaoh's legitimate grandson. Declare to your revolutionary fighters, whoever kills Pharaoh gets everything he wants.

- What about the position of commander of Pharaoh's fleet?

- What are you talking about, - Moses was surprised, not understanding, - what navy?

- I made contact with an old acquaintance of mine, a good man, we used to steal together, so he managed to be attached to the guard ship of Pharaoh's yacht, - Hosea began to explain, - when we break into the palace, Pharaoh will try to escape on his yacht. Am I right or not?

- If he is not killed, yes. Why didn't I think of that, - Moses said.

Hosea was smiling; he had thought of everything, it was not for nothing that his army always won in children's games.

- Tonight my friend will help my squad to capture this ship without any noise and if we do not kill Pharaoh in the palace, then when he tries to escape on his boat, my guys will attack him instead of protecting his person and will kill everyone on board.

As he finished his speech, Hosea looked at Moses with pride, but Moses did not notice his triumph.

- A beautiful plan, - he replied with glowing eyes.

- I know,' answered Hosea, 'so this friend of mine wants to be made commander of Pharaoh's fleet. What shall I say to him?

- He'll get the fleet, to hell with it, the main thing is to promise Hosea, and then we'll sort it out, - said Moses with a chuckle, - and then... maybe he'll get it. Do you understand?

They understood each other perfectly and laughed.

Hosea spent the rest of the day assigning roles, sending messengers, cursing, praising, and towards evening, he reported that everything was ready and it was time for them to move to the center of events, to the city.

Two hours later, after passing the checkpoints, they were sitting in the safe house taking the latest updates. Aaron arrived. He was obviously nervous and could not sit in one place.

- Sit down and don't flicker around like a mosquito, - Moses shouted at him. Sit down and have a drink. You're the one with the jitters.

As the sun rose below the horizon, riot squads swarmed to the outposts, the prison, and the town hall. A group of thugs smashed the wine cellars. The first fires broke out and first blood was shed. The first revolution in the history of civilization, which like all subsequent revolutions led to a deadlock of historical development, bringing great suffering and incalculable loss to all concerned, with all its attributes - blood, savage violence, looting and lawlessness - was beginning.

And in the meantime, a council of war was taking place in Pharaoh's palace. Two days earlier, Horum had reported to Pharaoh that according to his information, Moses had returned to Egypt and was preparing a revolt in the region of Gesem, where secret meetings were taking place calling for the overthrow of the existing order. In the present situation we should expect a bandit act in the very near future.

- Snake, - thought Pharaoh, - and what an unfortunate time you have chosen for me. There were only two thousand of Pharaoh's personal guard in the city, and the army was far enough away to come to the rescue.

Pharaoh's return army decree was sent to the troops, and in the meantime the council of war was deciding the immediate tasks of possibly repelling the attacks of the revolutionaries. It was suggested that Pharaoh should be sent to meet the army under the cover of a detachment of guardsmen, but Pharaoh did not accept this decision, nor did the following proposal to sail up the Nile in a yacht under the cover of a guard ship. As if to mock the imminent danger, Pharaoh decided to remain in the capital, hoping that the rebels would not have time to form their ranks before an army from Ethiopia arrived. After deliberation, the military council, represented by Pharaoh, decided;

1. Pharaoh's family and himself to move from the palace to the Main Temple under his protection.
2. Strengthen the security of the government buildings.
3. Execute all the most dangerous criminals in the city jail.
4. Issue a decree to mobilize the city's population.
5. Impose a state of siege in the capital.

Of this list only the first could be fulfilled. As darkness fell, the Pharaoh, with a small detachment of guards, secretly left the palace and arrived at the Main Temple. Work had already begun there to strengthen its defenses and Horum's men were reinforcing all the weaknesses they had identified. At that time a riot broke out in Gesem, and Pharaoh ordered to abandon the defense of the city and draw all available troops into the temple to repel the expected attack of the enemy. The night passed quietly, and in the morning Moses' troops burst into the city. In less than an hour the city burst into flames, blood was shed and the always quiet streets of morning Memphis were filled with the noise of battle, the screeching of those plundering and the savage shout of those being slaughtered, which sent shivers down your spine. By noon it was all over, the little pockets of resistance that arose in the city were quickly suppressed, and when Moses entered the capital, where he had not been for so long, it was as if the city had died out. No one came out into the streets to greet the new Pharaoh Moses! No shouts of welcome were heard, no grateful people were seen falling to their knees, only the breeze was blowing clouds of smoke from the burning houses, and the women were crying out. Moses' mood worsened sharply.

- Well, wait," he thought angrily of the people of Egypt, "I will teach you to meet your lord with dignity.

When he arrived to the palace, he first of all went to the throne room and sat down on Pharaoh's throne. This was the moment he had long dreamed of. He was on the throne! Strangely, he had no sense of joy, but instead Moses had a sense of some unhealthy excitement and a sense of the unreality of what was happening. Pharaoh, that's who's keeping him from feeling the solemnity of this moment. Moses suddenly realized clearly that as long as Pharaoh lived, he would always feel like a buffoon and an outcast on this throne.

- Where is Hosea, what of Pharaoh? - He yelled at his bodyguards, and stood up abruptly and went to his former room. Tremblingly, he pushed open the door, as if fearing something; he first peered in, and then cautiously entered. The room was empty. Apparently Pharaoh had ordered to throw out everything that might remind him of his grandson, and only the dust, lying thickly, indicated that no one had been in here for many days. After standing there, Moses headed back and as he passed the room that had once belonged to Pharaoh's son Ram, he decided to look there as well. Everything in Ram's room was in place, even the edge of the bedspread was slightly rolled up, as if its owner had left the room a second ago and was about to return. Moses even intuitively looked back at the door, and shivers ran down his spine at the reality of the feeling that Ram was alive and about to walk in here to throw it in his face - murderer. Moses became terrified, so he darted out of the room and ran into the throne room, where Hosea and Aaron were already waiting for him. Hosea, in contrast to Aaron, was cheerful and, to Moses' surprise, was wearing a dozen gold chains and a gold ring on almost every one of his fingers that made him look like a jewelry store clerk.

- Oh, I love pretty things, - he answered Moses' dumb question, and seeing that the latter was gloomy, he encouraged him; - don't overstitch Moses; I'll get Pharaoh all the same. Who expected that he would take refuge in the main temple? I'm from there now, a fortress, not a temple. I've been inside once, I know. We couldn't take it by raid, so we'll take it by storm. I've already made the assault ladders, a day or two and I'll bring you Pharaoh's bald head.

Hosea sprawled out in his chair and ordered me to serve him some wine. Looking at him and his demeanor, one would have thought he had spent his whole life here in the palace, so naturally he behaved.

-What a man, - thought Moses, - he is a fish in water in every situation; if you put him on that throne, you would not distinguish him from a Pharaoh.

In contrast, Aaron looked like a frightened dog cornered and about to be beaten.

Moses, with a displeased look on his face, asked: - "Brother, you look like a beaten dog. What is the matter?

- What on earth is going on, brother? - I thought we were going to be greeted with flowers, I thought the people would cheerfully accept the new and just government, and I didn't expect this blood. We look like a band of robbers, not liberators from Pharaoh's yoke. Is this what we wanted? Today I witnessed a terrible scene. A dozen men dragged a simple Egyptian out of his house and started beating him. The wife, who threw herself at them begging for mercy, was simply stabbed with the sword by one of them, while the rest, hooting, hacked her husband to pieces. When I wanted to stop the fight, they wanted to kill me, too, and if it hadn't been for my boys, I'd be lying dead.

- Well, don't worry too much and don't draw a general picture from one case, - said Moses grudgingly, - and we'll find those rascals and punish them severely. Listen, Hosea, take care of this matter and report to Aaron," Moses said with a turn of his head toward him.

- And, Aaron, you must be ready for the fact that we will destroy thousands that we will walk knee-deep in blood and stop at nothing to achieve our purpose. This foolish nation doesn't understand that we bring them happiness and prosperity. This is only the beginning and we will execute all those who are against us, no matter whether they have a sword or no weapon in their hands. Whoever's not with me is against us.

- A slug, - he thought of his brother, - you shouldn't seize power with such a person, but stand in the temple and comfort unjustly offended people. When I'm in power, I'll send him somewhere in the temple to serve, let him wipe the snot off the parishioners. Justice is the lot of weak men. Power always and everywhere wins because justice is toothless from its morality and conscience. It is weak, and God does not love the weak.

CHAPTER 9:

Volunteers

Just before his wife's delivery Nain was completely exhausted, and when the contractions began and sweet Fooige began writhing and moaning in pain, his heart was torn. His feelings of pity and helplessness superseded everything else, and the fact that he could do nothing to help her multiplied his suffering. To do something he prayed. Prayed to gods he did not believe in. The feeling of fear for Fooige and the unborn child created uncertainty in his mind, and he prayed, just in case, so as not to appear a hardened sinner in the eyes of the suddenly existing gods, to beg them to be favorable to his family. Now he was ready to believe in a devil, as long as it went smoothly, without any complications for Fooige and the child.

The mother invited a midwife, who immediately began to command as soon as she appeared on the doorstep. After examining the pale and moaning Fooige, she gibbered at Nain and chased him away.

- The old witch, - Nain thought angrily, and to distract himself somehow went to his father-in-law. Today was a day of rest, and as soon as Fooige went into labor, his father immediately ran away from the house to his matchmaker under the guise of calling for Monin.

The father-in-law and father-in-law, as Nain and thought, took advantage of the fact that the wives had no time for them, celebrating the birth of their yet-to-be-born grandson. The lack of control led to the fact that they were pretty tipsy and, in accordance with their condition, was having a conversation about women's nature and the role of women in men's lives. Nain's father stood on the fact that men and women have the same mindset.

- Since God created us in his image, so our thinking is the same, - he argued.

- And no, - Serbai said hotly, - can you imagine that our wives drinking wine behind a cucumber patch like you and I did last week?

- No.

- Why can't they drink behind the cucumber patch?

- I have no idea.

- What if you think about it?

- I guess they don't like cucumbers, - answered a groggy Bahan after thinking about it.

- Then that proves everything! If they don't like cucumbers, then their thinking is different!

Bahan was stunned by such a weighty argument and didn't know what to say, and his matchmaker, inspired by the crushing victory, brought the following argument.

- Besides, we have a small anatomical difference, here he pointed to the place below his belly, and if so, our thinking is also different.

- Prove it.

- And I will.

- I'm listening.

- For example, my little goat always speaks.

Then they saw Nain come in and they got excited.

- Well, - they asked in one voice, but Nain only waved his hand as if to say that nothing had changed so far and sat down at the table.

- Have a little drink with us, to Fooige and grandson, - his father-in-law suggested, but Nain refused. It was considered bad luck to drink for an unborn child, and so Nain looked disapprovingly at the two happy grandfathers, who, after drinking another mug, decided to continue the argument.

Then Boby, who could not walk, ran into the house.

- Nain, - he called out, running out of breath, - there seems to be a baby... mamma sent me... Fooige has just given birth. He disappeared as quickly as he appeared and only shouted from the yard: - It seems to be a girl.

Not expecting such a turn of events, the two brave grandfathers looked at each other perplexedly. Serbai grunted in annoyance and then suddenly said: - I like girls. Girls are better than boys; they have less to worry about and much more to caress.

Nain did not remember how he found himself at home, where his mother and mother-in-law took him to the room where Fooige was lying on the bed. She smiled wearily at Nain and with her eyes pointed to what appeared to Nain to be a tiny bundle lying beside her. Nain, afraid to breathe, leaned over it and saw the little wrinkled face with its eyes closed and he, having never seen a newborn baby before, was surprised at its size. The little girl's head was no bigger than his fist. Fooige was smiling, watching his reaction, and when Nain, smiling with a sense of relief that everything had finally ended so well, leaned over Fooige to kiss her, she whispered to him: - daughter looks like you.

At that moment, two contented grandfathers piled into the house. Trying to cover up the traces of the wine they had consumed, they began to congratulate their wives with a playful cheerfulness.

My little goat, - exulted the father-in-law, turning to his wife, - well, finally you have become a grandmother, let me kiss you!

My mother-in-law one look determined that he had been drinking, and angrily pressed her lips, smilingly replied: "Turned, you say in the grandmother? What, that I was a grandfather in your opinion?

- No, I was a grandfather, - Serbai replied, - although I wasn't, I've turned into one now, and you were my wife and you turned into my grandmother.

- I'm already his grandmother. And shame on you, matchmaker, - Monine said to Bahan, - Fooige hasn't had time to give birth, and you two dorks from Memphis market are already drunk.

- Well, what a joy, Monine.

- You can have all the joy, all the sorrow, as long as you're drunk.

- Come on, -Malis said, -What can you take from them, a man is a man, let's gather for the table.

Satisfied that Malis had interceded for them, the grandfathers began to look into Fooige's room, not daring to enter. Seeing the impatience of her father and father-in-law, Nain, took daughter in his arms, and carried her to them.

- Careful, Nain, - said Fooige, getting up on the bed, - don't drop it.

-What are you talking about, - thought Nain, - this bundle is dearer to me than anything in the world.

At night Nain was awakened by his father. Awake, not knowing what he wanted, he got up and went out into the common room.

- Quickly dress Nain and let's go to the city administration, - said his father with a frown - there is rebellion in the capital. Pharaoh and his guards are besieged in the Main Temple. A general gathering is announced, there is a possibility that the rebellion may spread to our city.

They washed and dressed quickly and made their way through the quiet streets of the night to the City Hall. Nain tried to find out what exactly was going on in the capital, but his father glumly replied that he knew nothing more.

In the town square, citizens had already gathered and guards were scurrying everywhere. Unlike the usual days when they were armed only with light spears, today all the guards wore armor, each with a short sword on his belt, and instead of a light spear, each with a heavy battle spear with a long shaft.

Father left Nain in the square and entered the town hall, where, except for the high-ranking officials, people were not allowed to enter. The town began to wake up and soon the whole square was filled with people talking anxiously as they waited for the head of the town to appear. Finally a group of high-ranking officials appeared on the porch, led by the governor. Among them Nain saw his father as well.

- Citizens of Great Egypt, - began his speech the governor, - a few hours ago, we received word that taking advantage of the fact that our army is on a campaign, the band of the outlaw Moses seized the Nile Delta - Gesem, the surrounding cities and the capital of our state Memphis. The Great Pharaoh has taken refuge in the Main Temple, and his valiant guards are repulsing the rebels' desperate attempts to capture Pharaoh. It is possible that the rebels will try to seize and loot our city. In connection with these events, I, by the power entrusted to me by Pharaoh, declare martial law in the city and the mobilization of residents in the militia to protect the city. Remaining loyal to the Great Pharaoh and Egypt, we must do everything to keep order in the city and exclude any attempts of a coup before the army arrives. All disobedience and violations of martial law will be punished by death. Long live the Great Pharaoh, long lives the Great Egypt!

The enlistment into the militia has begun. Bakhan, appointed by the War Council as head of supply for the militia, tried to get Nain on his staff, but he, seeing his father's desire to keep him away from possible hostilities, resisted. Nain, like an ordinary snot-nosed boy, not believing or understanding that he could be killed in war, rushed to enlist in the cavalry. The cavalry was already too much, and he was assigned to the infantry as an archer. Satisfied with his lucky position, Nain received a battle bow and a quiver of arrows. Judging from his childhood years, when he and the same boys hunted ducks in the reeds, Nain was not a bad shot, and more than once, proud of himself, brought home the loot, but when he tried to shoot with the issued bow, Nain immediately realized the difference between his homemade and this weapon.

Never mind, - he thought, - I'll practice for a day and then I'll shoot like a real warrior.

When he got to the dock guard unit outside the garden of his house, Nain ran home for a minute to kiss Fooige and tell his mother that his father would not be home until nightfall. Seeing him in his armor and with a weapon in his hands, his mother and then Fooige cried for some reason. Apparently, women perceive war very differently than men, for whom war is an opportunity to show valor and win glory, and for women war is associated with only one thing, death.

Only Boby was glad that Nain had become a soldier. He was under his feet, not allowing him to take a step, interfering with his mother's talk, and begging to be shot.

- Well, Nain, - he was begging, tugging him by the hand, - let me try shoot, just once, then all the boys would die of envy," and on receiving a refusal he started again, - well Nain...

Finally realizing that he had a bad brother who did not care about strengthening Boby authority among the neighborhood boys, Boby climbed on the roof of the barn, where his bow for duck hunting was supposed to be. Quickly retrieving his weapon, he returned, and began rushing Nain, who was finishing the soup his mother had heated up.

- Nain, I'm ready, let's go, your commander is probably waiting for us there, and you're eating here.

- And where are you going? - Nain wondered.

- I'll be your squire and scout.

- Wipe your snot out, warrior, - answered Nain's mother, - look at your bow, it can't even kill a sparrow.

Boby, missed his mother's remark, and stared spellbound at Nain's war bow lying on the bench. Sniffing his nose, he slowly got to it and tried to draw the bowstring. It wouldn't budge.

- When you are wounded or killed," he told Nain, - I will take it and shoot Pharaoh's enemies.

His words made Nain gasp, Fooige shudder, and his mother grabbed the broom with the words: - Bite your tongue, - she chased after Boby, who, without waiting for her reprisal, quickly rushed out of the house and lurked behind the fence, waiting for Nain to go to work.

The service was less interesting, even boring, and Nain's squad spent their time greeting and inspecting the boats as they approached. For the first few hours, the militiamen tried hard: searching boats, and suspecting whoever appeared at the wharf, but by late afternoon it had grown tiresome, and their vigilance had dulled. The militiamen hid in the shadows and speculated lazily about events in the capital. Only Nain wasted no time in practicing his archery on a dried gourd, and his faithful squire Boby brought him the released arrows. By the end of the third day, Nain's fingers, chafed from the bowstring, were aching with a dull ache; thanks to his training, he began to shoot, showing excellent results and his commander set Nain as an example to the other militiamen, who were lazily killing time over conversation. Life went on, and the fact that there was a rebellion in the capital had almost no effect here. It was as if nothing had happened and only in the air was felt that tension and anxiety which people feel before storm or tempest, but this anxiety was also gone with the entry of the chariots of Pharaoh's army into the city, which made a rapid march and with all possible speed rushed to the aid of the besieged Pharaoh. Six hundred chariots filled the streets of the small city, making it seem like it was not a city, but some huge military camp. An hour later, Pharaoh's battle flotilla arrived at the wharf, the sight of which made Boby dazed, and he swore to Nain that he would be a warrior-sailor when he grew up.

The chariot commander and Pharaoh's favorite Jew, Ace, finally decided to let the soldiers and horses rest until morning. After washing and eating a quick meal, he arrived at the town hall, where the leaders of the city were waiting for him. His whole appearance spoke for itself, and he did not hide the fact that such a long march was a hard test for his squad.

- As long as Moses' gang holds the capital in their hands, no one has the right to a break," he began his speech before the military council of the city. - Horses are breaking down, chariots are being blown to pieces, and my troops are badly tired. But they are eager to fight this band of rebels, and so I ask for your help with supplies and repairs. I could command you to do so, but I see that you yourselves are looking forward to the moment when Pharaoh's army outweighs the rapists and murderers. I ask one more thing, not all the soldiers could withstand such a rapid march and I need a dozen and a half men from your militia. The main army will be arriving soon, and your militia can join its ranks. And now, please go to work and try to finish repairing chariots before sunrise. After finishing his short speech, Ace instructed the head of the city to organize all the work, and went to the wharf to meet Pharaoh's general Ben, who had arrived with the flotilla.

Listening to Ace's report, Ben wrinkled his nose in displeasure, as if he didn't understand why Ice had to stay in town until dawn, but Ice paid no mind to this, for he knew that Ben was always displeased about something and he had seen him with exactly the same disgruntled face the day he defeated the Ethiopian rebels. After giving Ace a few minutes to drink some light wine, Ben ordered him to march in the morning, but not to the capital, but to the east, which surprised Ace unspeakably.

- You leave in the morning, and before you reach the capital, you turn to Epham, where you'll set up a barrier. I'll raise anchor in an hour and march on Memphis. I have not enough strength, as you understand, to defeat the rebels in all the territory they have seized, but I will take the capital and hold out until the main force arrives. When the main force arrives, we'll crush the ranks of the bastards and they'll flee the country from Pharaoh's imminent punishment. And there's nowhere for them to go but to the Median lands. I want Ace, not only to defeat them, but to exterminate every last scoundrel. Crush them once and for all, as they had encroached on Pharaoh and Holy Egypt. Your job, Ace, is to cut off their escape route and hold them off until I get there. Do what you want and do as you please, you are an experienced commander, but no bandit must break through your barrier into the desert. Is that clear?

It's understandable, but he wanted to fly to help Pharaoh myself. Now, instead, it will be necessary to hold the fleeing Moses by the tail like a naughty cat. Though the task seems easy only at first sight, try to hold back the rebels, who have nothing to lose, and who in agony will fight to the last. And probably Ben was right, and even if he was wrong, one could not argue with the bosses. So, having jumped up in his chariot, Ice got ready to go to check the squad's preparation for the march. At that moment a young warrior guarding the wharf caught his attention and Ice remembered that his archer had collapsed with a fever and needed a replacement.

- Eh warrior, - shouted Ace, - come here.

Nain and it was he, flattered by such attention from one of Pharaoh's generals, quickly ran up to the chariot.

- What is your name?
- Nain, - he answered loudly.
- How good are you with this toy, - he asked Ice, pointing to his bow.
- Good, - Nain suddenly lied.
- Hit it, - said Ice pointing to a lonely palm tree about sixty meters from them.

Nain saw that he had nowhere to retreat, so he took an arrow out of his quiver and fired without aiming. Either because he was sure of himself or because he had been practicing all these days, the arrow hit the target accurately.

- Not bad. Well done, - praised him the general and suddenly suggested - I need an archer, mine fell down in a fever, will you join me?
- I will, - joyfully agreed Nain, and all the time Boby who was hovering near him, not daring to even talk to such a big commander and hearing everything they were talking about, desperately showed Nain signs to ask the commander to accept him in his squad as well. Unfortunately, Nain didn't even notice the signs given to him, which upset the little fighter to tears.

Ace ordered Nain: - Hop into the chariot, - and trotted the horses.

As they rode past Nain's house, proud of himself and out of a desire to show off to Fooige, he asked Ace to stop for a moment to say goodbye to his relatives in case he couldn't get home before he left, but Ice didn't even look at him and rode past.

-There's a lot to do, - he replied after a little silence, - you will go out for a couple of hours at night, and we perform early in the morning.

And indeed, when the moon was already high, Ice finally calmed down and, having finished his countless checks, let Nain go home.

As soon as Nain entered the house, he heard the women sobbing. His mother and wife rushed to him, and went from sobbing to howling. She knew everything because of Boby, who always knew everything, boasted and told for everyone, that his Nain would serve as an archer with the commander himself, and how Nain had hit a palm tree from a thousand paces, maybe more.

Bahan, who had come home just before Nain, winced at the women's cries, endured a little, and then suddenly bellowed so loudly that they were frightened into silence.

- What are you howling like Nain is already a dead man! Shut up, I tell you! If it's not Nain, if it's not another man's son or husband who's going to fight for Egypt, then who? If I had been younger, I would have joined the army without a second thought. Sit down at the table, son, and you women set the table now.

The women stopped crying but and fussed around the table, and Bahan, himself worried about Nain, kept grumbling at them to hide his excitement from the others.

- What a cluck, - he went on grumbling.

Then his attention was caught by Boby, who was packing a fishing bag, which he always took on fishing trips, and in which he could find the entire fisherman's things: bone hooks, horsehair, dry bait and other stuff.

- What on earth are you doing up at night fishing? - Bahan switched to him; - don't you fellows have enough of the day? Go to bed now.

- I'm not going fishing, - Boby said, looking straight at his father; - I'm going to war with Nain. You just said it yourself, if not Nain or the other son, who will protect Pharaoh?

The father was taken aback, everyone froze, and there was silence in the house.

- What? - Burst out Bahan, - wait one sec, you will not sit on your ass for a week, and began to take off his sandal to prove it in practice, and Boby, without waiting for his evidence, grabbed a bag and jumped out of the house.

- You'd better come back, - his father shouted from the porch, - or I'll tear your ears off in the morning.

For the two hours that Nain was home, they took turns running out of the house and calling for Bobby, but he, apparently afraid of punishment, lurked somewhere nearby and did not make a sound.

It was time to say goodbye. Nain kissed his mother, hugged his father and stood for a long time, holding the weeping Fooige to him.

- Don't cry sweetheart, - he said, - you know me desperately. I'll be back soon, and then I won't leave you for a minute, and I'll bore you too.

The daughter was sleeping peacefully, and Nain stroked her hand:
-Sleep baby.

Nain picked up the sack the women had prepared for him, surprised at its weight, apparently they had tried to cram in as much provisions as the string would allow. Not wishing to upset them and shake the bag, Nain carried it on his shoulders and they left the house. Bahan decided to see his son off and look for Boby at the same time. Forbidding the women to see them out of the gate, or there would be a lot of howling, they walked with Nain to the meeting place, moving further and further away from the two weeping female figures standing at the home gate.

With the first rays of sunshine, Ace's detachment set out from the city, and Bahan returned home for a short time. He never found Boby.

CHAPTER 10:

The Collapse of the Revolution

The population of Egypt, on whose support Aaron had so counted, did not follow them, and the band of Hosea, which he proudly called the army of revolution, did not represent the whole people, but rather represented the worst, most adventurous part of the Jewish population. Even Aaron's father turned his back on him[1].

After Aaron inspirationally told his father the goals and objectives of the great revolution, he frowned at him and said: - Apparently I didn't hit you enough as a child, Aaron, or maybe I hit you a lot. So much that I beat your brains out if you can't understand one simple thing. Only a madman would think, that the live of the people depends directly on Pharaoh, whether he is good or evil. Only a fool, who unfortunately you are, can believe that waving a sword can change the way of life. Well, Aaron, you've chosen your path. Just remember, son, he who picks up the sword can never put it in its sheath again, he'll either have to fight or die. On that day Aaron had not understood his father's words, and only today, when Hosea's army failed to take the Main Temple after a week's siege, it was as if he had an epiphany and was horrified to imagine his future. Of course, they would sweep away. There's a mobilization going on all over Egypt, and as soon as Pharaoh's army approaches, and some say it's quite close, they'll all be hanged. All right, I deserved it by believing this "prophet" Moses, but it's a pity about my sons. It turns out that they will die just because their father turned out to be a brainless idiot and dragged them into this adventure. Maybe they will take the damn temple and put an end to this tyrant? It would be great, and then everyone would have a hope of salvation. But the fact of the matter is that the valiant Hosea's army began to disperse. If he only realized today the end that lay ahead of them, the men who were smarter than him immediately foresaw the future. And not only those who took up arms, but also those who did not support Moses. It became clear to everyone that by plundering and killing the Egyptians, Moses' army had made the entire Jewish population look like violent rebels in the eyes of Egypt, and if Pharaoh won, no one would be spared, neither those who was killing, or those who were against it. Try to prove after all that you are not a camel.

So every night dozens of wagons of clever people running away from a quite possible tragic outcome were pulled along the roads toward Elaph[2]. Their calculation was surprisingly simple, like life itself; if Moses gets the upper hand, we can always go back, and if Pharaoh, why risk our heads. Especially those who had soiled their hands in blood, those who had looted, left the ranks of the army and fled at the first opportunity. Even those who did not take part in the rebellion could not stand the temptation of getting rich at the expense of an Egyptian neighbor. Just before they left, they broke into their houses and took whatever they wanted from the unresisting victims[3].

- Maybe it's time for me to take care of the same thing and send my family to Elath, Aaron thought,-and time will tell what to do next. At least to pull my sons[4] and especially Eleazar, who has gone mad, from being a normal human turned being to a real pogromer, tirelessly doing evil deeds, as if he had been possessed by a demon, out of these events? - Let they go, - Aaron decided, and ordered his sons to be found and sent to him. They must be storming the main temple, and their might kill there. A messenger came and broke all his plans to talk to his sons about going to Elath: - Moses wants to see you, - he reported.

All that week Moses lived in anticipation of the absolute power that would very soon be in his hands. Everything started well, thank God, and even the fact that he couldn't kill Pharaoh at once didn't touch him much; Memphis was in his hands, and the main temple would fall not today, but tomorrow. But the longer the siege dragged on, the more anxious his soul became. They did not have the time they needed to complete the victory, and what they did have was wasted, and Pharaoh's army was bringing the end of this inexorable countdown closer by the minute. Each new day brought more and more anxiety, until today Moses suddenly realized that he had lost. Lost for the second time in the pursuit of power. What he thought was a revolutionary situation was actually a localized discontent among the Jews in a particular area of Gesem, and there had been no mass uprising of the entire Egyptian people. It seemed that they, the starving Egyptians, should be the first to take up arms and wrest the right to the land taken away years ago, and the right to control their own destiny. But it was a mistake and it turned out that the Egyptians in the person of Pharaoh saw not only the head of the state, but also that he was the embodiment of culture, religion and homeland, and to fight against it meant to fight against oneself. For Jews, who had not had time for 430 years to fully absorb the cultural heritage of the Egyptian people Pharaoh was only a simple king, and as soon as this king infringed on their interests, they did not hesitate went against him. As a result, without an overwhelming majority of the population, the Jews and Moses were doomed in advance to failure. Even if we imagine for a moment that the Main Temple is taken and Pharaoh is killed, a legitimate question arises: how long will Moses remain on the throne, a day, a week, a month? Pharaoh's army would come and everything would fall into place.

An army, that's the right tool to seize power! With an army you don't have to wait for that damned revolutionary situation, you don't have to wait for a favorable political moment; you don't have to put poison in Pharaoh's wine. You just have to move your army into the country where you want to be Pharaoh and the throne is in your pocket! Do I have an army? Those units that Hosea organized don't even come close to resembling its destructive power. An army is discipline, it is training, it is readiness to carry out the task assigned to it at any moment-that is what an army is! Can you call this mob of poorly armed rebels, who do not recognize discipline and military order, an army capable of carrying out his Moses plans? No, no and no.

- The main thing is that I've realized it and it means I have one more chance to seize the throne, - Moses thought, but for good. I'll form an army, I'll give it a chance to hone its fighting skills, gain experience, get drunk on blood and get a taste of victory and easy profits. And then, I will return here to Egypt, and do not expect mercy my Pharaoh. No matter how fate mocks me, I'll still be a pharaoh!

- Call Aaron and Hosea to me, - he commanded, - and be quick about it.

Perhaps he will scold me again and demand to take the damned temple at once, thought Hosea, when he was told that Moses wanted to see him at once. As he spurred his horse on, Hosea began to consider how to tell a good lie so that Moses would not get angry. To tell or not to tell the truth to him?

And the truth was that by the second day Hosea realized that they could not win the battle for power; they had too few forces at their disposal, and they scattered every night. It was not that the Egyptians did not support them, but the bulk of the Jews did not want to take up arms and die for the new leader Moses. In my ranks, Hosea thought unhappily, are either looters or stupid people who don't know why they are here and why they are shedding their blood.

- Go to the hell Moses, - thought Hosea,

- I won't tell him anything. Why should I hear him cry? I've earned enough, and it's time to disappear from here somewhere far away, not today, but tomorrow, for example to the island of Kaftar, or even to buy myself a small island with palm trees and women. With that kind of money I've looted in the last few days I'm my own Pharaoh, or at least Pharaoh's son-in-law, and let Moses fight alone for the happiness of the working people.

When Hosea entered the palace, he found Moses talking to Aaron. He was proving something to the seated Aaron, moving in circles around him and waving his arms in fever.

- Maybe you don't want to be my commander anymore either and want to defect? - Moses asked loudly as soon as he saw Hosea enter the room.

Hosea was frightened.

- He must have found out that I've hired a schooner and I'm going to run away? - Hosea's mind raced.

Trying to find out what Moses knew, Hosea decided to deny everything.

- What's the matter, Moses, the siege is coming to an end, and in a month or so I'm going to take it. Don't listen to the gossip mongers, they can't tell you anything about me. They're jealous of us and want to break our eternal friendship. They lie about everything.

- What do you mean, - Moses asked him without understanding, wrinkling as if he had a toothache, - what gossipers, which friendship?

-Which friendship? -Which, which, of course is unbreakable.

- Are you out of your mind? Unbreakable friendship, what kind of gossip? Are you drunk?

- No, but I'd like to be. Let's have a drink. Where's the mug? Pour it for me, Moses.

- I'll pour you a drink! I'll pour it for you!

Now Hosea couldn't understand anything and just shrugged his shoulders and winked at the gloomy Aaron behind Moses' back, saying, - Look at your brother, babbling like the devil.

- This a fool, - he said pointing to Aaron in an angry voice, - has decided not to help me anymore and is going to run away to Elath. And this is my own and beloved brother! How can I trust others when even my brother betrays me and the cause of the revolution in the most difficult moment?

- I am not betraying you, Moses, - Aaron tried to justify himself in a muffled voice, - I just didn't think it would come to this. I must be the kind of man who finds it hard to see all this blood and human suffering. All my life I've been plowing the land, and this revolution of yours is something else entirely. And I pity my family, what will happen when Pharaoh wins? They'll all be hanging.

- He is a real fool, - thought Hosea, - if you want to run away, run away why you tell this the first person you see? Slowly gathered his things and rushed away. Yes, Aaron the fool and he must have been born premature.

- All right, Aaron, - went on Moses, - if you run away into the wilderness, what then? What are you going to do there? Plow the sands and the dunes? Or are you going to do some trading? Why are you silent, Aaron, telling us your plans, maybe we will want to go and live in the desert?

- I don't know, I haven't thought about it.

- And you think about it, think hard. Think about how in a year you're going to die in this desert, and not you alone, but your whole family. Think, think, while Hosea and I drink wine.

Aaron sighed heavily at Moses' words. He must have imagined the plow being pulled across the sand by a camel, and from this bleak picture he lowered his head as if he wanted to hide it under a table. Hosea perked up; the wine in the palace was indeed excellent, and apparently Moses knew nothing of his escape plan.

- Do you think I'm an idiot? - Moses asked in a stern voice, turning to both of them. - Do you think I can't see that we've lost? Oh, shut up Hosea and don't try to tell me tales of our brilliant victory, which is just around the corner, - Moses almost shouted when he saw his protesting gesture.

- I see it all, and I know it all ahead of time. But unlike you foolish sheep, I know what to do next.

Here he paused, drawing more attention to himself, and after a little silence began to spell out his plan.

- We are retreating! Yes, yes, and you heard right. We're going into the Sinai desert and taking the entire Jewish population with us. All those sheep who take our bait. The more the better. The sheep are our future. There in the desert, we'll make first-rate fighters out of this crowd. Hunger will drive them to fight, and they'll be an army that can't be beaten. With such an army we shall conquer every land in the district from the Euphrates to Egypt, and its inhabitants, the Canaanites, the Philistines, the Phoenicians, and others, we shall put to the sword, cut them down to the ground.

Aaron, have you heard the Canaanites' boast that their vine must be carried on a stretcher[6] by two men? Well, I will give each of my warriors as much Canaanite land as he desires. We will build there a just state where Jews from all over the earth will want to live, and believe me, it will be paradise. So, I want to ask you right now, Hosea, do you want to be with me and continue to lead my army, and you Aaron want to be my main helper?

Hosea thought about it.

- I have a lot of money, - he thought, - so why do I need this fabulous land? I can lose my head at any moment. To hell with Moses and his army. I've got to escape, and I've got to do it today.

But this is his mind spoke, and his heart began to leap for joy, as it had been in the desert, when Moses had promised him the mountain of gold in exactly the same way. Apparently, the infectious lust for power had already penetrated into his mind, and like ordinary thirst it did not give him any rest. Why don't you give it a try? I can always escape. What if Moses was right and I would be a great general?

Hosea was used to making important decisions quickly. Just now, he thought for a second and got up from his chair. He filled his chest with air and said solemnly, as if swearing an oath: - I am with you, Moses.

Aaron knew Moses was right a thousand times over. Life was already crippled, so why make it worse. And as soon as Moses spoke of the fertile Canaanite lands, his whole peasant essence reached for the bait. He knew it would be blood again, he knew you can't build your happiness on the misery of another people, but the bait worked and drowned out the voice of reason. Aaron, too, stood up and, trying not to think about what would happen in the future, replied, - I am with you brother.

Apparently pleased with this outcome, Moses sat them down and began to outline a plan of action.

- First, we need an idea. If a person or a nation lives by an idea, no weapon can defeat it. Only another idea can defeat an idea. Our idea is religion. I thought long and hard about this and came to the conclusion that we have a good chance to play on people's belief in God. The ground has long been prepared and all we have to do is throw the seeds into it. We're just lucky that the Jewish people haven't forgotten their God, and that's what we're going to bet on, with you, Aaron, being the main conduit for my idea. Go to the people now. Gather a rally and explain to these sheep that Jehovah, the god of the Jews, appeared to Moses[7] and commanded to him to lead people out of Egypt into a new land where honey and milk flow[8]. Frame it roughly as saying that, when Moses was tending sheep in the desert, he saw light coming from a bush[9] as if it were engulfed in fire. It was as if a fire had descended upon this bush, but it did not burn. And when Moses came up, the voice was: - Moses, my servant, lead the Hebrews out of Egypt, into a new land, which I will give you forever.

Moses was a good actor, and when he reproduced the voice of God in a high, wailing voice, Aaron got goosebumps on his back, it was so real.

- They won't believe me, - Aaron said uncertainly.
- Oh, yes, they will, - Moses interrupted him. - After what we've done here, they all think of saving their own skins from Pharaoh's vengeance, and they'll grasp at this straw we can throw at them. In this hopeless situation, they'll start thinking, -what if it's true? They'll think about it, scratch their heads, and you'll see, they'll bite. Announce to everyone that in the morning we're leaving for the new lands that God is giving us. That's it, go, and I sure hope so.

After waiting for Aaron to come out, Moses turned to Hosea.

-And you Hosea, in order to cut off the Jews from staying here forever, must go through Gesem tonight with your goons and kill as many Egyptians as you can. Spare neither the young nor the old. This will not only encourage the Jews to flee with us, but also weaken Pharaoh's army in the future. Who knows, maybe we'll be back here soon. All right, let's do it.

After receiving his assignment, Aaron roamed around Gesem all day, preaching Moses' new idea. His three sons were with him and helped him organize rallies, while the fourth, Eleazar, did not even show his face and spent all his time with his new idol, Hosea.

When he met with the elders of the clans, Aaron confidently told them about Moses and his conversation with God and even invented a rumor that Pharaoh had supposedly decreed the execution of every Jew in order to win as many people to his side as possible. By evening, from the frequent repetition of these lies, he himself began to believe his own story. Finally he decided to get on with his packing and drove home. Elizabeth howled when Aaron ordered her to pack, and he, after shushing her, headed for his father's house. As he walked along the fence, Aaron saw that one of the stones making up the wall of the fence had chipped away and was ready to fall out. Knowing that he would probably never come back here and that he couldn't care less about the stone, Aaron wanted to walk away, but his natural sense of mastery took over and he bent down to try to put it back in its place. A neighbor's goat, grazing right there, seeing Aaron's bent ass, mistook it for a target and, getting on its hooves for acceleration, jumped forward with all its might and hit Aaron in the ass. Rolling over his head, the dazed Aaron could not comprehend what happen. When he turned around, he saw the goat, which seemed to him to be staring snidely at his defeated opponent.

- I'll kill you, - Aaron yelled in a fit of rage.

He was offended that some mangy goat had hit him sneakily for no reason at all, and his son, who was watching the scene, was laughing instead of sympathizing. Aaron sprang to his feet, gasping with rage and swearing at the cursed goat, rushed after it, burning with one desire to catch it and break its horns. The goat, seeing Aaron's angry face and evidently reading his black thoughts, ran away, while Aaron could not regained consciousness for a few minutes.

When Aaron entered father's house, he saw that father, who had been told well in advance that he must be packing, had no intention of leaving his house.

- Aren't you going to, - he cried, and the anger he had not unleashed on the goat had finally reached the top of his lungs and gone out to his parents, - or do you think that after all Will Pharaoh let you live? - Aaron shouted.

- After what? - as if he didn't understand what his son was talking about, his father asked him as he continued to quietly fix the clamp.

- Your mother and I did not kill or rob anyone; if you did it, then answer to Pharaoh. If I have to answer for the actions of my brainless son, then Pharaoh should answer for the actions of his grandson Moses, the legendary fighter for the happiness of the Jewish people. After a moment's silence, father said, - Ah Aaron, Aaron, how it pains me to see you, my pride and hope, sliding down into the deep pit from which there is no escape. How it pains me to see that with your own hands you have destroyed all that you had and created.

At that moment the mother, sobbing, rushed to Aaron.

- Son, she cried, - don't go. You will be lost there. I will throw myself at Pharaoh's feet and beg for you.

- She has become very old, - Aaron thought suddenly, hugging his mother, - and indeed, where am I taking them?

Well, don't grieve, - he said in a husky voice, - stay with God, but I can't. I'm going to say goodbye to the land, and you take care of it, and God willing, we'll come back.

Aaron wanted to comfort his parents by saying this, knowing full well that there would be no turning back.

The field greeted him with a sepulchral silence. The sight of it, the thought of not being able to harvest from it, broke Aaron's heart. Without going all the way around his plot, Aaron turned back, feeling that if he didn't leave now, he would never leave. Resentment came over his mind in a wave. Resentment at himself for abandoning the land himself, like that negligent mother who abandoned her child and that guilt made him want to howl like a wolf sensing death approaching.

Walking through the yard, Aaron rubbed his hand on the goat's bruised ass, and suddenly thought: - Isn't it Satan himself, in the form of this abnormal goat, who hit me, sneering at my fate and my vain attempts to deceive it?

1. Amram, Aaron's father died in Egypt at the age of 137. Bible. Num.26:59, E. Nyström's Bible Dictionary. P.18. The Bible does not mention the name of Amram even once during the 42 years that the Jews were in the wilderness, and according to the law, Aaron could not hold the office of high priest if his father was with him.
2. *Elath* or Eloth was an ancient city mentioned in several places in the Hebrew Bible on the northern tip of the Gulf of Aqaba.
3. The Bible. Exodus 12:35, 36.
4. The sons of Aaron: Nadab, Abiud, Eleazar, and Jothamar. The Bible. Exodus 6:23
5. The Bible. Gen.47:20
6. The Bible. Numbers 13:24
7. Jehovah is the name by which God calls himself in the Bible. It is also where he calls himself the One who exists. The Bible. Exodus 3:16.
8. The Bible. Exodus 3:17
9. The Bible. Exodus 3:2

CHAPTER 11:

Moses' Law

In the morning Moses' bandits set out from the capital in battle order[1]. The scouting party of Hosea's cutthroats marched in the front, the cover squad in the back, and Moses and the clan elders moved in the center of the whole unit.

On the way, they caught up with those who had left earlier, and they joined Moses' column, hoping for armed guards.

The women's tears dried up and they fell silent, the children were tired and not shouting and the whole column of people moving in silence looked something like a funeral procession that moved and moved eastward, without stopping to bury the dead.

They left on time, Hosea reported that Pharaoh's fleet was on its way to the capital and maybe now, the troops loyal to Pharaoh entered the capital.

There was no danger that Pharaoh would rush in pursuit, for Pharaoh's main forces had fallen behind, including his famous band of chariots, which posed a serious threat. Moses hoped that while Pharaoh was gathering his forces into a fist and rushing to catch up with the enemy, they would be far away in the wilderness, where without thorough preparation Pharaoh would not venture.

The events of the last few days had devastated Moses so much that it was as if he had fallen into hibernation. He looked about indifferently, thought of nothing, and answered all the questions of Hosea, who regularly came up to him for instructions, with a voice in which neither intonation nor expression was audible.

It was not until the third day that the death of the old Jew brought Moses out of his stupor. The slow-walking Jew behind the wagon had a heart attack and fell face first into the road dust without making a sound, as if he had stumbled. Afraid to lag behind the column, the sons of the dead old man quickly carried the father aside, and quickly buried him in a shallow hole. No one was surprised or disturbed by this, as if they were burying a dog, not a man, and the column and everyone in this mass of people knew, that it was only the beginning, and such grave mounds would mark the way of the column wherever it went.

- How will I be buried, - Moses thought, - like the great Pharaoh in the glittering pyramid, or like this old man in the roadside ditch? And if there is an afterlife, will the Jewish or Egyptian gods judge me after death?

Thinking about this, Moses remembered his childhood, when to him and Pharaoh's son Ram, the old priest had told him about the realm of the dead. I remember that he was struck by the fact that after death a man moves to an underground kingdom, where, just like on earth, it is warm and bright and where the same great river as the Nile flows, where the same fields and vineyards are. But, the priest said, only those who had done no evil while living on earth could live there. The god of the kingdom of the dead, Anubis[2], with the body of a man and the head of a jackal, - the priest said, - meets the dead man at the gate of the kingdom and brings him to the judgment of justice, where he will be judged by the great god Osiris. Standing before him, dressed in white, the deceased must recite an oath of his innocence. Every Egyptian knew this oath, and Moses automatically repeated it in his mind[3]:

I loved the gods,
I loved Pharaoh,
I loved my parents,
I loved the people,
I did not kill,
I didn't steal,
I didn't lie,
I wasn't jealous,

I was not the cause of tears,
I have done no evil.

The balance of the scales showed that the person who uttered the oath was not lying and was indeed a good and kind person. Such a dead person was given eternal life and allowed to live in the realm of the dead. If his heart outweighed the goddess Maat[4], he was a villain living on earth, and at the same moment, a terrible monster with the body of a lion and the head of a crocodile would swallow him.

I'd rather not be judged by the Egyptian gods; my heart will outweigh by more than a hundred Maat's goddesses; and fortunately I am a Jew, and it is the Jewish god Jehovah who must judge me. He is kind and always forgives everyone, and it makes no difference to Jehovah whether you are a murderer, a scoundrel or a good man, he gives forgiveness to all who believe in him[5].

At this point Moses' thoughts took an unexpected turn. Surely, in uniting the Jews who had left Egypt, Jehovah must be the cornerstone of his plans! But he must not be as kind and toothless as the Jews make him out to be. The people must fear his wrath and the chief sin for which he will punish them severely is disobedience. And they should obey God's appointee on earth, which am me. Cool! So, I have to think about the laws I will give them, supposedly in the name of God, and let them just try to break them! And I will put the Egyptian oath of the dead as the basis of the law.

Enlightened by this brilliant idea, Moses became joyful and began to consider the theses of his law.

Toward evening, his train of thought was interrupted by the noise of a panic-stricken column ahead of him. Unbeknownst to him, the column stopped. There was an unimaginable noise of people screaming in terror, women crying and children screaming. Hosea, who had just arrived, struck Moses with the awful news that Pharaoh's army was ahead.

- Where had it come from? - Moses thought with horror, - Will I have to die today in this accursed place, and will I never be Pharaoh?

Trying not to betray his fear, Moses ordered Hosea to tell him everything in order.

- Apparently Pharaoh also played war as a child, - Hosea began, - clever at warfare, almost like me. He outsmarted us and sent part of his army to intercept us, assuming in advance that we would retreat. And Moses, - he said calmly, - that part of his army is chariots! And I wondered why the fleet came to the capital, but the chariot troop didn't. It makes sense to me now.

- He understands now, - cried the horror-stricken Moses, - where were you before, you clever fellow, and what shall we do now?

Hosea paid no attention to Moses' rebuke of him, for he had evidently thought of a plan and listened calmly, smilingly, to Moses' furious behavior. Waiting till Moses was in the last stages of fear, Hosea told him his thoughts, and he did it as a good actor, showing with all his appearance: - Look, Moses, what a warlord I am. You will not fail with me.

- We have three possibilities, - he began, showing Moses three fingers to make him more understandable, seeing that Moses was quite dazed with fear, - first, to attack.

- Are you out of your mind, - Moses shrieked, - chariots are the elite of Pharaoh's army, and they will crush us in no time.

-You're right, - answered Hosea calmly, - I think so too.

- The second is to turn north into the Philistine lands.

- So? - Moses asked him, - Can we get away?

- No, - Hosea summed up, - these people under Pharaoh have a good army and will try to prove their loyalty to him. They have surely been informed of what is happening in Egypt, and I am sure the Philistines are waiting at the frontier to capture us and deliver us to Pharaoh[5].

- What is the third possibility? - Moses hastened Hosea, - Tell me.

-The third, - said Hosea admiring himself, - is to turn south into the narrow valley between the Red Sea and the mountains.

-You idiot, - Moses exclaimed disappointedly, - it's a trap and there's no way out; Pharaoh's army coming slowly will strangle us all in this mousetrap.

- Well, we'll see about that, - Hosea said merrily, mimicking Moses' poorly spoken Aramaic.

Moses did not understand and stared at Hosea.

- I know a certain place, Moses, - Hosea began, taking his time and enjoying Moses' attention, - where at a good tide and with a wind from the north or the east you can cross from one shore to the other without getting your feet wet. The Bedouins showed me this place when I was wandering about. There are always tides, so pray to Moses that he sends us a strong wind. Well, in the worst case scenario, - Hosea said after silence and giving Moses time to digest his plan, - we'll build a raft and sail to the other side in the dark, when no one can see us.

- But the others? - Moses asked, as if he didn't understand what was in store for the people.

- Oh, what do I have to think of every one of them? - Hosea grumbled, - I'd like to save my own skin, it's dear to me for some reason, and then he added, - and yours of course.

- Well, Hosea, - said Moses, after a short pause, - if we get out of this mess, I'll change your name. You'll be Jesus. Turn the column to the south.

1. Bible. Exodus 13:18
2. Anubis - according to Egyptian mythology, the god of the underground paradise after death.
3. The text of the oath of the dead was found in one of the tombs of Egypt. From the author: Agree that the oath of the dead reminds us like two drops of water of the Ten Commandments of the Bible. There is no doubt that this is yet another plagiarism of the biblical authors. It is safe to assume that other significant passages in the Bible were borrowed from Egyptian culture.
4. Maat - according to Egyptian mythology, the goddess of truth.
5. Obedience and faith in God are the red thread of the Bible. Just believe, and God will forgive you no matter who you are, murderer or scoundrel. Take the favorites of God, Moses and King David. These are the worst of scoundrels and murderers. So what?! They believe in God, so they are forgiven in advance for all the vile things they have done and will do! What do you think of the scene in the New Testament when the murderer hangs on the cross with Jesus Christ? As soon as the murderer said: - I believe, - and he immediately goes to heaven! A worthy reward for the murderer!

CHAPTER 12:

The Stable Boy's Assistant

- You said, daddy if not Nain and someone else's son would not protect Egypt, then who would? - Boby thought as he made his way through the quiet, sleeping streets toward the center of the city. And he wants to fight," he remembered with resentment the time his father had tried to beat him with a sandal. When I get to Memphis and do the deed, you'll see how brave I am. Then Boby imagined himself fighting bravely against the enemies of Egypt, against a hundred enemies. No, better with three hundred pogroms. No, better yet with five hundred enemies. Here he is getting into the thick of the battle, where the enemies are about to reach the encircled Pharaoh. Pharaoh is no longer able to hold back the onslaught of the enemy, and his guards are completely overwhelmed. The situation is critical, but at this crucial moment he, Boby, appears and saves Pharaoh from certain death. Victory is won and everyone rejoices, but at this very moment the enemy, who has pretended to be dead, jumps up and throws his spear at Pharaoh. No one is able to help Pharaoh, and only he, Boby, covers Pharaoh with his chest. Then Boby imagined that he, killed by this spear, was being taken to his mother, like the greatest hero of Egypt, and all the people on the way were crying, throwing flowers on the cart and pitying the dead Boby.

The scene he had made up made Boby sniff his nose, and he felt so sorry for himself that tears came out of his eyes.

But he didn't want to die at all, and he started to think over the situation when the enemy's spear didn't kill him at all, but only wounded him, and he recovered and became the most famous man of Egypt. Of course, the Pharaoh would reward him and offer to marry some princess of Pharaoh's family, maybe even an overseas queen, but he would refuse. Boby had long been fond of the poor fisherman Rabsak's daughter, and after thinking about it, he decided that he would never exchange her for ten princesses. Then Boby began to imagine how he, a hero of Egypt, would return home in a war chariot, and then this stubborn girl would immediately fall in love with him and daddy would give them a nice wedding.

Dreaming, Boby did not notice how he found himself in the center of the city, where soldiers and townspeople were finishing the last preparations for the march. Sitting in a dark corner between a fence and some crate, Boby watched the bustling people. Finally he chose a target. It was a camping wagon in which soldiers were stacking sacks of oats to feed the war horses. Waiting for the right moment, Boby swooped into the wagon and crawled like a mouse into a niche between the sacks. He lay still, trying not to breathe, and even when the soldier threw the sack into the van, which pinned him down, Boby did not make a sound. At last the packing was done and the food cart, without waiting for the chariots to appear, set off. Not half an hour passed, and from the monotonous swaying and the fatigue of worrying about Pharaoh and Egypt, Boby fell asleep unnoticed.

When he awoke, the sun was already high. The stuffiness had penetrated under the canvas covering the wagon, and he was unbearably thirsty.

Oh, silly, - Boby scolded himself, - I didn't think to take a drink with me.

Trying not to think about water, he began to look around his shelter. The wagon was small and lightly built, which allowed it to move quickly enough to keep up with the chariots and to provide food and water for the men and horses when they caught up with it. Cautiously making his way to the front of the wagon, Boby tried to see through a crack in the canvas partition separating the wagon from the coachman to see the man controlling the horses. Unfortunately there was nothing to be seen but the coachman's back, and after admiring that back, Bobby went to the back of the wagon, which was also covered by a cloak to keep the dust out of the wagon. Making a peek, Boby saw a similar van moving behind his van, followed by another and another and another, and this chain of vans went way back. After watching the movement of the vans for a long time, Boby began to think about the situation. Where to get water? Boby thought that the coachman must be even thirstier than he was, sitting in the open sun and swallowing the dust raised by the wagons ahead. - So there must be water somewhere in the wagon," thought Bobby, and decided to examine the wagon. But no sooner had he thought of it than the front curtain opened and the figure of the coachman appeared. It was a warrior in his fifties with what seemed to Boby to be unfriendly eyes. Without noticing Boby, who had his whole body pressed against the sacks, the coachman, holding the reins in his left hand, threw aside the sack nearest to him and drew out from under it a bag of leather, as big as a watermelon, a wineskin. As he opened the wooden plug, the coachman began to drink greedily from the bag, and Boby saw his Adam's apple go up and down, and trickles of water poured down his chest. As he watched this, Boby made automatic gulping motions with his throat, but nothing but dust entered his stomach. Finally, waiting for the coachman to get drunk enough, shut up the wineskin, tossed it on the sacks, and disappeared behind the partition, Boby rushed to the coveted water and grabbed the wineskin and began to drink greedily.

- How delicious the water is, - he thought, - and why hadn't I noticed it before.

Out of boredom, Boby decided to have something to eat and untied the fishing bag. There wasn't much to eat: two flatbreads, an onion and some dates. Without thinking about the future, Boby ate everything except the onion and, drinking delicious water from the coachman's supply, began to think about home. To his surprise, in spite of being an adult, he wanted to go home to his mother.

-Oh, I'm going to be in trouble when I get back. I don't know about mommy, - thought Boby, - but daddy will beat me up, maybe even with a sandal.

The only way to escape a beating was to be a hero. Thinking about it, Boby dozed off. He dreamed that he came home, and his good mother started kissing him. Then there was his angry father, who for some reason did not want to kiss him, but grabbed him by the shoulders and began to shake him hard, saying: - Where did you come from, you unfit boy.

From this shaking, or from fear of his father and his sandal, Boby woke up and to his horror saw that it was the coachman, not his father, leaning over him, shaking him by the shoulder, saying: - Where did you come from wretched boy in my wagon?

It turned out that the wagon had stopped for a short halt, to feed the men and water the horses. The coachman of the wagon, where Boby was seated, after having watered the horses, went into the wagon, where he always took shelter from the scorching sun during the march, and had a snack. Here, to his surprise, he found the boy asleep.

Boby, staring at him, told him that his brother Nain, the best archer in Egypt and the whole land. Now he is the archer of the greatest general of Pharaoh's army, commander of the chariots, so Boby decided to go to war, so that in case his help was needed he could save Nain and Pharaoh.

- Have you thought about your parents, you snot-nosed warrior? - The coachman asked him angrily. Have you thought how they're scurrying about the city looking for you, you wretched boy?

Then come the command to leave, and the coachman, who had not had time to eat, took a piece of dried meat and went back to his seat.

-Sit here like a mouse, - he ordered Bobby, - or I'll whip you. At night, when we catch up with the chariot troop, I'll take you to your brother and let him decide what to do with you. And if you have lied to me about him, I will harness you instead of my horses.

CHAPTER 13:

Brothers

Not two hours later, Nain became convinced that chariot riding did not live up to the romantic halo that surrounded these elite Pharaonic troops.

Even though the chariots moved at marching speed, he had to hold on to the railings the whole time so he wouldn't accidentally fall out of the chariot, and Nain imagined with horror what would happen to him if the charioteer let the horses go at full, fighting speed.

- How does an archer manage to shoot and throw darts without holding on to the rail, - Nain thought, shaking and swallowing the dust the horses kicked up, - does he have four arms, two to hold on and two to shoot?

Ace, on the other hand, seemed stuck to the chariot and paid no attention to the jolts. His body took the right position automatically, as if by magic.

Turning back a few times, grinning at Nain and his vain attempts to look dignified, the warrior called him to stand shoulder to shoulder and began to teach Nain some wisdom.

- The most important thing in our business, - he began, - is to learn how to handle horses. If I now entrust you with the reins, you will overturn the chariot even at this marching speed in a few minutes. It takes years to learn, and a more or less experienced charioteer is one who has ridden a chariot for at least three years. As long as I'm driving, you won't have to do it. Your job is to shoot. How do you do it with all this shaking? Don't worry, trust me, you'll learn to ride the chariot without holding on quickly, in a few hours your body will get used to what you think is a crazy jolt and your body will learn to keep its balance whether you're just standing there chatting with me, shooting or throwing a dart.

Nain smiled incredulously at Ace and pictured himself standing proudly in the chariot as it raced at full throttle. He'd no sooner had his back fully straightened than another bump proved to him that if he could learn to ride as proudly and at ease as anyone else, it wouldn't be as quickly as Ace had promised.

- In battle, - Ace continued his lesson, - you must listen to my commands. There are only two, so you don't have to strain your memory to remember them. The first command is port and the second is starboard. It's simple, when I tell you starboard you have to, you have to move over there and shoot from there, and when I tell you to port, you have to be over there in a flash and shoot from there. The thing is, I can always see better from where we're going to be in the most danger. Simple, isn't it?

-Simple, - Nain replied.

- Well, if you agree it's simple, - said Ace smiling, - let's start training.

- Starboard, - suddenly yelled Ace.

Nain had no choice but to follow the commander's command and on half-bent legs to the starboard side. No sooner had he fulfilled the first command than another followed immediately: - port side.

It went on for hours, and Nain lost track of time. He felt that he was jumping about in the damn chariot like a trained monkey, and that his ordeal was not likely to end anytime soon. At last Ace stopped the chariot, which meant a halt. Nain, on half-bent, wobbly legs, got down to the ground, and it seemed to him that there could be nothing better in the world than to walk on the ground. In the halt, the warriors who had witnessed Nain's training joked merrily and kindly about Nain. Nain was smiling through the force, and they, laughing, remembered how once they themselves had found themselves in a chariot for the first time and they, just like Nain, had been trained to keep their balance.

The rest was short, people quickly ate scones and, having watered the horses, the detachment continued their way. It was either because Nain was rested or because his body was used to the crazy jolt, but he felt much better after the break. To his surprise, his body seemed to exist separately from his consciousness and automatically, without a command from his brain, began to respond to the shaking, springing and bending at the right moment. By the evening Nain had completely mastered himself in the chariot, and the fear of falling out of it under the laughter of people evaporated, and Nain, like an important goose, proud of himself, freely dodged inside the chariot and, imitating Ace, looked into the distance from under arm.

As darkness fell, Ace stopped the horses and ordered them to prepare for the night. All day long the troop had been moving northwest, and Nain couldn't figure out how Ace was going to attack the capital, which was to the southwest and also on the opposite bank of the Nile.

- Maybe I've been so lucky to be a soldier that I get stupid and don't know which way is north and which way is south, thought Nain and ventured to ask Ice where they were really going.

Ice, unused to questions from soldiers, was initially furious at Nain's question, but when he remembered that Nain wasn't a soldier but a volunteer, he reluctantly decided to explain. First he told Nain a whole sermon from the rules for a soldier, who expressly forbade asking the commander what he was doing, and only then did Ice say that they were on their way to Epham.

- What about Pharaoh? - Nain exclaimed.

- Tomorrow the fleet will approach the capital and Ben, Pharaoh's chief general, will liberate the capital. Then an army will come and liberate all Egypt.

- Where are we going then? - Nain doesn't understand.

- We have another task, you a civilian can't understand military decisions, - answered Ice, - I won't explain you what we have to do, but I promise you a good battle in the future, so don't worry about the missed opportunity to excel. And don't ever ask me any more questions about the service, understand?

The messengers began to arrive and Ice went about his business: the reconnaissance report, the guard service report, the roundup and other important matters, and it was only an hour later that he began to go to sleep.

- What are you doing awake, - he asked Nain in surprise, - if it were up to me, I'd have had my seventh dream long ago. In four hours, the wagon train will come, and then you will have no time to sleep, you will have to water and feed the horses. Lie down; I don't want you to fall out of the chariot tomorrow!

He took a piece of felt out of the chariot and laid it out and immediately snored. Nain also lay down, and it seemed to him that he had just closed his eyes when the command sounded: - Wake up.

With difficulty Nain opened his eyes, took the oats, watered the horses and scolded himself for not going to bed earlier. Five minutes later, he was finally backed to his senses, only to shiver at the chill of the morning. Everything he was doing was familiar to him and did not leave much difficulty and even the horses obeyed him as their master.

- What military discipline means, Nain thought, even the horses didn't buck. When he had finished fiddling with the horses, Nain was just about to lie down to sleep the remaining minutes before the performance, when he saw a warrior approaching him, leading his brother by the hand.

- What am I asleep? - Nain thought, wiping his eyes, for it was obvious that there was no way Boby could have shown up here. But this was no dream, and Boby shrieked happily and threw himself around his neck. Stunned by his appearance, Nain couldn't understand why his brother was here.

- There's my brother, - Boby said pointing to Nain, - and you said I'd harness you instead of the horse.

Awakened a few minutes early, the disgruntled Ace was about to give the noisy men a scolding and was already on his elbow to come down on them when he saw the coachman silently observing the meeting of the two brothers.

- Hey, Genat, - he exclaimed, turning to the coachman of the cart,

- Who have you brought here, and what does it all mean? They stepped back from the barely lit fire and talked lively, and their contented voices made it clear that they knew each other well and were glad to see each other.

Boby, jumping from one place to another, told Nain about his escape to help Pharaoh and thereby so puzzled him that he did not know what to do next, and Boby, seeing his indecision, begged him to take him in his chariot.

- Nain, - he cunningly said, - talk to the commander, I will do everything, just take me with you. If you leave me here, I'll never find my way home and I'll be lost. What will you tell your mother then? I'll be lost for sure. I'll starve to death, and Daddy will beat you with a sandal for me. Come on, Nain, talk to the commander.

-You're a fool, you are, - Nain scolded him, - and the chariot can barely fit two men, or I'll put you around my neck? You'll see that Ace will order you to stay here now, he won't hold up his war band for some runny lad. What am I really going to tell my mother?

Ice and Genat talked and went back to the fire. Apparently the coachman told the story of Boby's appearance, because, looking sternly at him, Ice ordered: - For running away from home, I order Genat to whip you out as a delinquent soldier, but considering that you did it out of love for the Motherland and Pharaoh, I order you to be enlisted in the troop as assistant coachman of the food cart. You are at Genat's disposal. If I receive a single complaint against you, I'll have you thrown out at once. Did you understand?

- Never, I'm good, yes I will, yes I always will, - Boby babbled impatiently, elated with such news, but Ace would not listen to him.

- Go, - he ordered.

A delighted Boby waved to Nain and ran after Genat; while Ice lay down to take a nap for the hour before he got up: - You've got a desperate brother. He could be a good soldier. And you cannot leave him here, he will die. Let's go to Epham, put him in some family until the fighting is over.

Returning to his wagon, Genat ordered Boby to sleep, but he was excited about what had happened and his pride at being a soldier, lying down and dreaming of a future battle. In contrast, Genat snored as soon as his head touched the sack of oats. A couple of hours later the command to move was given and Genat jumped up and took his place on the saddle as if he had slept at least seven hours. Boby mustering his courage threw back the curtain and sat down next to Genat. He said nothing but glanced at him sleepily as he continued to drive the wagon. Boby soon guessed the secret of why Genat didn't seem tired after a night like that. He was sleeping on the move! After every minute, Genat would flick up his eyelids, glancing at the horses and the road, and then his eyes would slowly close. After a minute, he'd open his eyes again, make sure the horses were in place, and go back to sleep.

Boby wanted to talk to him like a soldier to a soldier, but, not wanting to disturb his commander's sleep, he kept quiet with great difficulty. Finally his nerves failed, and the moment Genat once more opened his eyes, he asked him to give him the reins. Genat thought for a while and, determined to test him, began to wrap the reins around Boby's left hand, and then, after watching Boby's skill at steering for a while and finding that he was doing well, he dozed off. Boby, honored by this, was puffed up like a turkey, and looked around proudly; wishing Nain could see what a fine charioteer he was.

- I can easily manage with a chariot, - Boby thought and said one more time woken up Genat: - And our commander is nice, he's smart, he knows who to take as a soldier, you won't be lost with me, - and seeing that Genat laughed at him, shouted at his horses, - well, don't spoil!

At another rest, Genat had a quick snack and disappeared for a short time, and when he reappeared, Bob saw that he had brought battle armor, helmet, and breastplate made of hippopotamus skin. When the troop set off, he, making sure that Bob could handle the horses, began mending the armor while purring a fancy song about the women of the capital. When the hardened skin of the armor would not yield to a sharp knife, Genat would start panting like his horse on the mount and quietly, so as not to hear Boby, but Boby heard anyway, said bad soldierly words that somehow made the skin begin to crumple nicely.

When deep into the night they had caught up with the troop and, having watered and fed the horses, Boby wanted to go look for Nain, but Genat, shouted at him, ordered him to sleep. And indeed, tired for the day, Boby did not have time to climb into the van, and instantly fell asleep, and when he woke up, the sun was already high. After reproaching himself, Boby climbed on the heel to relieve Genat.

At short halts other coachmen began to come to them who had heard about the young volunteer. Looking cheerfully at Boby, they chatted amicably with him, which made Boby very proud. They were all, for some reason, very kind, and brought some sweet dates or nuts for Boby, and always gave him a friendly pat on the shoulder. Everyone was interested in whom he was, where he was from, who his parents were, and one even asked if he had a fiancée.

- I do, of course, - Boby answered seriously.

- Really? - Also earnestly interrogated the old warrior, in whose eyes Boby saw a cheerful interest. He winked at the other coachmen standing there and continued; - Does she know that you love her?

- She does, - answered Boby, - I've tugged her hard by her hair several times.

They all nodded their heads in agreement; if one of the boys pulls a girl's hair, it's definitely love.

- Well, is she beautiful? - The old warrior persisted.

- Beautiful, - said Boby, and added, - like my mom.

Everyone laughed again, and Genat shouted at them: - Well, why you are attached to the boy, you rustling stallions, he's right to say that mothers are always the prettiest. Go back to your carriages, get out of the way.

Boby had lost track of time, and it seemed to him that they had been moving for ages. Finally, in the afternoon, a band of chariots suddenly appeared ahead, followed by a city of some kind. This meant that they had reached their destination and they could rest. Ace's chariot flew past their carriage, and Bobн managed to wave a hand at Nain, who smiled when he saw him.

The first thing Ace did was to send out a scouting party toward the capital to the west and begin deploying a detachment. He put 200 chariots positioned to cover all roads to the east, and he put the other four hundred chariots on rest, ordering them to rotate watches every eight hours. He placed the wagon train on the outskirts of Epham, forming a line of defense.

The soldiers, having quickly completed the necessary work, began to make fires of dung and small bush twigs to make the bean chowder they had not tasted on the march. Nimble Boby, it was not too difficult to gather dry branches and his and Genat's campfire was blazing merrily. Genat hung a copper kettle over it and began to conjure up his dinner. All the while he was looking slyly at Boby, and when they had enjoyed their meal, he reached into the wagon and pulled out the battle armor he had repaired on the march.

- Come here, son, - he called to Boby, and when the latter, amazed at the guess that it real battle armor for him, stood in front of him, Genat said, - it is unbecoming for a warrior to be without armor. Let's try it on. Having fiddled with straps, he has fastened the breastplate decorated with copper plaques, has shackled his feet in armor and finally has put a helmet on his head. Satisfied with his work, he stepped a few meters away and admired on the little warrior.

-So, - he finally said, - you are now a real soldier of Pharaoh's army, only a spear and a sword are missing.

Feeling himself the happiest boy in Egypt, Boby rushed from campfire to campfire, and showing off his armor. The elderly warriors, who made up most of the convoy, spoke warmly of his brave appearance, and asked Boby to sit by their fire, which was categorically impossible for him, as not everyone had yet seen him in such amazing armor. Everyone tried to shove something tasty into his hands, and one warrior, reached into his wagon and pulled out a trophy bow with a quiver and a dozen arrows. Boby froze in place and could not utter a word. It was a real work of art. Made of ebony, the bow was inlaid with silver, and the quiver had gold plates that depicted a battle scenes.

- Does he really want to give this treasure to me, - thought Boby, - if my father saw me with this bow and this armor, he would immediately forget about the sandals.

- This is a keepsake for you, - said the soldier, and his words made Boby's heart leap for joy.

Thanking the soldier, Boby rushed over to Genat and showed him the gift.

Genat spent a long time twirling it in his hands without ceasing to marvel at the beauty of the weapon, and Boby impatiently asked him to go look for Nain. He couldn't wait to brag. Genat reached into the van, fiddled around, and when he emerged, Boby froze with his mouth hanging open. Genat had put on his battle armor and instead of a simple coachman in a canvas cloak, Boby was facing a warrior, but that was not what struck Boby, but the fact that on Genat's chest, in the center of his breastplate, he saw a gold plate with the image of the Pharaoh's rod. This insignia was well known to any boy in Egypt, and it meant that its owner was either a warlord or an Egyptian hero awarded for special services to the state.

Let's go to Ace, - Genat said shyly, - I have a serious talk to him.

All the way to the location of the commander, the soldiers they met on the way respectfully looked at the sign of Pharaoh and bowed to his owner, and Boby was in seventh heaven with pride for Genat. The commander invited the deputies to dinner, and Nain helped set the table with Ace' personal cook, who had caught up their convoy. The improvised table was a feast of merriment. When Nain saw Genat, he opened his mouth at his Hero sign and bowed. The excitement at the table subsided, and everyone stood up to greet Genat, and Ice invited him to the table. At the same time, the commander invited Boby to the table. All the warriors at the table praised Boby's armor and passed his amazing bow to each other. After eating for appearances, Genat stood up, thanking everyone for the honor, and asked Ice for a few minutes. They stepped aside.

- Why are you all dressed up like you are going to parade, - said Ace, - or are you planning to retire again?

-I won't retire again unless you kick me out, - said Genat, - and I'm here, as you rightly pointed out, for a formal conversation with my commanding officer.

Genat stretched in a string, as it is a custom in the army.

-All right, go ahead, - Ace answered displeased with Genat's official tone, - I'm listening to you.

Genat hesitated, and then asked in a low voice: - Leave the boy to me under my charge. He won't be safer than with me anywhere, you know me commander.

Then, after a silence, he added: - His eyes are the same as Ned's, the same demons leaping in them, and I think it is his soul that has come back to me in the form of Boby.

Ace nodded at him and waved, - all right, take the boy. Satisfied Genat went to his chariot, ordering Boby to return before dark and no less satisfied Boby began to boast in front of Nain about his armor and the best bow in Egypt.

- You know, Nain, - he chattered merrily, - now my daddy won't beat me, and all the boys next door will die of envy.

- No, he will! I'd advise you to put a bib on your back to cover your ass, when daddy will beat you up.

- You're a liar, - Boby snapped, - daddy loves me.

-That's why he's going to beat you up, - Nain concluded.

They were sitting around the fire, when Ice joined them after letting the deputies go. Nain saw that the commander and Genat were good friends and asked him to tell them about the hero of Egypt and the deed for which he had been given the title.

Ace, ruffling by the branch, the embers in the fire, was silent, and then, as if recalling a long-forgotten past, began the story.

-If we tell about Genat, we must also tell about his best friend Ned. You know that according to the laws of Egypt, every tenth family must send their 17 year old son to the army for 33 years. So the village council, where Genat and Ned were from, decided to send them together. They were young at the time and, living next door to each other, had been friends since childhood. They ended up in a chariot troop. Ned became an archer and Genat a charioteer, and there were no better soldiers than them then or now. I remember Ned taking Pharaoh's first prize in the archery. He hit a papyrus stalk from a hundred yards away, and when his rivals protested and said that he put arrow to target accidently, Ned shot a second time and hit the target again. Well, no one could drive a chariot better than Genat. One, then a snot-nosed boy who volunteered to serve in the army, learned the art of driving a chariot from Genat and thanks to this knowledge many times he survived. That boy is sitting before you now; - Ace laughed, and began to rustle the fire with a branch. The branch hissed and snapped, and a bounced-out cinder fell on his hand. He brushed it off with his hand and blew on the burned area in a funny way.

- Do you know why my detachment is considered the finest of Pharaoh's army? - He asked and, without letting they answer, knowing they didn't know, he continued; - imagine two human warriors, an archer and a charioteer, who have been in the same chariot for years. They are so friendly that they are willing to die for each other in battle without a moment's hesitation. There is no other war band that fights with such bravery. So Genat and Ned were the best of the best. Once, long ago, when I was not yet squad leader, they saved Pharaoh from certain death. The Philistine warriors, when we were at war with them, surrounded his chariot and, killing the horses, tried to take him prisoner. That's when these two falcons came and attack them. They broke through to Pharaoh's chariot in spite of the fiercest resistance. Ned sent arrow after arrow without a miss, and Genat, skillfully handling his horses at great speed, was able to grab Pharaoh and throw him into his chariot. Without stopping, the three of them broke through to the main force, while I covered their retreat. For this feat, Pharaoh declared them heroes and adorned their breastplates with a golden rod. Of course, as in such cases, this rod is accompanied by a large cash reward, so these two friends, sent part of the money to relatives in the village, and the rest of them the whole squad was partying, almost a month, and I included. Ask the old warriors, who remember the case, and they will tell you more than I will.

- After a moment's silence, Ace continued: - And they were very different, Ned, a Jew by nationality, was cunning, and Genat, an Egyptian, a simple soul. Ned was like fire, unable to sit in one place, and Genat was calm as a boa constrictor. Ned, of course, was the ringleader. The others would have been prosecuted long ago, but nobody touched them, they were feared and respected. I remember a former chariot squad commander summoning them after another brawl in some town and asking: - You scoundrels, why you turned country tavern into ruins, eh? Answer me.

Genat was silent, and Ned immediately attacked, - they themselves are to blame, why they touched the drunken Genat, he was lying as a layer and could not even hurt a fly.

- Lying down? - The commander was surprised, - how could a lying man break the walls of the tavern? You son of a bitch, explain it to me.

- I don't remember, - answered Genat, - I remember them hitting Ned, and then I don't remember anything.

- He doesn't remember, and you what? - Asked Ned's commander, -or do you have a bad memory too?

- I'm sorry commander, I don't remember anything, only that they said that our commander a fool, - he lied, - so I got mad at them.

- What? -They said I am the fool? So, why didn't you give them a good beating? - Shouted the commander.

- We did, that's why you're scolding us, - and Ned was sly.

- You didn't give the bastards enough; you should have given them more. Get out of my sight, - shouted the commander.

After telling them this, Ace fell silent; he must have been remembering the fun times of the past.

- Where is Ned now, and why is Genat, the best charioteer, serving in the convoy? - asked Nain.

- A little over a year ago, we were fighting the Nubians, - Ice continued with a scowl, - and I don't know what happened, how it could have happened, but Genat broke the chariot. I don't know maybe he's get too old to react instantly, or what kind of accident that happens in warfare, but it happened in the middle of the battle. The horses galloped away, dragging Genat away because his arm was caught in the noose of the reins, and Ned was alone against a hundred. We finally put the enemy to flight and won, and, as usual, we looked for the wounded on the battlefield and buried the dead. Genat, after being dragged across the ground by horses, had no living place on his body, and he was running, looking for his friend. He found him. Ned lay on his back, impaled by a heavy spear. His eyes were wide open, and he seemed to be dead admiring the high sky, and a smile froze on his lips. It was he who rejoiced that his friend Genat had been dragged away from certain death by horses. So we buried him with that smile on his face.

At this point in the story, Boby sniffed his nose, and Nain saw two tears roll down his cheeks, leaving a wet trail. Nain looked reproachfully at his brother, as if to say that it was inappropriate for a soldier to cry, though a lump came to his throat.

- Immediately after this incident Genat, who had served his due time until fifty years of age, left the army and went to his village, - continued Ace, - but after a month or so he returned and asked me to take him back, but not as a chariot driver, but as a cartman. When I asked him why he was back, he said he was tired of peasant work, that his brothers and sisters had a life of their own, and that he dreamed every night of the chariot troop and his friend Ned.

At that moment the chariot of the scout commander drove up and Nain, so as not to disturb the commander, took Boby and led him to Genat.

CHAPTER 14:

The Calm Before The Storm

The sun had not yet risen, and Ice was on his feet. He got Nain up and ordered him to harness the horses. They ate breakfast and rode around the camp before it woke up. The soldiers slept peacefully as if gathering their strength for battle, and only the two hundred chariots on duty stood ready in the darkness, ready to rush into battle at any moment.

From this pre-dawn darkness and unbroken silence Nain could not believe that in one day the whole quiet and sleepy camp could turn into a boiling cauldron with shouts of people, rumbling chariots and moans of dying people.

Taking the scout commander and several chariots of the escort, Ace drove the chariot westward toward the far advanced patrol party.

Nain admired the dawn that had begun. The sun had not yet awakened and was somewhere over the horizon, but the eastern part of the sky was crimson, as if they were warning people that they were expecting a miracle any minute and that the sun god Ra would rise from the horizon to greet the whole world. And indeed, at first a small blindingly bright edge of the sun appeared, and then it shone triumphantly with its entire disk as if it had been ejected by a catapult. Night died and day was born.

Nain had admired the miracle of sunrise before they had traveled fifteen kilometers to the patrols. The patrol consisted of twenty riders on fine horses. These men, in case of danger, were to notify the main forces without to get fighting.

The scurrying patrol leader told Ace that all was quiet ahead and that he was expecting three scouts he had sent a few miles ahead. And, indeed, not ten minutes later, three riders appeared ahead. When they spotted the chariot of the squad leader, they headed straight for him.

- The rebels are within ten klicks of here, - the older sentry reported, - and camped. They were not prepared for combat and look like ready not to attack until noon at the earliest.

With orders not to engage the enemy patrol, Ace turned back to camp. It was clear to him that the rebels could strike his position, if not by noon, then certainly by evening. All the way back he, in his mind, arranged his chariots, his small number of infantry, and his convoy in such a way as to best oppose the enemy. Upon arriving at the camp, Ace assembled his deputies, and ordered the preparations for battle to begin.

- I decided not to wait for Moses to strike and the first to begin military action, to put it simply, we must be the first to attack the enemy, - he began, - according to the data I have the number of the enemy column of up to two hundred thousand people. They are mostly unarmed civilians who pose no danger to us. Moses has about ten thousand fighters who have no experience in combat operations. If we adopt defensive tactics, with three thousand first-class warriors, we can hardly hold back the onslaught of this hulk. The enemy, exasperated by the fear of Pharaoh's army coming at his heels, can break through in any one place and retreat into the desert. Therefore, as soon as the enemy column approaches to a distance of three kilometers, we will strike at his right flank with all the chariots we have. I understand your bewilderment, - he continued, "experience of fighting tells us that the most effective is to hit the chariots in the center and then crush the flanks, but in this situation it will cost us a lot of casualties. So by striking from the right flank, and crushing it in a few minutes, we will sow terror and panic in Moses' ranks. The whole crowd will rush to the left, and we will drive them into the narrow valley between the Red Sea and the mountains. The rest is much easier, the main army will come up, and we'll kill all the rebels in this mousetrap with no way out. Don't touch the unarmed, cut down only those who resist. One last thing. You have a chance to distinguish yourselves, whoever captures Moses alive, will get a good reward and quite possibly a star will fall on his chest, - hinting at Pharaoh's golden rod, Ace finished with a smile.

By noon, a sentinel who had ridden in reported to the astonished Ace that the rebels had turned and were heading south toward the Red Sea.

- What's the matter, - thought Ace, - have they gone mad? Why are they climbing into the mousetrap themselves? Or maybe they don't know the terrain and don't understand it? Or has Moses lost his head from fear of his famous detachment, and his army is completely demoralized? Well, so be it, they're making it easy for me.

Having waited just in case until morning, and having made sure that Moses had really gone into the valley, Ice ordered to move closer to the enemy and his detachment, coming to the entrance to the valley, blocked the exit from it. Now they had only to wait for the main force, which, according to the reconnaissance report, was moving swiftly to their aid and was one day's journey away.

A day later, by lunchtime, the advance patrol of Pharaoh's army appeared from the west. In a couple of hours, Ice would have to report the situation to him personally.

Ace had never been the sort of servant who was afraid of authority, but receiving Pharaoh in his detachment was no joke. This was no Pharaoh's inspector, with whom you could drink wine and finish your inspection without leaving the tent. He quickly summoned his deputies and ordered them to put everything in order, just as general commanders usually do before a general inspection.

- I'll skin you if you don't, - Ace threatened them.

The soldiers were in a huddle all over the camp, and the squealing commands of the commanders could be heard, especially the younger ones who'd never had Pharaoh in their element and they began to panic.

They began to frantically rush the soldiers, and some of the most cowardly commanders began to clean the horses and rub the brass plaques on the chariots themselves, helping the soldiers.

Everyone put on their ceremonial armor, and Nain saw the golden rod of the Pharaoh on Ace's breastplate. Catching his eye, Ice remarked that he had not received it as an Egyptian hero but as a warlord.

- I'm no hero of Egypt, - he smiled, - but my squad has the highest number of heroes, thirty-two.

Finally, ahead, Pharaoh's gilded chariot appeared, moving under the cover of his personal guard's mounted hundred. The chain dogs, Ace called them for their suspiciousness and willingness to chop up anyone at the slightest suspicion. The entire force of Ace dropped to their right knees with bated breath, and all bowed their heads. Unlike the civilians, who had to fall face down at the sight of Pharaoh, the soldiers, according to the custom, had to greet Pharaoh by standing on one knee.

As they approached Ace, Pharaoh, himself driving the chariot, stopped the horses and invited him into the chariot. After handing him the reins, Pharaoh ordered the guards to stand still and asked to Ace to show him his eagles. Everyone knew his love for the chariot squad, and the commanders of the other squads were always jealous of Ace.

Ace had long known that Pharaoh had a phenomenal memory. Even as a young man, Ace had been amazed that Pharaoh could remember the names of nearly every warrior in the chariot squad. Even today, Pharaoh ordered him to stop in front of each hero's chariot and, calling their names, ordered them to come up. And when they, red-faced with excitement, approached, he asked them questions about their personal lives, from which he could judge that Pharaoh remembered the history of each of them well.

And in fact, Ace had long noticed that the people of Egypt were completely ignorant of Pharaoh. One could judge from those appearances of his in the streets of the capital that he was a superhuman. The whole ceremony of his appearance to the people was designed to assure them that before them was God living on earth, and the people, falling face down in the dust, thought that the Great Pharaoh could neither laugh, nor cry, nor worry. Everyone was sure that this God was in no way inherent in simple human qualities, much less human shortcomings. It had never occurred to them that Pharaoh was human like them, that he could love, hate, worry, suffer and be merry just like an ordinary human.

Here Ace remembered how once, Pharaoh came to his squad for a combat readiness inspection. After the inspection and training attacks, Pharaoh took part in an archery competition. The soldiers succumbed to him, and he won the grand prize. Knowing he was a lousy shot, Pharaoh couldn't understand why his glorious falcons didn't do well. He was about to give Ace a good scolding when he realized that the warriors missed on purpose, to please him and take the grand prize. He scolded Hayes, who only shrugged, - What can I do if the soldiers love you? Pharaoh cancelled the results of the shooting, got out of the competition and asked the soldiers to show him the real shooting they were capable of. It was here that the soldiers showed real ability, and Pharaoh was pleased with the results shown. He was especially impressed by the winner, Ned, who hit the stem of a papyrus twice from a hundred yards. Presenting him with the main prize Pharaoh asked him if he could hit the eye of his opponent from a distance of one hundred and fifty meters.

- Come on, my Pharaoh, let's try, - Pharaoh slyly suggested him, - maybe I will hit.

- No, I believe, - laughed Pharaoh.

In a cheerful mood, Pharaoh gathered the senior commanders in the tent and traditionally summed up the check with a big feast or, simply put, a drinking party.

Ace knew that Pharaoh was a great lover and connoisseur of good wine and specially kept a couple of barrels of Philistine wine in his tent. The wine was clearly to Pharaoh's taste, and when everyone had dispersed, he went on and on tasting it, and then he decided to get some air. When he came out of the tent, he saw a soldier standing on guard, and ordered him to give him his spear and go to rest.

- Sleep, my warrior, - he said, - and I will do your service.

For half an hour Pharaoh faithfully performed the duties of the guard.

He paced in marching order around the tent, and would not let anyone near it, demanding the password. With great difficulty, Ace managed to outwit the obstinate sentry and lure him into the tent, where Pharaoh, with the next cup, forgot that he was a sentry and had a duty to perform.

The next morning before his departure he smiled at Ace embarrassedly and praised the bloody Philistine wine, and after his departure Ace gathered the commanders and ordered everyone who saw the drunken Pharaoh to keep his mouth shut, otherwise I'll skin him.

- Where is Genat, - suddenly asked Ice Pharaoh, - I couldn't find him in the ranks.

Ice briefly reported and Pharaoh, becoming angry, ordered him to rejoin the convoy.

- A hero in the wagon train? The best charioteer of my army! I will put you in the cart, - said Pharaoh, fervently, - you will cartwright, not commander of my best troops.

The wagons of convoy stood apart from the troop, and the cart soldiers knelt down in fear at Pharaoh's approach. There was no occasion yet for Pharaoh to inspect the wagon train. When a frowning Ace stopped his horses in front of Genat's wagon, Pharaoh ordered to Genat to approach. -I don't remember you having a grandson, - Pharaoh was surprised, looking at Boby, and apparently still angry with Ace, ordered, - Give the reins to Genat, he will now be my personal driver. In half an hour the council.

Genat moved the horses at Pharaoh's nod, and at that moment Boby jumped into the chariot and stood beside Pharaoh, to the horror of Ace. Apparently he didn't know what he was doing. Pharaoh was not surprised, put his hand on his shoulder and ordered him to touch it.

Angry as hell Ace went along the wagons to Pharaoh's tent, which had already been erected for him. At this unpleasant moment for him, a ram that had jumped out of one of the wagons got under his feet. Ace knew that the soldiers bought rams and kept them in the wagon for special occasions for meat. He knew and looked past this little infraction, but at that moment the ram was the last straw that set him off, and he kicked the ram and yelled: - Go to hell!

- I have no right to throw away such charioteers as you, Genat, - said Pharaoh as he stepped down from the chariot at the prepared tent. - You will be my personal charioteer while I am here. After the council I will go to inspect the enemy positions, and meanwhile you can rest. - And you, - he turned to Boby, will ride with me in the chariot. Tell me who you are and Pharaoh gently stroked his head.

Boby listened to Pharaoh with bated breath. Standing in the chariot beside Pharaoh, for some reason he felt that this would happen and he would surely take him with him, as if it had already happened to him in a dream and now that dream had come true.

After washing his face and taking a snack before the council, Pharaoh recalled the events of the past few days, and suddenly caught himself thinking that this roast duck was fragrant and delicious. Then he realized that he was beginning to calm down and finally come to his senses from the nightmare he had seen since the liberation of the capital.

There was no home in Memphis without a dead man[1]. On the last night; Moses' goons executed any Egyptian in their path. They spared neither the young nor the old. Such grief seemed impossible to bear. People did not fall down before him, as they once did when he returned to his palace, but when they saw Pharaoh; they stretched out their hands to him and asked for one thing, revenge. Revenge; punish with your power the subhumans that raised their hands against the civilian population. This boundless grief turned into animal bitterness, which blinded the people. In the capital the pogroms began on the Jewish families who had not taken part in the riot and who had not supported Moses. They did not think of leaving, remaining faithful to their homeland. The Egyptians, blinded by a sense of revenge, went about their wicked business without realizing what they were doing. Pharaoh ordered that the pogroms be stopped at all costs and threw everything he had at his disposal. But it was not easy to calm the people, and it was not until evening that the burning of the Jewish houses, the screams of the beaten and the screams of the women ceased in the capital.

A sense of shame seized Pharaoh. He, the first leader of a country, could not prevent the most disgusting and shameful thing for any country: a civil war.

- I was lucky, if you can call it luck, - he thought sadly, - that the civil war has not taken the most disgusting form, when not only one nation goes against each other, but also brother against brother.

Of course, everything had not happened out of nowhere, and such a serious reason as the famine that had arisen in the country had played its fatal role. But he, the Pharaoh of this country, where was he at this time? What exactly did he do when the two nations, Jewish and Egyptian, instead of rallying together, rushed to tear the piece of bread from each other's mouths?

- I have overlooked, - Pharaoh scolded himself, - but the main culprit is not me, but this beast, this scoundrel who wanted to seize power I must punish Moses, I must teach a lesson for the future to those who are ready to destroy their country for their own selfish interests. Men like Moses are scarier than any natural disaster. By fishing in the murky waters of natural disasters and social errors, they inflict on the country a blow of such devastating force that a catastrophic earthquake cannot.

The council of war did not last long. It was decided to attack the enemy at dawn, and to do so by the appointed time to draw troops to where Moses' camp was located. Pharaoh's plan was for Ace, with all the power of his six hundred chariots, to attack the enemy's center, while Pharaoh's infantry was to finish off the flanks.

At this the council was closed and the whole camp was in motion. The detachments moved hurriedly to the positions Ben had indicated. The easterly winds were disturbing the soldiers, and when it got too strong and turned into a storm, cussing was heard everywhere, but no matter what; Pharaoh's army was inexorably in its initial positions.

1. The Bible. Exodus 12:30

CHAPTER 15:

Crossing of the Red Sea

While waiting for the wind to blow, time dragged on slowly and a minute seemed like an hour. All was in vain; there was no wind and the sea was deep enough to think about crossing. Moses' situation was not just threatening, it was catastrophic. The scouts reported that Pharaoh himself had arrived in the troops, and we should expect his chariots to attack any minute.

There was terror in the camp of Moses. They all knew what was coming. Curses were heard everywhere against Moses, and only armed guards held back those who wanted to seize Moses and give him up to Pharaoh in exchange for the lives of their loved ones.

At last Hosea arrived. Under his leadership, about seven kilometers away, a small group of men were secretly building a raft that could hold a dozen people. Just as Hosea appeared, a welcome east wind began to blow. At first Moses saw how the wind, as if testing its power, began to throw grains of sand at the men; and after half an hour it howled like a wild beast and drove the waves of the sea southward.

- Well, Hosea, - rejoiced Moses, - as soon as you appear anywhere, everything begins to form, as if by magic. If this beautiful wind doesn't die down or change its direction, we can leave at nightfall. What about your raft?

-Almost ready, - answered a smiling Hosea, pleased with Moses' praise. - If it doesn't work out here, we'll leave quietly at nightfall. I can't let Pharaoh tear you to pieces, Moses; I'm used to bail my friends out of trouble. Hosea was telling these lies in good conscience. He did not want to come back here, but to lift sail and gone away by raft, and only the east wind had begun to change his mind.

Moses summoned Aaron, and when he arrived, frowning and unsociable as usual of late, Moses began to explain his plan to him.

- Aaron, if we are lucky today, and the wind opens a sandbank through which we shall flee from Pharaoh's army, and then all who do not know what really happened will think that the greatest miracle, which only God can do, has taken place. Centuries will pass, and people will believe this tale and marvel at the power of the God of the Jews, Jehovah. Go Aaron to the people and tell them my words, tell them that God has appeared to me tonight and said will open the waters of the sea to those who believe in him and his prophet Moses. Tell them to be ready to depart by nightfall. Do not take anything unnecessary and the ten kilometers that separate us from salvation, we must go in one breath. Tell them that if anyone does not believe the prophet Moses, let him stay here and know the wrath of Pharaoh.

Know this, Aaron; it will not only be my glory, but also yours. You are my brother, and that means that you are involved in my work and God's work. Go Aaron and bring God's glorious message of our salvation to the people.

Hosea, listening to Moses, could not hide his astonishment.

- He's lying, - he thought, - I am a crook myself, and I have seen crooks, but there are none like Moses. Don't play dice with him; he'll leave you without pants.

Moses was on a roll; Hosea had not seen him so cheerful in a long time. He was joking and joking, and then all of a sudden he got angry and said:

- You know, Hosea, - he said, - you're wrong to think you can outsmart me. I foresaw that you would leave me here and go on the raft alone. Then Moses laughed pretentiously, and, wagging his finger at him, continued, "My loyal men would have killed you at that attempt".

- Stop joking, - Hosea seemed genuinely offended, - why would I leave you? Never! Let Pharaoh cut me, let him bury me in the ground, but I do not betray my friends. I wish I were dead if I lie.

- You are a cheater, I know, - said Moses, - but I believe you. I believe you so far.

- Oh, oh, oh, - Hosea sneered to himself, mocking Moses, "I have provided for everything, and you would have been killed". Ha ha ha ha. I don't think so! Those three men that you sent to build the raft and kill me if I escaped are no longer alive. They slipped while building the raft and fell right on the axes. They fell three times each.

As night approached, an atmosphere of nervousness gripped the whole camp. The people believed and disbelieved Aaron, but since there was nothing else for them to do, everyone prayed to God in his heart, and asked him to open the waters of the sea and deliver them from Pharaoh's punishment. The tide began and the water began to recede. People stood beside the water with bated breath. The level was going down and down, and the strong wind kept pushing the water southward like a huge pump, and suddenly a miracle happened: the bottom was exposed, and a sandbank appeared, reaching from one shore to the other[1].

All night people, wagons, cattle were moving along the shoal, which was not more than 50 meters wide. It was forbidden to make any noise on pain of death. The cunning Hosea had ordered the fires to be kept lit to assure the Egyptian sentries that the camp was still. A barricade of wagons was erected behind the last retreating men in case the chariots suddenly attacked.

1. From the author. Here, dear reader, I would like to give the full verse from the Bible describing this event. Read it carefully:

The Bible. Exodus 14:21

And Moses stretched out his hand upon the sea, and by a strong east wind and Moses stretched out his hand over the sea, and by a strong east wind Jehovah caused the sea to blow all the night. And he made the sea dry land, and the waters were parted.

Please pay special attention to the words; *And by a strong east wind!*
So God's miracle was just a strong east wind.

CHAPTER 16:

The First Battle

The night before the battle Nain had not slept. The anticipation of the upcoming battle roused his mind, and he could not come to his senses from excitement and fear. No, he was not afraid to die, he did not even think about it, he was afraid that in the first battle he might do something wrong and disgrace his name.

And then there was the crazy wind that blew in, howling in every voice that made Nain's soul ache.

In the morning, Nain helped the cartmen to water and feed their horses, checked their weapons for the hundredth time, and, seeing that the other warriors getting ready for battle, put on his armor.

- Well, Nain don't fail today, - he ordered and asked himself.

Junior commanders scurried around the camp, chariots were lined up. Everything was ready. Finally, Pharaoh appeared in his gilded chariot. With one last look at the battle-ready army, he raised his rod, and then sharply lowered his arm in the direction of the camp of Moses.

Breaking the silence of the morning, thousands of voices shouted f - a - a - a - r - a - o - h - h, letting the horses go at full speed.

Nain waited anxiously. Waiting for the first enemy to be killed to appear.

- Who will it be, - he thought, - a young warrior, a peasant, who, like himself, had just stepped on the path of war, having left his stubble? Or would it be an elderly Jewish merchant who took up a sword to defend

Moses? Or will it be a frightened craftsman who has already regretted a hundred times the workshop in Egypt, where his great-grandfathers were still working? Who?

Nain didn't know that the process of waiting for a fight could be so painful and terrifying. The excitement grew and grew until he was unable to think, and his throat, hoarse from screaming, refused to make any sound but a wheeze. He couldn't understand why the chariots had suddenly stopped, why there was no enemy, and why Ace was yelling at him.

- Let go of my fucking shoulder, - Ace's scream made sense to him, and Nain found that he was standing there, clutching onto Ace's shoulder, unable to unclench his fingers. It was only when Ace whipped him that the world slowly began to make sense to Nain, and he understood the meaning of the word - gone.

- How gone, - Nain couldn't understand, - what about the fight? Was that really all?

This little respite allowed him to pull himself together, and when the command to go forward sounded, Nain's excitement suddenly passed, and the excitement of the hunter seized him. Catch up! Catch the fleeing enemy and wipe him off the face of the earth!

The rugged sand and the shoal that led to the opposite shore indicated where to look for the enemy, and six hundred chariots rushed in that direction. But the wheels of the chariots were sunk in the wet sand, and the dash with which they had just moved was gone[1] and when Ace' chariot ran into a blockage of carts, the column halted. The hotter ones tried to go around the blockage, but as soon as they turned off the bank they plunged into the water. It was deep enough all around. Ace ordered the blockage cleared, and the warriors who had fled began dragging the wagons aside and throwing them into the water. In the fever, no one noticed that the wind, desperately holding back the tide, had died down, and that the great quantity of water which it had driven southward with its power was at first frozen in place, as if contemplating whether to return, slowly at first, and then, picking up speed, gushing back. The water quickly swallowed the shoal and began to rise rapidly, and in a few minutes, the distraught people saw a wave of at least two or three meters high approaching them from the south. Like a tsunami, the wave struck the mass of people in the sandbank and crushed everything and everyone in a playful way, and dragged them into the sea, toward Epham[2].

Nain, when he saw a wave coming, was not frightened. As a boy, he had drowned in the Nile more than once, and learning to swim more than once had helped him in such critical situations. The main thing he had learned from his previous experience with water was not to panic. Quickly took off his armor, Nain, unlike many who, clinging to the chariots, waiting for the wave to hit, threw himself into the water and swam, trying to get away from the chariots. He sped as fast as he could, knowing that the main thing now was to dodge the impact of the wave-drawn chariots. The wave caught up with him, and gently lifted him onto its crest, carrying him a few dozen meters before it dropped and left, taking the stunned men, horses, chariots, and carts with it. Nain caught a piece of thill from cart and, trying not to let it out of his hands, he waited to see what would happen next. No matter how good a swimmer he was, Nain was well aware that he would not make it to shore without this piece of wood.

At first Nain saw heads of men and horses all around him, but as time passed there were fewer and fewer of them, and after an hour it seemed to Nain that he was the only one slowly drifting to shore.

He did not know how long his swim lasted, an hour, two, five, but when the shore was at hand his strength finally left him, and if it had not been for a piece of wood he would probably have drowned. At last his feet hit the bottom, and Nain, still afraid to throw the wood, staggered ashore with it. He rested on the sand, and could not believe that he had survived the ordeal. After taking a break, Nain waited for the other swimmers and to his delight, he began to notice people's heads on the surface of the water. At first they seemed to him as small dots, but soon he began to distinguish the faces and, rushing to one or the other, helped the exhausted people to get out of the water. Then dead bodies began to be swept ashore. Lots of them. The survivors walked along the shore, dragging them out of the water, looking at the faces, and when they found their friends, they shook their heads sorrowfully, praying for the repose of their souls and for their salvation.

Nain began to look for Ace, but he was nowhere to be found, neither among the living nor the dead.

1. The Bible. Exodus 14:25.
2. The Bible. Exodus 14:28.

CHAPTER 17:

Moses' Triumph

It was a triumph. Moses had not felt so happy in a long time. To the people, crossing the bottom of the sea seemed such an incredible miracle that everyone without exception believed that he Moses was the true messenger of the great god Jehovah, and all his opponents shut up, succumbing to the universal joy of deliverance from death. All this pride was pouring out of him, and he himself suddenly believed that he was a prophet and had every right to control the destinies of these people according to his own genius. Twenty-four hours ago, from a frightened tsar, he had turned into a majestic husband, telling those around him, - Look, here I am, the cleverest and the most handsome one you have. Pray to me, I am your god and savior. The strange thing was that he had completely forgotten that the crossing was possible only by Hosea's knowledge and the chance coincidence of a strong easterly wind and a low tide. He began to believe that it had happened only because of him and no one else, and even the small annoyance that he was not yet Pharaoh did not prevent him from living today.

Sister Mariam, gathered all the women, and they made a divine procession, thanking God and his prophet Moses for saving their souls[1].

- Well, sis, did you eat it? - Moses thought gloatingly, watching this procession, - from now on you will know how to speak to me, you snake. It wasn't that Moses didn't like his sister, he couldn't stand her. By her tone, by her attitude, Moses sensed that Mariam knew what he really was. She knew that he was nobody that he was just Pharaoh's former grandson, and in the few conversations they had, she spoke to him easily and without respect, as if he were a brother, not the greatest man of our time.

Even the perpetually frowning Aaron seemed to come alive and was now sitting by Moses, chatting cheerfully with Hosea, whom from this day forward Moses had become called Joshua[2].

- Stop talking, - Moses said irritably, - seeing that they don't give him the attention he deserves. First, you, Joshua, owe it to me to scout out a place where we can stay for a long time. The main condition is water. Look anywhere you want, but find me such a place. Secondly, in one hour we're getting off and going into the desert. The danger of Pharaoh coming after us is very great, and I don't want to lose my head here. You, Aaron should go to the people and start inculcating in them that only the god Jehovah and his prophet Moses, can lead them to happiness. Indoctrinate them that all of today's difficulties are temporary and that in the future; our people will have a great deal of God's grace. Tell them day and night that your brother Moses is God's anointed, and everyone, without exception, must obey me unconditionally. Don't forget to mention yourself, - he said with a smirk, - you are my brother and you are also a partaker of God. Go, Aaron, time is of the essence, tell the people the truth.

- Yes, I almost forgot; - added Moses; - tell Mariam that she was very right to organize the divine move. Learn from her, Aaron, how to work with the masses. If you convince a woman of something, consider that you have also convinced her husband, for she will always persuade him in bed to do as she pleases.

- Joshua, - Moses said after Aaron had left, - you are already squinting your shameless eyes at the Ethiopian in Ananias' cart. Don't even think about her. I like her myself, and I don't care what you've done in the past for me. Do you hear that you are quiet?

- Oh, shit, - thought Joshua, - he's like a goddamn righteous man, and he wants to be a saint. That Ethiopian woman was really something. Slender, as if carved from an ebony trunk by the skilled hand of genius, she attracted the attention of many, if not all, men, and in truth, Joshua had his eye on her long ago.

- Who are you talking about, - Joshua decided to play hide-and-seek just in case, - I have no idea.

Moses did not support his game.

- Don't play dumb, - Moses said, wrinkling his nose, and ordered, -you'll bring her to my tent tonight.

- What shall I tell Ananias?

- Nothing, - said Moses; - what do you want me to tell you? You have to kick his ass if he objects and bury him in the sand.

When Joshua left Moses, he went to negotiate with Ananias, and all his good spirits evaporated.

- Well, - he thought grimly, - I'd rather have a piece of bread torn out of my mouth than a girl like that.

1. Bible. Exodus 15:20,21
2. Joshua is an Aramaic name, literally translated - savior.

Joshua, unlike Moses, is not only a biblical character, but also a historical person. The historian of the past, Procopius, cites in his book *History of the Vandals* an inscription found in Mauritania belonging to refugees from Palestine: - *we are those who fled from the robber Joshua*.

CHAPTER 18:

The Hero of Egypt

The tragedy that happened before Pharaoh's eyes stunned everyone with its cruelty. Everyone froze and was silent, not knowing what to do. Pharaoh sank into the chariot and stared at one point as if he were petrified. Boby, who was with him in the chariot, wept and repeated only one thing: - Nain.

The commanders, led by Ben, stood around and waited aloof for a command, but it was as if Pharaoh had forgotten everything.

- What are you standing here, - Boby suddenly yelled at the commanders, - go and look for the people.

Strangely, the people obeyed, and the Pharaoh's cavalry rushed along the shore in the direction where the wave had washed away the group of chariots.

- Let's go look for Nain, - Boby said to Genat, who glanced at the silent Pharaoh and moved his horses.

- Don't cry, - Boby suddenly said, smearing tears on his cheeks, turning to Pharaoh, - my father told me that men do not cry. We'll find all the living and bury the dead, and we'll build new chariots and then they won't get away.

At these words Pharaoh woke up.

- To the camp, - he ordered Genat.

He was silent all the way, and when the chariot stopped at his tent, he asked Boby again.

- Shall we build new chariots?

Boby nodded affirmatively, and Pharaoh dismounted and ordered: - Drive Genat ashore, look for his brother.

Seeing Pharaoh's chariot, the soldiers knelt down and then followed it with astonished eyes, seeing in the chariot a little boy instead of the Great Pharaoh.

All day long they searched for survivors and buried the dead. Of a chariot troop of a thousand and two hundred men, little more than a hundred were left alive. Pharaoh decided not to pursue Moses anymore and return to Egypt. He would die himself in the desert, he thought of his grandson. They decided to wait one more day and leave.

All night long Pharaoh dreamt of his dead son. Ram seemed cheerful and comforted him by saying that the death of the chariot troop did not mean the death of the whole army.

- I, will be a good helper to you, - said Ram steering the chariot of fire. Then Boby appeared beside him and together they drove off into the distance.

- He must be happy there, - thought Pharaoh as he woke up, - but it's a pity I don't see much of him in my sleep.

His lousy mood of yesterday had given way to one in which he wanted to work hard. And then a report came in that they had found Ace alive, and Pharaoh, already knowing what he was going to do, order that Ace and Genat be sent to him. Ace's legs were broken and a few minutes later they brought him on a stretcher. At the sight of Pharaoh, Ice tried to get up, but Pharaoh gestured for him to sit.

Ace began to tell how he had been stunned by some cart.

- I do not remember anything, Great Pharaoh; - I remember water, and then the stars above my head when I woke up. I do not know how I found myself on the shore, how long I was there, I do not know anything.

- We are going back, - Pharaoh began to say slowly. We were unlucky yesterday, but we will be lucky tomorrow. Only that tomorrow we must bring closer by hard work, not by waiting for luck. You, Ace, must build a new chariot troop within a year. I know it is too short a time for so much work. But it is a short time for the lazy, not for you. You have to make it in one year.

He was silent, waiting to hear what Ice would say.

Listening to Pharaoh, Ace took his words as an order to be answered. He tried to kneel down, and seeing that he could not do so, only bowed his head respectfully.

- I will do everything, Great Pharaoh, - he said excitedly, - I'll tire myself and my soldiers, but in a year's time, you'll have a first class chariot corps ready to do any job. I couldn't find a better helper than Genat, - he added, realizing that Pharaoh had summoned the two of them for a reason.

- No, Ace, you will form the band, but I want to entrust Genat with other, more important work.

At these words Genat knelt down, waiting for Pharaoh's order.

- Many troubles have happened during these two years, - Pharaoh began to say instead of orders, "we have lost many soldiers and gained many orphans. Thousands of new orphans fight their fate every day for their bitter lives. Some of them will be taken in by relatives, some by temples, and the rest, most of them, will wander around Egypt, clinging to thieves and joining their ranks.

Here the Pharaoh paused and, raising his voice as if before an attack, said,

-You Genat will gather orphans all over Egypt. You will be their father and mother, and you will raise from them soldiers loyal to the Motherland and to Pharaoh. You shall make Egypt a family for them, and if you have neglected even one orphan, I shall ask you severely.

There was silence. Genat was silent, and Pharaoh, who was not accustomed to not being answered, looked at him sternly.

A whirlwind of thoughts raced through Genat's mind. He was a professional soldier and had never had a family of his own. But, ever since Boby showed up in his convoy, Genat realized that it was family he had been missing all his life. It was the children he missed, the ones he would teach, and the ones he would take care of. He missed their affection, their arms wrapped around his neck, and he realized that in the army he had lost a lot and that he had secretly dreamed all his life of being a father. What Pharaoh was talking about was not family, and they would be other people's children.

- Would I be able to be them instead of a father, - he asked himself, and he already knew the answer.

- Yes, I can. I love children, as we all do, not because they are my own or someone else's, but because they are children.

- I'll do your bidding, - Genat wanted to say in a military voice, but the lump in his throat made his words quiet and intermittent.

- Sometimes, we old men are taught to be wise by the deeds of our children, - having ordered to pour wine for all, Pharaoh continued, - when I learned the story of escape to the army of Boby, when he comforted me in a chariot after the death of the group, when at night I thought what to do next, I clearly understood that the future of Egypt belongs to our children. Tonight a simple thing became clear to me, as long as there are boys in Egypt who run away from home to defend their homeland, Egypt is invincible! Our task, the state and all parents, is to set them on their feet, to help them understand where the truth is and where the lie is, and then no Moses will be able to lead them astray.

Pharaoh waved his hand, and Boby was led into the tent by his order. Taking a few steps forward, he knelt like a warrior, waiting for Pharaoh's order. To tell the truth, for some reason Boby was not afraid of Pharaoh at all; he seemed to him as kind as his father. The same soft voice and the same warm eyes.

- What are you going to be, - Pharaoh asked Boby sitting down beside him.

- I don't know yet, - Boby said honestly, "I wanted to be a fisherman to catch such fish that people would be surprised, and I wanted to be a priest. But now I don't. Nain says it's bad to be a priest, you can't get married then. And now I've decided to volunteer for the army, like Ace. But I miss my mother so much. After this campaign I'll stay home for few days, then get married and then join the army. Nain won't go to the army. Nain wouldn't leave his wife and he'd come home. Then Ace will need another archer. Will you take me in your chariot? - He said to Ace.

- I will! I'll take you for sure, - said Ace seriously, and then, with a sly squint, said, - but there's room in the chariot for two, where are we going to put your wife?

Boby thought for a moment, then concluded: - She'll be riding in a convoy with Genat.

Everyone laughed.

- But when you come home, - Pharaoh asked him again, - will your father beat you up or not?

- He will try, - Boby answered slyly.

- How can he try? - said Pharaoh in amazement.

- And I always, - cheerfully answered Boby, - when father wants to beat me, I run to my mother and press against her leg and whine, - Mommy, mommy, mommy. Then she presses me to her leg and doesn't let me be beaten.

Everyone laughed again, and Pharaoh took the ring off his finger and gave it to Boby.

- This is for your love of Egypt, my boy. Show it to your father and tell him that I ordered you not to be punished. Well, when you grow up, this ring will open any door for you. I don't know what you will be in the future, but one thing I am sure of is that you will be a good citizen of our great country. Then he clapped his hands and a small armor was brought into the tent.

- This is your ceremonial armor, - said Pharaoh, - close your eyes and don't you dare peek until helper will not dress you.

As the servant tightened all the straps and Pharaoh allowed his eyes to be opened, Boby saw that Genat and Ice bowed their heads respectfully before him. On his breastplate Boby flaunted Pharaoh's golden rod.

CHAPTER 19:

The Return.

Only now, as the army returned to Memphis, did Nain feel how much he missed Fooige. He was hurrying the time and it seemed to him that the column was moving too slowly, but nevertheless, with every meter he passed his soul sang in anticipation of the long-awaited rendezvous.

No matter how much Ace tried to persuade him to stay with his unit, Nain did not agree. In the short time he had spent in the army, Nain realized that service was not for him. Nain wasn't attracted to military campaigns or battles where he could make his name famous, or a good soldier's pay.

But Genat's offer appealed to him, so much so that he almost accepted. Genat offered him a teaching position at his military school for orphans.

-You know Nain," Genat persuaded him, "all soldiers are illiterate. But what about the soldiers, even the commanders do not know the basics of writing and counting. It would be great to teach the orphans, not only to fight, but to help them learn the sciences. If you accept my offer, I'll take care of the rest of the formalities. And we'll settle the question of housing for you and your wife.

- Why do soldiers need to read and write," Nain asked, - they have another job to do.

- You're so incomprehensible, Nain. Don't you see that people have already understood that war is a great misfortune, and I believe that in the next hundred or two hundred years they will stop this senseless and cruel occupation. Where will the soldiers go then, eh?

Of course, Genat is right, and someday, wars on earth will end. But hey, he's had not enough for a hundred and two hundred years! No, it's too short a time for people to understand the cruelty of war. But in a thousand years, maybe. At that time the people will indeed be different, much smarter. They won't let their pharaohs do the bloody fighting. But the fact that people must be taught, not just how to fight, Genat was absolutely right.

At that moment Nain suddenly realized that it was his calling to be a teacher. He imagined himself walking around the classroom and explaining counting, writing, and history to the students, and he felt so good, as if he were really a teacher and had his own school.

- His own school, - Nain thought, - that's what he wants!

Enthralled by this idea, Nain began to think through every detail of the decision that had not yet been formed.

Of course, there were schools at the temples, but they only taught arithmetic, preparing tax collectors for Pharaoh. No, that is absolutely not what he wants. He will open a school where there will be more than just counting; there will be everything, history, architecture, knowledge of the world. He will find assistants who will pass on to the children all the latest advances in science. Whatever it costs him, he will open just such a school.

Preoccupied with this idea, Nain did not notice how they approached Memphis, and crossing the Nile pushed all his thoughts of the school to the back burner. Then there was the parting with Ace and Genat, Boby's tears, and his promise to Ice to return to the unit.

When Nain and Boby finally got to the bazaar, another problem came upon them. The story of Boby's escape into the army had gained publicity, and incredible rumors swept through the capital as if the little boy had saved the drowning Pharaoh and pulled him to shore. As soon as they appeared in the market, people saw the golden sign of Pharaoh on Boby's chest and crowds of people gathered around them. Everyone dragged them to his shop, inn, and workshop, asking them to do them the honor of being a guest. Taking advantage of the offer of the owner of the little tavern, Nain dragged Boby there, and ordered him to remove his armor. Boby vehemently resisted his brother's decision, until Nain threatened to beat him.

-Don't you realize that they won't let us pass now, - he angrily reprimanded Boby, - every inhabitant will drag us to his place, and when will we get home? In a hundred days?

After waiting for the people outside to disperse, Nain and a sorrowful Boby, dressed in a simple semi-hiton, moved through the bazaar to choose gifts for the whole family.

At the bazaar they met a neighbor from their hometown, lame Irta, who had come to the capital on business and was hurrying back home. The delighted countryman briefly told them the news of the town and reassured Nain that all his relatives were alive and well, but he upset Boby by saying that his father had long ago prepared a twig to meet him.

- A hero will not be beaten, - Boby told him bravely, and, taking advantage of Nain's gazing at the beautiful tunic for Fooige, untied the sack and showed his neighbor the golden rod.

- So it was you who saved Pharaoh? - Asked Irta. He had heard the legend of the young savior of Pharaoh circulating in Memphis. - Let's go home now, what a joy for our city!

The day was drawing to a close, but Nain did not buy any presents yet and he, not daring to go home without decent presents, decided to go home the next morning. No matter how much Irta persuaded him to set sail with him, Nain refused, and the Irta hurrying to the wharf, kept looking around, and looking back, searching for the little hero with his eyes.

In the next morning they set sail, and Boby referring to the fact that there was no crowd on board the boat, put on his armor and waited for their home to appear.

- Nain, - he pestered, not leaving the side of the boat, - when will it be?

- Leave me alone, - Nain grumbled angrily as he pestered him for the hundredth time. - I've told you a hundred times already, tomorrow, for dinner, and tonight we'll spend the night in a little town halfway home.

Nain understood his brother well; he remembered his return home after the temple escape and was only angry for appearance's sake. He was himself impatient to get home, and knowing he still had a long way to go, he glanced ahead as if he could see his home shore there.

When at last the next day their dear city appeared, Boby shrieked with delight, and Nain was surprised at the number of people on the wharf.

- Probably a wedding, he thought, but he was wrong. It was welcoming them!

Nain didn't know that neighbor Irta, who had sailed home yesterday, had brought the whole town to its feet.

- People, listen to me, - he shouted before he could get off the dock.

Listen and rejoice, our city has given Egypt heroes. Immediately he began to tell the details he had learned in the capital, not forgetting of course to add from himself, about the two sons of Bahan who had saved Pharaoh and his army. Attracted by the noise of the crowd, more and more people joined in, rapturous voices and cheers were heard in honor of Pharaoh, Egypt, his hometown, and Bahan, father of the sons who made their city famous. After a brief moment on the wharf, the people marched to the home of the heroes. Frightened, Malis and Fooige couldn't understand why people had gathered at their house, why they could hear the cheers, and why everyone was talking about Nain and Boby.

The next day the whole town gathered at the wharf, which could not hold a hundredth of the people gathered there. The head of the town and the whole town council arrived at the wharf.

Bahan hugged his wife and waited for the long-awaited boat to arrive with his sons. He thought that there is no greater happiness for any father than to meet his hero sons. You can look proudly at everyone and think - look people, these are my sons!

Malis thought about happiness, too. But for her, as for any mother, it lay in the fact that her sons were coming home. It didn't matter to her that they were heroes; the important thing was that they were coming home.

Fooige, too, thought of happiness, and by happiness, like any other soldier's wife, she meant the end of her husband's arduous wait and the return of her beloved.

The ubiquitous boys, who had sailed down the stream in the morning on a reconnaissance mission, flew to the wharf in their light boats, shouting at the top of their lungs: they are coming!

CHAPTER 19:

The Battle with the Amalekites

- Joshua does it, Joshua fined it, and Joshua provides it. Joshua and Joshua. This Moses has got a nerve, - thought Joshua, - He's blaming everything on me, while he's having fun with his Ethiopian woman.

There was much to do, and every day brought new worries. The main problem was water. There was nothing to drink, not even a wash. And the heat! People living in Egypt seemed to be used to it, but in the desert it was something else! From the morning there was such a sweltering heat that the people seemed to be floating in this hot air, and there was no escape from this hell anywhere. Finally Joshua's men came upon the valley of Wadi el-Sebai, at the foot of the hill of Jebel Musa[1], which met all the conditions Moses had set for it. From east to west the valley stretched for four kilometers and was nearly six kilometers wide. The snow melted in the mountains and fed the valley with water, and the vegetation, so necessary for the cattle, flourished in this fabulous corner of the Sinai desert. All would have been well, but there were people living there. A tribe of Amalekites[2].

- They have lived, and enough is enough, - said Moses and Joshua threw an army into the valley. Few of the Amalekites managed to escape, the rest were slaughtered. Every last one of them was killed including the women and children.

- That's the way we have to do it Joshua! - Moses rejoiced, - without pity for these subhumans. That's how we're going to conquer the land. Everyone under the knife, no one will be excluded and the descendants will say thank you to us. Especially to me.

So, on the third month of wandering through the cursed wilderness, the people began to settle down at Mount Musa and the shock of the overwrought fear of the chase began to slowly pass. The Jews who had escaped from Egypt before the revolution, hearing of Moses' camp, began to flock to him from all over the desert, and the enraged king of the Amalekites, Haman, who had declared holy war on Moses for exterminating his people in the valley of Mount Musa, began to destroy the Jewish convoys on their way to join with Moses. Of course, Moses was displeased and again ordered, - Joshua, it is your duty to teach the filthy Amalekites a lesson.

Saying is one thing, but executing is another. The attackers acted in small groups of about a hundred men, and Joshua was exhausted from intercepting these groups. They would suddenly appear and, after scattering the Jewish refugees, quickly disappear into the desert. It seemed easier to catch wind in the desert than to catch them.

Joshua was angry at the failures, and when luck would strike and they would discover an Amalekites camp in the desert, his warriors ripped out their hearts away from the chest. So brutal were they that Joshua's own blood ran cold as his boys cut down everyone, regardless of age or gender. But these were half-measures, and Jesus finally figured out how to trap the Amalekites. As bait, Jesus stationed three thousand soldiers near Rephidim[3] disguised as peaceful settlers. There was never any water in Rephidim, but the Amalekites captives, who had been brought there on purpose, were surprised to see how the Jews were getting water from the freshly dug wells and planning to build a city there. They did not know that the wells were empty, but at night Joshua's boys brought water from afar in leather sacks to draw it in the morning in full view of the astonished captives. Then Joshua allowed the captives to *run away* and only had to wait for Haman to come here to defeat the Jews before they could gain a foothold in this strategic, water-rich desert location. Moses did not like this plan.

- Too much trouble, - he said, but Joshua insisted, proving that *to invite in* the Amalekites was easier than chasing their flying bands through the desert.

And Haman took the bait! Intelligence reported eight or ten thousand men moving toward Rephidim. After sending a message to Moses, Jesus began to prepare for battle, and in the evening Moses himself came to him in company with Aaron. Questions began to be asked, but Jesus refused to answer. He had no intention of introducing Moses to the battle plan:

- He would not understand anyway, - he thought, - he did not play at war in his childhood; he is a coward and dumb. He will only get in the way with his silly advice.

The morning before the battle, Joshua placed Moses and Aaron at the top of the hill, thus giving them a good opportunity to observe everything that would happen at the foot[1], while he himself was wandering among the soldiers for the hundredth time, instructing his assistants what they should do during the battle. Finally a cloud of dust appeared in the distance, indicating the approach of the enemy, and in a few minutes a myriad of horsemen struck the center of the detachment of Jewish infantry, trying to cut it in half. Jesus was aware of this favorite tactic of the Bedouins and built his plan with this in mind. It seemed that the infantry would be overturned by such a heavy blow, but they, obeying Jesus' order, only fought back and, not taking up the fight, began to retreat to the hill on top of which Moses was stationed. Watching such a joyless start to the battle, Moses began to panic.

-What's going on? - He thought with fear, -why are we retreating? Another half an hour and I'll have my head bashed in. Where the hell is Hosea, I mean, Joshua? Maybe it's time to get out of here.

The moment he began to seriously consider how he could get out of this mess, the infantry, pinned down on the hill, and finally began to offer fierce resistance to the Amalekites. A hard battle ensued, but there was no hope of saving the Jews. The superiority of the Bedouins was obvious. It seemed that in half an hour the last Jew would be killed. As the Jews met with desperate resistance, the rear of the Amalekites began to press on the front lines, and the whole mass lost its advantage - speed. At that moment, one of the two groups of cavalry led by Joshua jumped out from left side of the hill and crashed into the back of the unexpected

Amalekites. Panic erupted in their ranks and they struggled to rebuild their ranks. But the next moment, a second troop of cavalry jumped out from behind the other side of the hill and struck the Amalekites in the right flank. This settled the matter. In the resulting panic, Haman, king of the Amalekites, was killed and his army, caught in the iron grip of Joshua, threw down their weapons. But Moses ordered not to take prisoners, and the beating of the demoralized enemy began. Only after a couple of hours, when not a single Bedouin was left alive, were the soldiers able to catch their breath.

Joshua, having had time to assess his losses, finally went up the hill to Moses. Pale and apparently still in the throes of his cowardly experience, Moses said:

-- Well, well done, Jesus, - he shouted as he greeted Jesus, - you will do well under my guidance.

Not the least bit saddened by the news that the whole company of infantry who had valiantly met the Amalekites were killed in battle, Moses, apparently feeling guilty for the Ethiopian woman taken from Jesus, whispered in his ear: - - We'll find you a woman like mine, you'll love her. Let's go celebrate our victory.

1. From the author. The Sinai Mountains consist of three mountain ranges and the westernmost one is directly Sinai. It has two peaks, the northern one called Safsafe and the southern one called Jebel. At the foot of Mount Musa is the valley of Wadi el-Sebaye. According to researchers, only in this valley could refugees from Egypt stay. According to the Bible, they spent a whole year there.
2. A nomadic tribe in the Sinai Peninsula. Were totally exterminated by the Jews. Apparently, some of this people lived in the cities. We can tell this from verse 15:5 in the first book of Samuel.
3. The site of the battle between the Jews and the Amalekites. Bible. Exodus 17:8
4. The Bible. Exodus 17:10.

CHAPTER 20:

Aaron's Sons

- I must talk to sons, Aaron thought.

He felt that something was amiss with them, and that the friendship that had existed between him and the children had melted away like smoke. In the tent of his sons he found only Nadav and Abihud. The day had just begun and they were already drunk. So drunk that they could not speak. Apparently they had been drunk all night and had had time to take a good hangover. Aaron spat in annoyance, and knowing that it was no use talking to them in their condition, he went to Moses. All day long, as he went about his business, Aaron contemplated the conversation he would have with the children, and when he went back to their tent in the evening, he already knew how to guide them to the truth, although, to be honest, Aaron himself did not know where to look for that truth. Especially after that day.

Enough time had passed and outwardly everything seemed to have settled down, but when Aaron looked at his hands, it seemed to him that they were still covered in blood. Aaron hated to think of it, and whenever he remembered it, he tried to forget it, but the memory of the night was always there, and he scowled and swore at it with displeasure.

Just now, he remembered how perfectly the day had begun and how terribly it had ended.

Moses, having taken to making laws, left the camp, and pitched his tent on Mount Musa, and had been there for forty days[1]. Not wishing to be disturbed, he forbade all to disturb him on pain of death, and even posted guards at the foot of the mountain. What he had been doing there all these days, Aaron did not know; maybe he was really writing laws or something else, but in the camp the people decided to celebrate the feast of the sacred bull Apis. After an amazing trek across the bottom of the Red Sea, the faith of the Jews in the God Jehovah increased enormously, but the people, having lived in Egypt for many years, had absorbed the culture of the Egyptian gods and were unwilling to forget them.

The Egyptians and the Jews alike revered the bull Apis as a symbol of the stability of life, and the annual celebration in his honor was one of the most joyous feasts, in which people asked the bull Apis to give them a stable and, most importantly, a satisfying life.

A few days before the feast, the people made an image of the young bull Apis and, placing it on the platform they had built, asked Aaron to consecrate the idol[2].

- I wish I hadn't done that, - Aaron thought, - maybe it would have been all right.

Immediately after the consecration the feast began. The people, exhausted by their hard marching life, for a while forgot their wounds, illnesses, hunger, and as if they had plunged into their former lives. Songs, dances and jokes were heard everywhere[3].

The feast was in full swing when Moses appeared in the camp.

- It was as if the devil had brought him into the camp on this particular day," thought Aaron, "and he could not have stayed on the mountain one more day.

The first thing Moses did was to attack Aaron.

- How dare you idiot to consecrate the calf, - he shouted, - or don't you understand that we must by all means beat any gods out of people's minds except our Hebrew god Jehovah. Today they celebrate Apis, and tomorrow they want to go back to Egypt. Is it so hard to remember that the people should have one god and only one of his prophets, me Moses.

- People, - cried Moses, climbing up on the platform, - these are the laws of the one and only right god Jehovah, which he has given you through me forever[4].I command you to disperse. Go and get on with your business.

That's where it all started. Old Isaac climbed up on the platform and addressed the people, who clearly did not want to stop the feast.

- People, - Isaac shouted, - aren't we free to make our own choices? Don't we have the right to believe and worship the gods we like? Why should anyone order us to believe or disbelieve as they see fit?

The boisterous crowd greeted old Isaac's speech with applause, and Moses, seeing that they wouldn't even listen to him, suddenly shoved Apis the bull from the platform.

Get out of here, you foolish people, - he shouted menacingly.

Without letting him continue, Isaac in turn pushed Moses so hard that he flew after the bull Apis. His stone tablets, on which Moses had written the laws, fell out of his hands and was shattered[5].

Aaron rushed to pick Moses up, and he and Moses and his bodyguards were hurt in the scuffle that broke out.

Moses was furious.

- Me, - he shouted as he was dragged out of the crowd, - the anointed of God himself, me who saved everyone from destruction, me, the smartest man of our time, was beaten by mere men? Joshua, where are you?

His face was twisted with anger.

- Where is your lazybones? Get me a couple hundred now.

Joshua did not reason. He had never seen Moses so furious and quickly disappeared to do his bidding.

Aaron, seeing that this could end badly, began to calm Moses down.

- Don't be hot, Moses, - he began, - every man has the right to choose his own god.

Moses cut him off.

- You fool, Aaron, - he shouted, - you fool, because you don't understand that it's not about God, it's about power. This crowd has to believe in the God we point them to, and if we don't show them whose boss now, tomorrow they'll not only beat us up, but they'll throw us the hell out of here. I won't let them choose their god, and now they'll see whose god here, and you, if you don't back me up now, I'll blow your head off without a second thought that you're my brother.

Not ten minutes later, a crowd of armed men gathered around Moses and a crowd of unarmed supporters gathered around the platform to continue the feast.

It was all set for the usual village brawl that Aaron had seen more than once in his life, and which usually ended village festivals. Usually there was one scenario for such fights: after a good drink of liquor, the two neighbors would meet, and while they were talking drunk, one of them would suddenly remember with resentment that his companion had kicked his beloved dog three years before. Out of his great love for his dog and his great resentment for this act against his neighbor, he would slap him in the face, and the latter in turn would slap him back. After a fight, they scattered in different directions and began to gather allies from among the same drunken friends and relatives. After an hour, in an open place, usually outside the village, two camps were buzzing and the fair claims of one neighbor to the other were being clarified. In the course of this clarification, old grievances of other participants surfaced and, after a good swearing, the parties proceeded to a fight, which usually involved all the male population of the village. The drunken men fought, desperately breaking each other's noses, and at the end of the fight it was always unclear who had won. In the morning, when they sobered up, the brawlers would shamefully look at each other, smile remembering their exploits of the previous day and swear that nothing like that would ever happen again. - Forgive me; neighbor, - they said, - the devil made me do it. They smacked their hands and continued to be friends. But on the next great feast, everything would happen again. The root of all these fights was, of course, drunken prowess, and no goals were set by the warring parties. It was a kind of cruel entertainment for quiet village life, and people warmly regretted the broken noses of their opponents the next morning.

- He who is for Jehovah's God, - cried Moses, - come to me!

Without a second's hesitation, he strode confidently to the platform. There, with their sleeves rolled up, Isaac's supporters were waiting for them, looking forward to a fist fight. Isaac's two sons pushed their father aside and stood in front of the approaching Moses.

- Moses, - said the eldest, - why do you insult my father? - If you don't like our customs and our festivals, nobody stops you from celebrating your own, and I will not allow you to raise your hand against St. Apis and against my father.

So the village fistfights usually began, and the grievances of one side were made. Now the script was for Moses' supporters to voice their grievances, but instead, Moses drew his sword and chopped Isaac's eldest son from top to bottom. The crowd gasped, unable to believe their eyes, and Aaron, clasping his eyes, chopped Isaac's second son. A massacre ensued. The unarmed men ran through the camp, trying to get away from the blood-crazed executioners of Moses. But it was all in vain as they came upon them and hacked and hacked and hacked. In a couple of hours the camp was deserted, everyone crammed into their tents in terror, but Moses' thugs went around the camp, dragged everyone they didn't like out of their tents, and killed them in cold blood[6]. By the end of the day thousands of hacked-up human bodies were lying everywhere you looked, with relatives weeping over them. There were no wounded, they were just being finished off.

Aaron cursed again, remembering how he had wielded his sword like a madman, and pushing that terrible memory aside, he went into the tent with his sons. He found them at the table. Nadav and Abihud were about to take a hangover, and Aaron, furious at their crumpled faces, brushed the wine-filled mugs off the table.

- You have lost your sense, - he shouted, - you are drinking intoxicated for weeks. Soon you will turn into animals. A man has to work, don't you? What do you do for a living?

Abihud grunted and began to pick up the mugs from the floor, while Nadav, frowning at his father, lowered his eyes and quietly said: - When I was little, I loved to watch you toil. I loved to watch you walk behind the plow in the field and your sweat-wet shirt clinging to your huge back. I dreamed that when I grew up, I would plow the land the same way, and my shirt would stick to my back the same way.

Then he was silent, and Abihud picked up the mugs and poured the wine into them. As he did so, he eyed his father cautiously and made sure he didn't flick them to the floor again.

- Shall I pour it for you? - He asked his father, and Aaron, stunned by Nadav's words, did not know what to say.

- Pour, - he ordered, and drank the wine in one gulp.

After a while he asked in a low voice: - Why have you brethren become so unhinged? Moses made our kind priests for all the people. You hear me, for the entire Jewish people. We have a great responsibility to instruct our people, to preach God's laws and our ideas, and you seem to have lost your minds. What are you doing, my dears?

Aaron was silent, giving his sons time to answer his question.

- Father, - said Eleazar, entering the tent, - give them a good thrashing, for they are out of hand.

- Shut up, - Abihud shouted at him, while Nadav boldly looked into Aaron's eyes and said, - as I see we have to preaching and not deceiving.

- What? - Aaron did not understand.

- You and Moses, - continued Nadab, - what did you say and promise the people in Egypt? A sweet life, didn't you? Milk rivers? And what have we got? The people are groaning with hunger, with disease, with your tyranny, and they are dying like flies in this cursed desert. You promised freedom from Pharaoh's rule and a just society. And what do we have in reality? Yes, Pharaoh did not oppress our people as Moses did. Remember how he and you chopped up the people for the mere desire of the people to worship the god Apis. Is this the freedom we dreamed of? And this is only the beginning; wait a little while and you yourself will shudder at your and Moses' treachery.

- Do you know what happens next? - He asked Aaron with a sigh, and without waiting for an answer he said, - A civil war, that's what. Moses will execute anyone who dares to say a word against his crazy plans. How can you not understand that he is anxious for power and will not spare me or you or anyone else in his quest. I am sorry, father, that I succumbed to all these vile lies and left Egypt, but I am especially sorry for you.

- You must have listened to uncle Korah's speeches[7]; - Eleazar said with a chuckle, - this idiot is also urging the people to return to Egypt. Wait a little while, and we'll beat his horns off, so that he won't muddy the waters.

With these words, Eleazar poured himself a glass of wine, and after drinking it, he continued.

- And you know, Nadav, I feel absolutely nothing sorry for my past and you know nothing about life if you think that plowing the land is better than bossing people around. There you whip two oxen pulling a plow, and here you can whip everyone under you. And all your foolishness comes from pity. You've always been a compassionate person. You pity the people, it pains you to see them suffering. Oh, oh, oh, what a pity. But Moses says otherwise, the firmer we rule this flock, the more they will obey.

Abihud swung his head around briefly and struck Eleazar in the jaw, knocking him to the floor. Aaron rushed to Abihud by the look of him that he wouldn't stop at one punch, and Eleazar got up and backed toward the exit and gritted through his teeth: - Well, we'll have another reckoning, brother.

- Go to your Moses, - said Nadav, while Aaron, upset by his sons' fight, did not know what to do and just held Abihud.

To be honest, Aaron himself did not like Moses' behavior in recent events, but to be even more honest, he felt that the pervasive contagion of power was beginning to take hold of his soul as well. If the first time after he had fled from Egypt he remembered every day his past life, his land, his oxen, and he longed to return to his former life, now it was gone and he no longer thought about it. Aaron was more and more absorbed in the work of ruling the people, and the reverence and fear with which the people treated him began to honey on his heart.

Maybe Moses was right when he said that the people were stupid and ignorant of what was good and bad for them, and that only they, the divinely chosen leaders, could ensure their happiness and prosperity. May this happiness not come now, may many not live to see the light of day, but it is impossible to build a future without sacrifice.

Or maybe his brother Korah is right in accusing Aaron and Moses of usurpation and tyranny[8]. Maybe he is right to say that a happy future cannot be built on the bones of thousands and thousands of people, and that Moses' plan to seize the fertile foreign lands, if it succeeds, only at great cost and without any guarantee that they will not be thrown out by the local aborigines in the future. Maybe Korah is right when he says that only the native land on which their ancestors lived and died can provide the strength in their people and that strength and deep-rooted love for the homeland will always help the people survive the hardest times in their history.

Maybe so, but now what should we do? Go back to Egypt? Korah did not kill and the Pharaoh will forgive him, but me?

- Eh, life," sighed Aaron and pounced on Abiud, "why did you hit Eleazar, eh? He's your brother, and you're supposed to respect and love each other, and you're like dogs.

- You didn't hit him enough as a child, so you have to make up for it now," Abihud replied. All he thinks about is who to kill and where to steal from. What kind of a man is he?

- What is there to understand, - said Nadav, - his is like his uncle, Moses.

- All right, stop scolding your brother, help him to define his life, he is still young, he does not understand many things, - Aaron interrupted them, - and stop drinking. Nothing can be fixed, life goes on, and you have to get wise.

Aaron got up and did not find anything else to say, but went to his tent.

1. The Bible. Exodus 24:18
2. The Bible, Exodus 32:5, 6.
3. The Bible. Exodus 32:18
4. The Bible. Ex32:15,16
5. The Bible. Exodus 32:19   From the author. Tablets are stone slabs on which, according to the Bible, God wrote ten basic laws for the Jews. According to the Bible, Moses broke them into pieces by his own hand. It is not clear how he could do this to God's writings. But that's not the point. In 1902 the Code of Hammurabi*, the king of Babylon who lived 2,000 years before Christ, was carved in stone. This codex contains laws that *suddenly*, many years later, form the basis of the *Law of Moses*. Another plagiarism of the great prophet Moses is on the face of it.
6. From the author. This is one of the most striking passages in the Bible and I want to bring it to your attention verbatim. Bible. Exodus 32:26, 27, 32:26 And Moses stood at the gate of the camp, and said, Whoever is for Jehovah, come to me! And all the sons of Levi were gathered to him. 32:27 He said to them, "Thus says Jehovah, the God of Israel, Put every man his sword on his hip, walk through the camp from gate to gate and back, and KILL EVERYBODY YOUR BROTHER, EVERYBODY YOUR FRIEND, EVERYBODY YOUR KIND. This is the truth about God! Kill, kill, and kill. Disagree - kill, do

something wrong - kill, say the wrong thing - kill. A clear formula for taking power:
1. The planting of faith in God (an idea).
2. The appearance of a prophet.
3. The ideological (religious) brainwashing of the people.
4. Seizing power.

Do you want to seize power? Use the formula of the Bible.

It seems to me that in the aftermath, many scum of the human race have done their dirty work using this exact biblical formula. To them, the Bible and Moses set a clear example of how to seize power and fight dissent. The holy church fathers sent out crusades ordering the killing of anyone who did not believe in the *right God*, Stalin ordered the killing of those who did not believe in the *communist God*, Islamic leaders ordered the killing of *wrong people*... Moses, Muhammad, the Holy Inquisition, Hitler, Stalin – and who will be the next prophet?!

In my book, I did not describe the next event that struck me, when a nation exhausted by famine began to complain about its plight. The Bible.Num 11:1. How did God solve this problem? Simple! He exterminated part of the camp by fire. But that didn't help, so when the people asked for meat again, he *had mercy* and sent them a huge flock of quail. Why is that in quotation marks? Because as soon as the people ate the quails, God made them sick. And many died. God called their desire to eat a whim! Imagine a father who has a child who wants a meal, and the father prepares a piece of meat and sprinkles poison in it, to kill the child's desire to eat.

7. Korah is a biblical figure, cousin of Moses and Aaron.
8. The Bible. Num.16:3

CHAPTER 21:

Eleazar

- Well, wait a minute, - Eleazar kept saying to himself as he headed for Moses, "I'll show you how to beat me. They are called brothers! You see, they feel sorry for the people, but they don't feel sorry for me.

After waiting for Moses to be reported and allowed in, Eleazar had already made a plan to settle accounts with his brothers.

- What do you want? - Moses asked him grudgingly, taking a break from reading the papyrus.

Eleazar thought once more and, no longer doubting whether he was doing the right thing, began to tell him.

- Nadav and Abihud are going back to Egypt, - he began, - and now in their tent they are persuading my father to go with them. They also say you're a crook and there's nothing to do here.

- Well, what about your father? - Moses asked grimly.

- He wouldn't agree and is trying to talk them out of it, but they are standing their ground and have decided to go.

- Well, what do you think? - Moses asked Moses, having ordered his servant to find Joshua.

- Well, what is there to think about! What was I doing in Egypt? Who was I there? And here, thanks to you, uncle, I am a real man.

Moses liked Eleazar's answer and smilingly rubbed his shoulder.

- Well, do you believe in our God Jehovah? - He asked Eleazar with a sly look in his voice.

- Yes, yes, I do, - Eleazar said hurriedly.

- Will you die for this faith?

- I will, uncle.

- What a fool, then, - said Moses with emphasis.

- What do you mean? - Bewildered Eleazar asked, - this is our God and we must die for him.

- That's right, my nephew! Today it benefits us to believe in Jehovah, and I do, and tomorrow, if I have to believe in the gods of Egypt and scold the god of the Jews, I will do it without a second thought. God is just an idea, and if the situation changes, God must be changed. There must be one god for you. That god I am your uncle and you must serve only me. Do you understand?

- I understand, - Eleazar answered smiling and added, - and if the situation changes, - he hesitated. Suppose you lose your power, would I have to change God?

- You'll go far, - Moses said, squinting his eyes, - like me. Just don't think I'm going to lose power anytime soon.

Joshua, who appeared in the tent, only shook his head and laughed as he listened to Moses' instructions to Eleazar. Even he, who was used to Moses, was disgusted at the leader's open hypocrisy.

- Why are you smiling? Am I not right? - Moses asked him.

- Am I right, and who can argue? - Joshua answered with a question, and looked around as if to see who was arguing with Moses.

- Stop fooling around, - Moses interrupted him in a sullen tone, - and he told Joshua everything he had learned from Eleazar. What shall we do?

- The hell with them let them run away, - answered Navin, - good riddance.

- They will be gone tomorrow, and the day after that the crowd will come after them.

- What would you have me do with them, - Joshua asked with a grin, -kill them?

- Yes, that's right.

- But...- Joshua hesitated, - they are your nephews.

- He, who is not with me, - said Moses, - is against me.

And in a different voice, a voice full of anger, he commanded: - 'Tonight you will send your men. Two brothers must be dead by morning. And everything must be cleaned up, understand?

- I will, - answered Joshua grimly, and glared at Eleazar.

Moses caught his gaze and, as if he had come to his senses, ordered his nephew. - Go, Eleazar, and remember who your God is.

When Eleazar went out, Joshua frowned, - He will warn his brothers.

- So much the worse for him, then you'll kill him too.

In the morning a fire broke out. The tent of Aaron's sons[1] was on fire. There was nothing to burn in it, and when the fire ate the tent, the people found two burned bodies. Apparently the brothers were drunk and had forgotten to put out the lampstand. Aaron came running in, unable to believe his sons were gone. Moses came too. He stood for a moment and then said with a frown, - they drank too much.

Then he called for Mishael and Eltzephan and told them to bury the bodies of Nadab and Abihud like dogs outside the camp[2].

- They were not worthy, - said Moses, and added for Aaron, - and you will not weep, or God will punish you too[3].

1. The Bible. Leviticus.10:2
2. Mishael and Eltzephan are biblical figures, cousins of Aaron. The Bible. Leviticus.10:4
3. The Bible. Leviticus.10:6

CHAPTER 22:

Korah

Moses' camp moved slowly across the desert toward Canaan, destroying everything in its path like a swarm of locusts. Any settlements along with their inhabitants and livestock were devoured by this mass of moving people, and it was impossible to tell if it was an army or just a mob of hungry settlers. It was a monstrous conglomerate hitherto unknown to the world, a moving state with its institutions, including courts, armies and political parties. This unusual and newly baked state was no exception to all known states, and within it there was a fierce struggle. A struggle for power.

And the beginning of this struggle was there, at Mount Musa, where Moses put down with the sword the first rebellion of a part of the Jewish people. That part sought to assert its right to liberty and was not at all like a political party, and the revolt itself was spontaneous. But little by little, month by month, as this driving state developed, as more and more controversy arose, two main parties were formed in this state. The Moses Party and the Korah Party[1]. The goal of the Moses Party was the conquest of strategic Palestinian lands and the subsequent construction of an independent Jewish state on those lands, the goal of the Korah Party was the return of the Jewish people to their homeland. As always, between these two parties, there was a layer of people who were undecided. The same people were either for Moses or for Korah. It all depended on the situation of the day.

Korah led the people who wanted to return to Egypt. The former life in Egypt was favorably different from life in the wilderness, and there were many who were willing[2].

Korah was never eager for power. He never thought he would one day be the leader of a group of people.

- Why did all this happen, - he thought as he gathered for a meeting with the elders of the clans, - why did I leave Egypt so dear to my heart? It's all my desire for justice, that's what.

When Pharaoh raised the tax on the land, it seemed to Korah the height of injustice, and sincerely believing it, he gave in to the sweet speeches of Aaron and the new leader Moses.

Only here in the wilderness did he realize his mistake, which was that Pharaoh was right! In making this decision, Pharaoh was not thinking of a particular group of Egyptian society, but of the whole state, and was trying to consider the interests of all. Only now did Korah realize how hard it was to make this decision, and how much time Pharaoh had spent to find the best way.

A few weeks ago, Korah had sent a faithful man with a letter to Pharaoh, and the fate of the entire Jewish people depended on his answer.

Korah was about to leave when Aaron walked into his tent. They greeted each other warmly as cousins should, and began to discuss the latest news. Korah could see that this was not why Aaron had come here, just to have a chat, and he spoke as if he were doing it mechanically, without thinking. Apparently he was thinking of something worth his time.

Korah had known and loved his cousin since childhood as an honest and industrious man, and he could not understand why Aaron continued to support Moses. So now he came asking to obey, Korah thought, and he was not mistaken.

- Korah, brother, - Aaron began from afar, - what have we to share with you? You know very well that I respect you. You're my brother, and I'm willing to do what I can for you. But you can't do that, Korah. You have divided society. You have led the people into turmoil, and God forbid there should be a time when people will turn on each other with a sword. You really can't do that, and I'm asking you to come to your senses.

— No, Aaron, — Korah answered, — it's you who must come to your senses. Look around you with your eyes wide open and see what is going on around you and you will understand the horror of this situation. Look at the suffering of your deceived people! Think why your sons died. Do not tell me again that it was an accident. Don't tell me, I won't believe it anyway, because I know Moses killed them. And you, how could you let them be buried like some vagabonds. And poor Mariam? At the mention of his sister's name, Aaron shuddered mechanically. He remembered how he and Moses had come to her to ask for her help. Things were heating up in the camp, and Moses was planning to hold a procession in support of himself just as Mariam had done after crossing the Red Sea. They desperately needed the support of the women, and Moses had high hopes for his sister. He dragged his Ethiopian woman to Mariam as well, thinking that the women would quickly find contact with each other and it would help the cause. The storm began as soon as they entered Mariam's tent.

— Get out of here, you slut, — Mariam shouted when she saw the Ethiopian woman, and the latter, looking wildly at Moses, dashed out of the tent.

— She is not a slut, I live with her, and there is nothing unusual here.

— And why did you leave your wife and children, eh? Two sons are growing up without a father, and you hunt for every skirt in the camp," said Mariam with bitterness in her voice, "do you think that people are blind and do not see what you are doing?

— Have you heard about my new law permitting divorce[3]?

Everything that comes from me comes from God, okay? So it's all right here, I gave Zipporah the divorce letter and let her live her life as she knows it. And I will think about my sons, don't worry, the time will come and I will raise them, and now I have no time to deal with them, — answered Moses with pathos.

— So it's God's fault, — said Mariam indignantly, — he is the one who has legalized divorce and debauchery, and you are only doing His will. Moses, you're a scoundrel!

— That's where you're wrong, Moses, — Aaron interjected.

He did not like the look on his sister's face. The squeamish expression on her face as she looked at Moses. Knowing well the character of Mariam, Aaron decided to appease her by rightly criticizing Moses.

- You abandoned Zipporah even before you returned to Egypt, brother. You abandoned her and now that your father-in-law, ashamed of what he is doing, has brought her here[4] and you are not doing a pretty thing by messing with this Ethiopian woman.

As Aaron spoke, Moses' face poured with blood.

- Who are you people? - He suddenly yelled in a way that scared Aaron out of his wits. - I am the meekest man on earth[5]. I, I," he gasped, - how dare you speak to me as if you were an ordinary man, not a prophet! How have you not yet understood that God has chosen me to be the first man after him, and you must call me lord[6]! Do you understand me, Aaron? - Turning his head to him, Moses asked angrily.

- I understand, my lord, - Aaron answered quietly, his head bowed.

- Have you understood me? - He asked Mariam.

This only added fuel to the fire of scandal.

- Go away, you wandering dog, - she said, pointing to the exit, firmly and contemptuously, "and don't you ever set foot here again.

No one had ever spoken to Moses in that tone of voice, never! He became furious and jumped up to Mariam and knocked her to the ground with a single blow to the face.

- Snake, - he yelled, and started kicking her wherever he could.

Aaron dragged him away from his sister, but he was also struck by Moses. Only his bodyguard, who had run in on the noise of the fight, could stop him hanging on his hands.

Blinded by rage, Moses beat Mariam so badly that the leprosy-stricken men looked better. The bruises and abrasions went away after a week[7], but apparently kicking her Moses damaged some internal organ, and Mariam began to stunt and would no longer get up. Every day when he inquired about her health, Aaron forced himself to visit his sister, but each time he found a valid excuse not to do so. He was ashamed to look her in the eye. Ashamed that he had failed to protect his own sister.

- You are sorely mistaken that the men behind me are capable of raising a sword to their fellow tribesmen," came the words of Korah, which brought Aaron out of this shocking recollection. - Moses is the one who can be expected to throw his executioners on people who want to live their own way. But, Aaron, I warn you. What happened at Mount Musa will not happen again. The people are ready to defend their choice, and if you again try to impose your decision on us with the sword, we will defend ourselves, and we will not allow you to trample on the right of free people to choose the way we think is right for us. So tell that to Moses.

With these words, Korah stood up, indicating that the conversation was over. Aaron walked silently toward the exit and was already standing on the doorstep when Korah added in a quiet voice: - I have great hope for you, my brother Aaron. I trust that you will not allow the strife, and I trust that you will not allow Moses to repeat the beating of the people. The people still trust you, Aaron, - Korah said, looking straight into his eyes, and added quietly, "and they pity you.

The rally was closed, and the guards did not allow anyone in except the two hundred and fifty delegates of the people[8], all of whom were well-known people who had great prestige among the people and were in favor of the return[9].

- How I miss Pharaoh's answer," thought Korah as he prepared for his speech, - if he would just forgive us, the people would go home tomorrow.

- When I think of the fate of the Jewish people, - Korah began to say to the assembled delegates, "I remember our history. Over four hundred years ago, Jacob came to Egypt and settled in the land that has become our homeland. There were only 70 Hebrew souls with him[10], and from them the Jewish people multiplied and were filled with Egypt by the Jews extremely[11]. Think about it, does a bad life make a people multiply? Think back to how we and our ancestors lived in Egypt and compare it to our current bitter life of wandering[12]. Our whole journey from Egypt is marked by mounds of graves, which go on and on behind us, and there are not a few of them. How many people have we lost to famine, disease, and the sword of Moses? A million? Two million? Three? I don't know the answer, but I do know one thing, that our descendants will count all the fallen in this wilderness, and they will bill Moses and the God who blessed it all. People will still learn the real truth about this black streak in the life of the Jewish people.

Brethren! It's time to decide, and I want to share my thoughts with you. Am I right? I don't know, my dear compatriots, but I am certain of one thing, that the Mosaic plan leads to a dead end from which there is, and can be, no way out. Look back, Pharaoh after Pharaoh tried to take these lands. More than a thousand years went by in these unsuccessful attempts, and what? Where are these pharaohs? They are gone, and the people who inhabit these lands live and multiply. And now, Moses is suggesting that we repeat the error of the Pharaohs and embark on this destructive path of an eternal state of war. A war of annihilation that will last for thousands of years. Do you want for yourself and your descendants to live in an eternal war camp? I do not! And so I have decided this hard question for myself and am going back to Egypt. I do not know how Pharaoh will meet me, how my neighbors, the Egyptians, will meet me, but it is better to die there, on the banks of the Nile, so beloved by me, than to be one of the grave mounds here in this cursed desert. I have decided, now you decide.

Giving the floor to the next speaker, Korah hurried to the guards, who wouldn't let a man he recognized as his ambassador to Pharaoh into the meeting. Ordering him to pass, Korey reverently took the rolled up papyrus with Pharaoh's seal on it.

- Well, at last, - he sighed with relief, - thank God, just in time.

He broke the seal and opened the letter. The more he read it, the happier he felt.

To Korah.

We, the Great Pharaoh of Upper and Lower Egypt, by the Grace of the gods forgive you and in your person the entire Great Hebrew people.
You, Korah, and all those who wish to join me in my power, are free to return to your homeland with all the rights and the obligations of the citizens of the Great Egypt.
Our mercy is given to all but Moses and his brother Aaron and there are no gods who will spare them from the punishment they deserve.

Pharaoh of Upper and Lower Egypt.

Korah's heart jumped for joy. At last our suffering had come to an end! It would not be long before they would see the fertile and native lands of Egypt again. The lands that had fed, and would continue to feed the people.

- Is it really possible?! What joy, - rejoiced Korah. - We must read Pharaoh's answer to the people now.

Korey began to make his way to the rostrum from which Dathan the son of Eliab[13] was speaking, looking forward to how tomorrow the people would turn back to Egypt with songs, but at that moment he heard the noise of horses galloping at full gallop, and in a minute five hundred horsemen were cutting unarmed people into the crowd of delegates.

In less than ten minutes, everyone who had gathered for the rally was dead[14]. The letter of Pharaoh to the Jewish people was trampled into the sand by the hoof of someone's horse, and the Jewish people never knew of its existence.

1. Dathan, son of Eliab is a biblical figure. A companion of Korah. The Bible. Num.16:1
2. The Bible. Num.16:35
1. According to The Bible. Num.16:1, in addition to Korah, his group included men of prominence and eminence, leaders of society, for example: Dathan, Abiram, Pelephah, etc.
2. The Bible. Num.14:3
3. The Bible. Matthew 19:7, 8
4. The Bible. Exodus 18:5
5. The Bible. Num.12:3
6. The Bible. Num.12:11
7. The Bible. Num.12:14
8. The Bible. Num.16:2
9. The Bible. Num.14:4
10. The Bible. Exodus 1:5 222
11. The Bible. Exodus 1:7
12. The Bible. Numbers 20:5
13. Dathan, son of Eliab is a biblical figure. A companion of Korah. The Bible. Num.16:1
14. The bible. Num.16:35

CHAPTER 23:

The Fratricidal War

Immediately after his conversation with Korah, Aaron went to Moses. He was in the worst of moods, and the foreboding of disaster was burning his heart.

In the tent Moses and Joshua were discussing animatedly, but when they saw Aaron enter they broke off as if on cue.

- It's time, Moses, - said Joshua, - and now is the time to do it, so I'm off.

- As soon as you're settled, - Moses shouted after him, - come to me at once.

Joshua nodded at him and hurried off.

- What was the talk about? - Aaron asked Moses and poured himself some wine.

- I told to him about the quarantine camp for the lepers, - Moses said noncommittally.

Aaron had become a different man lately, and Moses was loath to tell him that he had sent Jesus to destroy the gang of wicked men led by Korah. Moses had long wanted to get even with them, and then, as a gift of fate, the rally they had planned. Moses simply couldn't pass up such a chance to destroy all the leaders of this gang in one time and one blow.

- As soon as this whole group is left without leaders, all the speeches against me will be over at once, - thought Moses, - and if I tell that to Aaron now, he might derail the whole affair. He has become very touchy lately, and it may be time to replace him with a tougher one. His son Eleazar, for instance. ...Is he young? Yes he is, but loyal as a dog and listens to me with his mouth open.

Meanwhile, Aaron finished his wine and poured himself another.

- Let's get drunk, Moses, - he suggested. - Let's get so drunk that we forget who we are and where we are, so that at least for a short time all this business and worries disappear. I'm sick of it all!

Moses looked at Aaron in surprise.

- I've never noticed your need for wine before," he said, "well, if you want it, go ahead and drink it, but I have a feeling it will be even worse for you in the morning. Do you know why? Because you take everything to heart. Relax, Aaron. Look at it from the outside. You probably think I don't care. You're wrong. I do care. I have a heart too, Aaron, and it's not made of stone. But I see a purpose, and that purpose keeps me from paying attention to little things. I see us conquering fertile lands, I see us building cities, I see our descendants enjoying a carefree life and thanking us for all we have done for them.

Aaron listened to Moses and thought; - Does he really believe what he says himself? Once upon a time in Egypt, Aaron himself had to say all these things to the people, and he believed sacredly in everything he said. But now! Things look very different now. That life in Egypt, which they had not appreciated, now seems the only right one, and this other one, which they had only dreamed of, now seems like some illusion, something unfulfilled, and, most importantly, unnecessary to anyone. No heart aches about this ghostly life in the future, and it is not at all believable that it, this sweet life, will ever come.

It is better to really get drunk and not think, or you can go crazy. Only now did Aaron understand why Nadav and Abihud were getting drunk in their last days. They had no future! They didn't trust Moses, and they didn't trust their father!

- That's what Nadav wanted to tell me when he remembered how he liked to look at my sweaty back, - Aaron suddenly guessed.

- Moses! Let them by the way they're going, - he said suddenly. - Let them go to Egypt, and maybe luck will smile on them there. I spoke to Korah today, and he told me plainly that they don't want strife. They, Moses, think differently and they have different dreams. They have a different idea, and an idea cannot be defeated, it can only be destroyed by the sword.

- That's what I'll do, - Moses answered, listening to the growing noise outside. - I'll beat the crap out of them and lead them to a happy life. With a sword, a whip, a flint-iron, everything I have.

At that moment, Joshua came into the tent.

- That's it, Moses, we chopped up them like cabbages, - he said excitedly, - tomorrow we will have more work to do. I can always smell what's coming next and tomorrow is going be total war.

He paid no attention at all to Aaron, and the latter, listening, could understand nothing.

- They won't come to their senses today, I can tell you that. They'll start rallying in the morning, getting themselves all hot and by lunchtime they'll get organized and give us a fight. We shouldn't wait for that moment, Moses, but as soon as they start their protests, we should, we have to strike first thing in the morning time without waiting for them. They're strong enough to get us in trouble, but there's no one else in charge to command them, so I'm a hundred percent sure we'll win. Make up your mind, Moses, and right now. I need your order and I have a lot to do before tomorrow. Well?

Joshua immediately disappeared, and Moses poured Aaron another cup of wine.

- You wanted to get drunk, didn't you? - he asked, - so drink! You understand, I think, what happened in the camp. Well, Aaron, you're not leaving this tent till morning. I don't want any more trouble with you. You stay here and don't move! With your pitying heart, you're just a snotty boy, not a warrior for my cause.

- Guards! - He shouted, and immediately two armed mighty men from the personal guard appeared in the tent, glancing anxiously at Moses.

- If my brother Aaron tries to leave this tent without my permission, cut him down, even though he is my brother and the high priest. And if he escapes, I will order you to cut off his heads. Is that clear?

- Yes, sir, - they said at once in surprise, and Moses smiled impudently at Aaron.

In the morning, everything happened just as Joshua had predicted.

All night long the people in Camp Korah (standing apart from Moses' camp) were mourning the dead, and in the morning the angry people formed a huge rally. Calls to arms were heard and most of the men began to arm themselves. The shameful moment in the history of any nation was approaching, when a civil war was breaking out. It had long been felt coming, and it had begun there at Mount Muse, but now all that was missing was a spark, and yesterday's treacherous murder of Korah and his supporters had caused a huge firestorm, which, like a stack from a direct hit of lightning, had set everything in flames.

Without allowing the enemy to organize, Moses' army moved on the Korah camp. The civil war had begun. Brother went on brother.

Joshua, who had no experience in civil warfare, was wrong in his predictions, and his hope for weak resistance from the Korean supporters failed. Korea's followers, strengthened in their faith in their just cause, fought without sparing their lives. The fierce battle had been going on for hours, and no advantage was seen on either side. It seemed that the two armies would die before they knew who had won. And is there a winner in a civil war? And was it even possible for a brother to kill his brother and rejoice in his victory?

And then, out of the blue, Aaron[1] appeared among the living and the dead! Waving his thurible, he walked as if he had lost his mind, not paying attention to the fact that his head might be cut off at any moment.

- Brothers, stop," he repeated, waving his censer and bowing to the fighting men.

Either the men were tired of waving their swords or they had seen the light, but immediately behind Aaron's back the battle ceased and the opponents diverged, forming a corridor twenty meters wide.

Having passed through the whole field of the battle, Aaron divided by this corridor the warring men, and they, as if realizing what a great sin the do stood in silent expectation. None of the commander's urging had any effect; the men were unwilling to continue the battle.

Finally, the elders of the clans from both sides came up to Aaron, who was standing in the middle of the warring parties and kept waving the thurible.

- How could you do this? - Aaron addressed them. - How could you raise your hand against your brothers? You are charged with a great sin!

The sin of the blood that has been spilled, and the disgrace of all time! What will you tell your grandchildren? How you killed your relatives and friends? Be silent, all of you, there is no pardon for you!

The elders were silent, staring at their feet, while Aaron prayed. His example worked on them, and they, too, prayed fervently, rocking from heel to toe and bowing with every forward motion. Finally Aaron spoke, in such a confident voice that the elders stood still and listened breathlessly, not daring to blink.

- By the authority of the high priest, given to me by God himself, I order you to disperse. You Koreans are free to go wherever you want, and you Moses supporters must not hinder them. I beseech you never to raise a sword against one another again, but, on the contrary, to help your brethren in every way in case of trouble. God is one, and he loves you all, so love one another. Amen.

With his last words the elders bowed low to Aaron and hurried to the waiting men.

Surprisingly, the battle ceased, and the battlefield was filled with weeping. The dead were mourned. Korea's supporters alone had lost nearly fifteen thousand men that day[2]. Moses lost no less.

A day later the Korans withdrew and left, and Moses' camp, after standing for several days, moved along the Salish Sea, preparing for battles with the local tribes.

1. The Bible. Num.16:48
2. The Bible. Numbers 16:49

CHAPTER 24:

Aaron's Death

Aaron finally stopped listening to what Moses told him and became a real threat to Moses' plans to subjugate the people to him. After Aaron stopped the bloodshed and released Korea's supporters by his unilateral decision, his authority grew tremendously, and the people reached out to him with all their problems. Moses could clearly see that his brother was becoming the real leader of Jewish society. On top of this, Aaron stopped talking to Moses, and, after Mariam, who had not yet recovered from her beating, died in Kadesh[1], he demonstratively moved his tent to the other end of the camp.

Moses no longer hesitated. A week earlier he had ordered Joshua to prepare and carry out an assassination attempt on Aaron.

- Whether it is will the Amalekites who suddenly attacked Aaron when he will out of the camp, or whether it will just robbers, I don't know, but Aaron must go to his death in the next few days. Do you understand?

Joshua was not at all surprised by this order. It was as if he had known for a long time that it was going to happen someday, he said briefly:

- Let's do it, - as if he were talking about a lamb prepared for slaughter. They never talked about it again, but Moses waited every day to see what kind of death his own brother was going to face.

But everything did not go as planned, and Moses was even glad that everything ended so well after all. Of course, if you can call his brother's death a stroke of luck.

In the afternoon, while Moses was talking with Eleazar, a worried Joshua came running in.

- Moses, we have a problem, everything is going wrong, - said Joshua. - Everything we've been going for is gone. Why did I make an army? I don't care, Moses, let's run in different directions at least today. You know I have gained nothing, and I have nothing to lose.

- I do not understand you. Speak up clearly! - Moses yelled at him.

He had never seen Joshua so helpless, and fear began to creep into Moses' heart.

- Aaron! All Aaron!!! - Joshua muttered. - I just talked to him. He's completely out of his mind. He's going to do the procession tomorrow. Tomorrow everything will go to hell! And I haven't gained anything!

- What procession? - Moses didn't understand. - What are you talking about?

- He said that the sword and fire we brought from conquering foreign lands would surely come back on the heads of our descendants. He said that tomorrow he would ask the people to give up our idea of taking these lands by force. And I have nothing behind me, I have not saved, I have not gathered. He also said...

But Moses interrupted him:

- He said, he said... Why do you keep saying the same thing, like a parrot? Remember what I told you a week ago, and you still haven't done it, and now you're fussing like a fire.

- There wasn't the right occasion. He's become cautious, he is suspicious. What's going to happen now, Moses, because I've gained nothing.

- Shut up! - Moses bellowed. - Where's that old goat?

- He went up the mountain to pray.

- Come on, Eleazar, - Moses said as he decided something, - Let's go talk to this peacemaker.

When they got to Mount Hor[2], they saw Aaron kneeling and appealing fervently to God. Moses looked around; there was no one around.

- Is this how you repay me? - He turned to Aaron in an angry voice, and Aaron got up, not wanting to kneel down in front of Moses.

- For all that I have done for you, Aaron, for all that I have given you, and you have decided to repay me with treason! Thanks, brother; I guess I've got a snake on my chest.

- What did you give me? - Aaron asked him calmly. - All I got from you was guilt over my father and mother, before my sons who died in the fire, before Mariam, who was finished off by you, before all the people who I deceived. What more have you given me? What have you given to others? You have plunged the people into such misery that it is a wonder we are all still alive. This is not enough for you; now you want to attack the lives of our descendants. You want to condemn them to a life in which our grandchildren and great-grandchildren, generation after generation, will have to defend their families with swords in their hands or flee from their bitter fate all over the world in search of peace and a piece of bread. Is this what you are preparing for them? Well, Moses, I will no longer allow you to deceive the people, and tomorrow I will anathematize you. Then let the people decide what to do next.

- Apparently, I will have to do to you what I did to your sons, - Moses said angrily.

Knowing that Aaron would be hurt to learn that his sons were not died in fire, but simply murdered, and that his son Eleazar was involved in this murder, Moses added, - and Eleazar, like that night, will help me do it with you.

He watched with sadistic pleasure as Aaron's face turned red, as convulsions ran through him, and as he began to gulp air with his mouth wide open.

- Did you help kill your brothers? - Aaron wheezed, grabbing the pale Eleazar by the chest.

Tears spurted from Aaron's eyes, and he gritted his teeth in unbearable pain so hard that Eleazar thought his father's teeth were about to crumble.

The distraught Aaron grabbed Eleazar by the throat and began to choke him as if a disgusting viper had got into his hands. Eleazar's eyes popped out of their sockets and his head became foggy, but at that moment Moses stabbed Aaron under his left shoulder by sharp blade.

- Damn you three times! - Aaron wheezed, falling at the feet of Eleazar, and it was unclear to whom he had said this, his brother Moses or his son Eleazar.

Joshua's men quickly disguised the dead Aaron and buried him on top of Mount Hor. Well, Moses appointed Eleazar to take his father's place. And Eleazar became the high priest of the Jewish people[3]. A high priest sounds proud, doesn't he?

1. The Bible. Numbers 20:1
2. The Bible. Numbers 20:25
3. The Bible. Numbers 20:28

CHAPTER 25:

The Enemy of the People.

As soon as Abram woke up, he knew at once that he was going to be in a bad mood today. He must have gotten off on the wrong foot.

Damn life! How can you call it a life? How can you compare life on the banks of the fertile Nile with life in the desert? The desert has no beauty - it is in the heart of a Bedouin. So says the proverb, but where and whence is it to be found in the desert, and even in the heart of a Jew, when he absorbed with milk of mother the gentle breeze from the Nile, the smell of papyrus and the feeling of joy that people have when they look at the waters of the great river. And what about the desert? Everywhere you look there is sand, sand, and barchans, which are also made of this nasty, eternally squeaking sand. And water? There is no water at all, and even if there is some, it can be found only in rare wells, which are so deep that one can't see the bottom even in the daytime. And is it possible to compare sweet water of the Nile with brackish and disgusting well water? And anyway, that was not the point, but the fact that his life had changed as soon as he moved in with his son. There, in Egypt, he was the master, he had his own business, and that made him feel the flow of life itself, and here he turned into an unnecessary old man. He wasn't wanted to believe it. Abram seemed fine to himself, but his children and grandchildren, of course, did not say so, but their behavior and attitude show that you, Abram, are outdated, you are the past, you are an old wreck and it's time for you to go to your death.

- And the water here is really rubbish, - Abram cursed, getting ready to go for firewood, - I'd give anything, within reason, of course, for a mug of good water from the Nile.

Picking up small branches, Abram didn't immediately notice the four sentries coming toward him.

- Have you gone mad, old man! - It is the Sabbath[1], and you have broken the law1, - shouted one of them, stopping. Arrest him; - He commanded the others.

The next day a judge, who should to judge Abram came to Moses. He clearly did not know what to do.

- Moses, - he appealed, - the Sabbath observance law that you gave to the people has come into effect, but there have been no precedents yet, and now I don't know what I should do about old Abram[2].

- I should pardon him, - Moses thought, - after all, the first man convicted of breaking the Sabbath, and by pardoning; I will show mercy to this old man. Let the people know that I too have a heart. The generous Moses sounds great. Let it be declared, that Moses in the name of the God of Jehovah pardons the old man, but it will be the last mercy for breaking the sanctity of the Sabbath.

Suddenly Joshua, who had come to Moses in the morning on business, said in a hard voice:

- Moses, we must be firm in keeping our laws that God has given to the people through you. You are well aware that by giving life to one, we will provoke others to break the laws. It is my deepest conviction that mercy must not be shown, and this old man must die so that others are not incriminated.

Moses listened with open mouth to Joshua's speech.

- What's the matter with him, he thought, is he sick? He is so cunning that he never speaks his thoughts out loud.

Moses did not know that yesterday when the old man was led to his arrest, Joshua had recognized the old man as his former accomplice in contract murders, and he was determined to make the last person who knew his past disappear forever.

Moses looked intently at Joshua, as if trying to get a glimpse into his thoughts, and gave a short order: - Execute the old man!

- That's right, Moses, - Joshua rejoiced, - you are as fair as ever.

He laughed to himself at Moses, but you couldn't tell by his serious face, and only the devils were jumping in his eyes.

But Moses didn't notice anything. He was suddenly struck by a new idea that occurred to him.

- How could I not have thought of this before, - Moses scolded himself, - how could I not understand that the ideological opponents must not be destroyed by the army, but by the hands of the fooled people. It is only necessary to sow suspicion, fear, envy and hatred in the society, and then all failures, diseases, hunger and any other misfortunes can be blamed on the shoulders of these very opponents, or rather, enemies. Only for everyone else, they too must become enemies. Not mine, not anyone else's, but the enemies of the people. It is only necessary to show that there are people among us whose aim is to sabotage and who only dream of making life hard and unbearable for the people.

Moses stood up.

- Declare, - he said to the judge, - that this old man has willfully broken the law given to us by God, and has thereby incurred his just wrath upon the entire community. By these actions he has harmed our religion and all the people. Condemn him to death as an enemy of the people[3].

- Joshua, - Moses commanded, - you are to assemble the people for a show trial of the old man, and you, Eleazar, are to memorize the speech you are to make after the execution.

An hour later poor old Abram, who could not understand why he had been branded an enemy of the people, was stoned.

The high priest Eleazar stood in front of the old man's bloody corpse and addressed the crowd.

- People, - he said fervently. - The nearer we get to the land which Jehovah God gives us for eternal use, the fiercer is the resistance of the people who seek to hinder us in this righteous cause. Can we really call them men? They are the scum of our society, pests and enemies of the people. Look around you carefully, and you are bound to find Pharaoh's accomplices lurking.

If a sheep suddenly died, think whether your neighbor, in his desire to do you harm, poisoned it. Or if someone's child has died. There is no greater grief for a parent than this, but before you bury him, consider whether he has been jinxed by a hidden hydra in the neighborhood. If your brother or son is reviling our laws and our leader Moses, are they not enemies? And if you have the slightest suspicion that someone is harming society, you should immediately report it to your superiors and judges. Whoever does not do so is himself an enemy of the people and deserves to die. People! Be vigilant for our interests! Death to the enemies of the people!

Moses listened to Eleazar's fervent speech and was proud of his nephew. He had not made a mistake in appointing him high priest.

It was a hot season for Joshua's special band. Every night arrests were made, and in the morning the enemies of the people were hanged outside the camp[4]. The repression first affected the upper ranks of the Jewish people and all the chiefs of the clans, the judges, and their assistants were executed. Moses removed anyone who could pose any threat to his sole authority. At Sittim alone[5] 24,000 enemies of the people were executed[6]. The revolution continued.

1. The Bible. Exodus 31:14
2. The Bible. Numbers 15:34
3. The Bible. Num15:36
4. The Bible. Num.25:4
5. The Sittim is land not far from where the Jews crossed the Jordan.
6. The Bible. Num. 25:9

From the author: Apparently, every revolution develops according to the same laws and they have the same stages of development. Reading this part of the Bible, it is as if you are transported back to the time of the 1937 repressions in the USSR. History is repeating itself and repeating…

CHAPTER 26:

The Reckoning.

Joshua heard absolutely nothing of what Moses was saying. Looking into his eyes and pretending to listen attentively, he was thinking about something else entirely. Today, as he passed through the camp, Joshua caught a glimpse of an older man, and that glimpse kept on bothering him. He was sure he had seen this man before, but he could not remember where. It seemed to be nothing unusual, he had caught hundreds of glances in just one day, but this look was special, and some sixth sense told Navin that there was something wrong here, something very important, and he could not get rid of this feeling.

- Do what you want, Joshua, but you must have a few of our spies in Pharaoh's security department, - Moses ordered him. - We must know all his plans for his war preparations, and you must spare no expense in bribing him.

As soon as Joshua heard Moses say the words security, he instantly remembered that look and who it belonged to. Of course he is! It was the former head of Pharaoh's security service, Ochos. Abruptly, Joshua stood up, headed for the exit, and in response to Moses' surprised look, he said:

- I'll do as you order, don't worry, Moses, but right now I have a squad to check on right away. There's something wrong and I want to get to the bottom of it personally.

- All right, go, - he shrugged, - but remember that tomorrow at noon I expect you on Mount Nebo[1]. I want to discuss with you the plan of the invasion and the crossing of the Jordan.

- I cannot be mistaken, - thought Joshua as he left Moses, - there has never yet been a time when my memory has failed me. But then how can I explain it? There was a rumor that Pharaoh had Ochos executed for the death of his son. And the face, overgrown with hair, as if it were not his.

But the look... No, it's him, it's his eyes!

Jesus sat silently on his horse and rode slowly toward the tent where he had already been told this man lived.

- What am I risking? - He thought, - Will I fail? That is out of the question! Would I be received as he was? What can they do, they fear me just as much, if not more[2]. And it had become dangerous to work with him: he could be put on trial as an enemy of the people. Apparently, the time had come, and God himself had sent me a helper.

When he heard the noise of the men approaching, the man with Ochos' eyes came out of the tent and frowned at Joshua, as if expecting trouble from this visit.

- What is your name, - Joshua asked him, and when he heard Hamat answer, he nodded his head. Hamat is Hamat.

- Now, Hamat, - said Joshua firmly, - get on this horse, - and with a nod he motioned for one of the guards to release the horse, - and come with me. We must talk.

The old man bit his lip and looked around without turning his head.

- Now, now, don't be silly, Hamat, don't draw attention to yourself, - added as he saw the old man assume a defensive posture.

Apparently, after thinking and deciding, Hamat mounted his horse easily for his age and, pretending not to care where he was going, followed Joshua.

So that Hamat would not be tempted to flee, Joshua's guards took him in their ring, wondering to themselves what Joshua would want with this unassuming man.

In his luxurious tent, Joshua removed everyone and offered Hamat a taste of wine, but he refused.

- Where do you come from and what are you doing here?

- I live by the grace of the gods, - Hamat began memorably. - I have no family and wander around the world. I once owed a great debt to a man, and now I am looking for him to repay it.

- Am I not the man you are looking for? - Joshua asked with a sly look, to which Hamat shook his head in disapproval.

- I know who you are looking for... His name is Moses, isn't it?

Hamat was silent.

- I also know your real name. Your name is Ochos. Don't try to do anything, - Joshua quickly added when he saw Hamat tense up and clench into a ball as if preparing to jump, - but listen to me carefully. Then Joshua's voice dropped to a whisper.

- Tomorrow, at noon, Moses and I agreed to meet on the Mount Nebo. I'll be a little late, so you'll have time to pay your debt. Just keep in mind, Ochos, the guards will check the summit before Moses sets foot there. One last thing... ...you're not getting out of there alive, I'll have to kill you. Understand?

Ochos, and it was really him, looked at Joshua in amazement. The man he feared the most had suddenly become his ally.

- Why are you doing this? - He asked Jesus quietly.

Joshua wanted to make up something more improbable for Ochos, but then he changed his mind and told it like it really was.

- I don't need him anymore. And dangerous, - he added, - our prophet seems to have gone completely mad. He's so mad that it's scary even to me to see his crazy eyes.

After a short silence, Joshua remembered the past related to Egypt and suddenly said cheerfully: - I used to have a different name. Now I'm Joshua, and in Egypt they just called me Hosea.

- So it was you who shot the high priest? - Ochos wondered.

- I did, - said Joshua, pleased that Ochos remembered his past services.

...For the first time since he began his hunt for Moses, Ochos had a real chance to do his bidding and wash the stain off his conscience. Moses was very careful. It was a stroke of luck. Tomorrow he would die, too, but that didn't bother him. His life had always belonged and belonged to Egypt, and outside that sphere it was of no value to Ochos.

In the evening he climbed Mount Nebo. He looked around and found that there was absolutely nowhere to hide. Not a bush, not a crevice. The guards would spot him at once and then all the days of waiting would be in vain. Nervously walking in circles around the bare bloody summit, Ochos examined it inch by inch, and finally his attention was caught by a small hollow in which a teenager could hardly fit. Kneeling down, Ochos began to palpate the hollow. To his delight, it was filled with small stones, and he began to shovel them out. After a couple of hours of hard work, Ochos enlarged the hollow enough to accommodate an adult of his stature.

In the morning, Ochos climbed to the top of Nebo with Dathan's miraculously surviving son, Elisha. His family had all been killed by Moses, and Ochos took the boy under his wing.

To all of Elisha's questions, Ochos only brushed aside, keeping a watchful eye on what was happening at the foot of the mountain. When the riders appeared below, Ochos took the ring from his finger and gave it to Elisha.

- You are already adult man, - Ochos began, - and you must understand me. I am going to kill Moses here. You hate him for the death of your kin, and I, my boy, hate him no less. He must die, and he will die. And you must sneak into Egypt and give this ring to Horum. He is Pharaoh's chief of security. Farewell, my son, I hope you will grow into a worthy man.

I will stay with you, - said Elisha firmly, - and I will help you. What if you can't kill the beast? Then I'll sink my teeth into its throat, and I'll be killed, but I won't unhinge my jaws.

- No, Elisha, you are too young and you must live. As for help, yes your help is needed; - Ochos replied as he approached the hole he had dug the night before. Cover me stone me so that no one will notice anyone hiding here, and then hurry to get out of here. And don't worry about the hangman's punishment, son; he can't get away today.

Moses was in a great mood this morning. A few more days and they would cross the Jordan. His dream was slowly taking shape. No one, not even Joshua, really knows what he is up to. All this talk of Canaanite lands flowing with milk and honey is just a cover for his real plan. They had passed through the desert, and by plundering and killing civilians he had trained his army to be brutal. Now he will enable it to plunder these lands, he will enable it to live easily and unconcernedly. If anyone will break a sweat, it will not be from working the plow, but from the hilt of a sword. Well, then he will throw his army into Egypt. I will defeat Pharaoh's glorious army, and the throne will be mine. That is the ultimate goal!

As Moses was getting ready to meet Joshua, he began to think about a candidate to replace him. There are no words for it, Joshua is a good general, but he is too smart. Joshua was already starting to show me his teeth, but what's going to happen next?

- Well, he must die, - Moses thought, - in the next battle a *accidental arrow* will surely strike down the brave commander. Well, I'll decide who will take his place later.

He climbed to the top and waited until the guards, having checked everything, left, he pondered, waiting for Joshua. He was late, but Moses didn't care. He was admiring the magnificent view of the land of Canaan. Soon these lands would be his, then Egypt, and then he could throw his army onward. Maybe he would become ruler of the world. Why not?

There was a sound of footsteps behind him.

- Why are you so late? - Moses muttered grudgingly, without turning around, - Where have you been hanging around?

-I was indeed too late when you dog killed Ram, and I had to wander a long way to find you, - Moses suddenly heard the horrifyingly familiar voice of Ochos. He turned sharply and, with eyes dilated with horror, stared at the hardly recognizable chief of Egyptian security. In his hands Ochos held a sword.

- Look closely, Moses, - he continued, - do you recognize me?

Moses could not say anything, he only nodded his head.

- I have come to punish you for the death of Pharaoh's son, for the plunder you have committed in Egypt, and for all the blood you have shed. I find you guilty and in the name of Pharaoh I sentence you to death by Egyptian law. Pray, Moses!

The first thing that came to Moses' mind was the idea of invoking God. He fell to his knees and in a voice trembling with terror he spoke:

- Know, Ochos, that the Lord has sent me to do these things, and not of my own free will have I done everything. The voice came to me from above, and I was obliged to obey.

Knowing Ochos very well, Moses knew immediately that he could not be bribed, so Moses decided to start this divine nonsense in order to somehow win a few minutes. While he was fooling Ochos, the tardy Joshua would approach, and then there would be a chance to stay alive.

But Ochos interrupted him.

- I know your God. Your God, Moses, has several names: meanness, abomination, and savage cruelty. One wonders how nature could put so much wickedness and hatred into one man.

With these words, Ochos drew his sword over Moses' head, but he didn't have time to use it. Apparently the thought that he was about to die and never become Pharaoh made Moses sick. He clutched his chest and, like a beached fish, gulped for air with his mouth wide open. His eyes misted over, froze, and he collapsed on the ground.

After waiting a moment, Ochos turned Moses face up and felt for a pulse. Moses was dead.

- Too late again, - he sighed in frustration, - this bastard had escaped my retribution. But though he died not by the sword but by fear for his miserable life, justice had finally been served.

- Now it's time for me to remove the stain from my conscience, - thought Ochos. He pointed the sword at his breast and, falling on it, exclaimed:

- Meet me, Ram!

1 The Bible . Num.16:28.

Horum received a report that some boy was persistently asking to see him, claiming that he had important business with Pharaoh's chief of security. The guards tried to drive the stubborn boy away, but he would not leave.

- Very well, bring him in, - Horum said to the guard as he continued reading his delivery. A few minutes later the emaciated boy was brought to him. He was very emaciated and looked like a traveler who had come a long way.

- I must speak to Horum, - the boy said, sniffling his nose and staring at him impatiently. Horum got up from the table and approached him.

- I am Horum, who are you?

- My name is Elisha and I have this to give you, - the boy reached into the folds of his torn clothes and held out his hand to Horum, clasping something in his fist. When he opened his fingers, Horum saw a ring on his palm. It was the ring of Ochos!

Taking the ring, Horum hurried to Pharaoh.

On entering Pharaoh's chamber, Horum found him at his desk, piecing together some blueprints. Silently, as he approached the waiting Pharaoh, Horum placed the Ochos ring on the table. Pharaoh eyebrows rose high, betraying his excitement; he clearly recognized the ring.

- What does it mean? - Pharaoh asked excitedly.

- I do not know all, - answered Horum, - but I know one thing for certain, that even the dead man Ochos has done his duty, and that your sworn enemy Moses is dead.

1. The place of Moses' death. The Bible. Num.33:47
2. The Bible. Isaiah 4:14

CHAPTER 27:

Nain's school

This always happens! It seems like you're trapped in a vicious circle, and there's no way out. Everything goes wrong and, whatever you do, nothing works. But, at one moment, good news comes, and then another and the world seems to you so good and well-organized and you in it as a fantastic hero that can do everything.

Only yesterday Nain was tormented by the fact that his idea to open a school finds no support and all around are problems. There was no place to hold classes, no school supplies, no nothing at all, and, in general, it seemed that no one needed the school.

But this morning the governor of town summoned him and promised to allocate some money for the school, and by lunchtime he was informed that the head priest of the local temple had agreed to allocate a room for classes. It's finally moving forward! It wasn't even about the money or the room, the main thing was that his idea had been recognized by officials!

Word of the soon-to-be-opened school spread quickly through the city and in the afternoon people streamed to Nain. Rich Phineas was the first to rush in. He plumped his fat body on the flimsy couch, wiped his forehead sweaty from walking, panted, looked slyly at Nain and offered him a large sum of money to set up the school.

- I always knew that a respectable husband like your father would raise a worthy son, - he said. - Take the money, and if you need more, just tell me, Nain. We've had enough of sitting in the dark. I've lived my life, and I can't even count money, I'm illiterate. So at least let our sons gain wisdom - intelligence. Then he stopped his speech and paused and asked:

- You will take my sons to your school, won't you?

- You cannot count your money, not because you are illiterate, but because you have so much money that you cannot count it," thought Nain, but said aloud: - Of course, your sons will be first on my list. Satisfied with this answer, the rich man Phineas got up and went off to his business, making as much noise as when he appeared, and other people rushed to Nain.

The poor fisherman Rabsak, their fisherman neighbor, also came. He hesitated for a long time to enter Nain's room, crumpled his tattered headdress in his hands and could not dare to cross the threshold. Nain, seeing him through the open door, invited the poor man in.

- Sit down, neighbor, - Nain offered, pouring him some water. Rabsak bowed politely and, after drinking the offered water, shrank his gaze. He seemed to have forgotten why he had come here, so quiet and detached was he sitting in his chair. Then, apparently coming to his senses, Rabsak began to speak slowly.

- You know me, Nain, all my life I have done nothing but catch and sell fish. And my great-grandfather and grandfather and father did the same. My sons will live by fishing, too. I guess that's the fate of our family. We have never been rich, but I am proud of my work and try to raise my children to be honest people. But my youngest, Rogaw, your Boby's friend," Rabsak said suddenly, - he's not like that, Nain. He helps me, no words, but I look at him when we're choosing a net, and I see he's not a fisherman! He's not our kind of fisherman.

Pulling out the net is the most exciting part of our job. I've pulled thousands of nets out of the river, and still, as if for the first time, my heart sinks with excitement. But he doesn't have that fisherman's excitement, the thrill of waiting to see if the catch is caught or if the net is empty. Of course, he cares whether there is a fish or not, but not the excitement of a fisherman, when you see a fish beating in the net. ...Strange him with us. He's always asking me questions that make my head spin: is the Earth big, do people live on the moon, and all kinds of other questions that only priests can answer. What can I, a lifelong fisherman, tell him? So my wife and I were wondering if you would take him to your school.

Maybe he'll grow up to be a priest and be happy. I want our children to live better than we do, Nain, and be happy. But we have no money, Nain, but I will, - said Rabsak, - bring fresh fish every day for your Fooige. You'll never be short of fresh crucians with my nets. And my old lady bows low to you, - said Rabsak, as he stood up and bowed low to Nain. Nain was much moved by this simple speech of the old fisherman. He stood up towards Rabsak and held out his hand.

- Of course, my dear neighbor, I'll take your little boy, - he said confidently, -and we'll still buy fish only from you. And your crucians are really wonderful!

Nain had no idea that the good news was not over today. As soon as he returned home, Fooige, having admired him playing with his daughter, showed him her new work. During this time that Nain had lived with Fooige, he had developed a different appreciation for art. Nain saw that the game of colors can convey a person's state of mind, all the splendor of the existing world and inspire him to solve the most difficult problems.

- When does she find the time? - Nain thought as he looked at her new work. In the painting the women were rinsing the laundry in front of the Great Nile. Nain admired the life-like painting and felt the precise power of the great river. A feeling of tenderness for his native land filled Nain and he felt proud to be living in this particular country. And from the women who were rinsing their laundry, there was a certainty that life would never end, that centuries would pass and they would still be rinsing their laundry, still gossiping, doing their work, and still bearing children, continuing to live forever, generation after generation.

- You're a genius, - Nain said, and saw the happy twinkle in Fooige's eyes. - I wish I had a gift like yours. Then I'd paint a picture like that, like... well, in a word, so that everyone would admire it as I admire you.

- Nain, - Fooige began uncertainly, - what if you gave me a lesson at your school? If you find my drawings good, maybe I could instill in your students a love of drawing?

At these words, Nain's mouth dropped open in amazement.

- How clever of you, my dove," he said at last. - Of course it is! You're right, our children should not only be able to write and count, they should understand art, to see and appreciate the beauty of the world.

- How glad I am, Fooige, - said Nain, embracing her, - that you understand me and want to help me. How thankful I am, and how I love you!

But that was not the end of the good news!

Suddenly, and as usual, with a noise, Boby burst into the room.

- Nain! - He shouted. - Hide! There's a priest from the Main Temple at the wharf asking for you. I'll sic the dog on him now, and you run for your life.

Nain was taken aback by the unexpected news, and mechanically he felt a sense of fear. In the next moment he realized that he had absolutely nothing to fear, but went out onto the porch in a slight excitement left by the unexpected fright, and a scared to death Fooige ran out after.

From the porch, Nain saw the approaching figure of a man in pink robes. The man, leaning on a staff, stopped in front of their house and looked at Nain from under his arm. It was Sokh!

Nain rushed forward, knocked Boby who had fallen under his feet, and flew over to the old man and hugged him tightly.

- My friend, Sokh! How glad I am to see you! - He said at last, when the excitement had subsided, - where did you come from?

- Here I am, as I promised, to look at your sweet little Fooige, the one you were willing to die for, - Sokh said, wiping away his tears. - Well, show her.

- There she is, on the porch, waiting to worship you," Nain answered, pointing and shouting, "Fooige, mother, Sokh has arrived!!!

Her mother ran out after Fooige, wiping her hands on her apron, staring at the stranger. As Nain led Sokh to the porch, she and Fooige bowed low, as was the custom, to the priest.

- Please come into the house, - his mother invited him in, and, beckoning Boby, she told him to run after his father.

... The revelry for the arrival of the dear guest went on till late at night. The mother and father, knowing how much this man had done for their son, tried their best to please him. The mother kept trying to put a new dish on his plate, and the father got a thirty-year-old wine. Well, Sokh kept talking and talking and talking...

And Nain's father-in-law got drunker and drunker. By the end of the evening he said that he respected all priests of the world and from that moment he took a vow of celibacy.

- Let's go home, my priest, - his mother-in-law said, pulling him from the table.

Nain and Sokh sat down in the gazebo. Sokh took his time to tell him the news of the temple and said hello from Mack.

- And Buck was killed in the siege of the temple, - he sadly told Nain. - He sadly told Nain, - Mack, who was already a very private person since his brother's death, had stopped showing his face in public and smiled for the first time when I told him I was coming to see you.

Well, Nain told him about his future school after the news, to which Sokh was overjoyed.

- I was not mistaken about you, my boy,- the old man said, suddenly agitated. - You don't know what a great thing you have in mind! I have no words to express my gratitude, and I wish I were old enough to help you properly. But I can still help you. I will make copies from the papyri of the history of Egypt, and you will teach the children from them, and I believe that all the knowledge they acquire will help our country in the future.

- And your Fooige is indeed a beauty, - Sokh said after a pause, suddenly changing the subject. - But that's not so important. What matters is that she loves you. You can't fool me, old man, and I can see that. I'd die at the bottom of a deep well for her.

Here he laughed, - you old and sick priest is dreaming about beautiful women. Only it's too late, I guess it's time to believe in God.

- Have you, - Nain wondered, - become a believer?

- No, of course not. I know too much about religion to believe in God. I'm just talking about the time in any man's life when he wants to believe in an all-powerful God.

- Is there such a period?

- There is! Have you ever noticed, Nain, that it's mostly the elderly who pray for their sins in temples, and that there are very few young people there? - Sokh asked him.

- I have.

- Do you know why? Young people don't have time to think about God and death; they have to get on with their lives. And death... when is it going to happen? They've got their whole life ahead of them, they think. But old people in the end of their life, when they have only a little time left to live, they start thinking about the inevitable end, and they become frightened. They can't accept that when they die they will never see this world again. They cannot accept that the world will continue to exist, people will continue to live and love, the sun will continue to shine, life will go on, and only they will never be in this beautiful world again. Never! They don't want to accept it! Their soul protests! They want to stay in this world, maybe in another form, but to stay and keep their own selves. That is where they fall under the influence of religion. Not only have our Egyptian gods offered eternal life, Nain. All the religions of the world are the same and use the same idea, eternity of life. - Believe in God, - the priest whispers, - and you will have eternal life in paradise. There you will meet your relatives and friends, and there you will stay forever.

- What if it's true? - Old people begin to think. - What if God exists and can save me? Maybe... ...maybe... suddenly... And they run to the temple, they become good people; they try to please God, cherishing the idea of eternal life. They cling to faith like a drowning man clings to a straw.

So, Nain let me tell you, as long as there is death, there will be religion.

- I believe, - Nain exclaimed, - people will conquer death. That day will come to earth. But probably these will not happen soon. So what to do about religion? How to destroy this myth?

- Oh, you young people! You only want to tear down the old. How to teach you that there are grains of wisdom in the old. So take all the best that has gone before you, and all the bad, cruel and unjust will go to the dustbin of history. Religion, Nain, is not only evil. There is good and love in it, too, but that's the trouble, religion is all about loving God, not people! What do you leave behind? - That is the greatest question no God can answer.

After a few minutes of silence, Sokh asked: - Do you remember, Nain, that old papyrus in which we read of the death of Egypt?

Nain nodded his head affirmatively.

- I have brought you a copy of that document," and with these words he handed the papyrus to Nain. It was already dark in the courtyard and there was no way to read it again, but Nain didn't need to, he remembered it by heart.

Egypt, Great Egypt was dead.
There were only a handful of people left alive.
It's been 40 years since the Nile spill out last time.
Where is this great river? Nile is gone.
This is a pitiful stream instead of the Nile.
The gods have turned their backs on us.
There is nothing to feed the children and the people have killed
Them. People eat people.

- I've been looking for a long time for a continuation of this story, - Sokh said, - I really wanted to know why this tragedy happened, but, unfortunately, I couldn't find it. However, I found the last part of the message and brought it to you. Read it.

Nain took the papyrus and asked Fooige to bring the lamp. The whole family came into the arbor with her, and Nain stood under the lamp he had brought and hung and began to read.

I am dying. But I am calm. I know that YOU, the descendants of the great pharaohs, will restore our culture to its former glory. Let not today, let not tomorrow, but YOU raise from the knees of Egypt dear to my heart, and not God, but YOU belong to the future of our land.

www.ingramcontent.com/pod-product-compliance
Lightning Source LLC
LaVergne TN
LVHW091533060526
838200LV00036B/590